"Megan Kinney delivers a comp[...] forgiveness, and redemption with lik[...] characters who endure tough challenges. Strong action and a great plot twist make *Dakota Courage* a must-read."
—Sharee Stover, *Publishers Weekly* best-selling and award-winning author of Love Inspired Suspense

"In *Dakota Courage*, Megan Kinney takes you on a heart-twisting ride that keeps you turning page after page. The romance is compelling, and the jeopardy is palpable. The backdrop of the Sturgis Motorcycle Rally adds a unique element that carries the story from a fast-paced start to a picture-perfect ending. Loved every minute."
—Janis Jakes, author of *The Bounty Hunter's Bride* and *A Rose in Winter*

"Megan Kinney's *Dakota Courage* catapults the reader on an emotional ride as a woman struggles with coming to terms with who she once was to who she is. Gripping and poignant, this book is a must-read for anyone wanting hope that a traumatic past doesn't have to stop one's hopes for tomorrow."
—Parker J. Cole, speaker, radio host, and author of The Daughters of Black Gotham series and *The Once and Future Queen*

"Weaving redemption from beginning to end, *Dakota Courage* is a roller-coaster ride filled with suspense, romance, and family. Megan Kinney's strong voice shines as she reminds us that past mistakes do not have the power to dictate the future and that our faults, experiences, and history do not determine our worth. Tackling such sensitive topics as manipulation, sex trafficking, and kidnapping, *Dakota Courage* tugs at heart strings. Readers will be left with renewed hope and encouragement that will stay with them long after they close the book."
—Beth Pugh, Selah Awards finalist and author of the Pine Valley Holiday series

Dakota Courage

by

Megan Kinney

IRON
STREAM
FICTION

Birmingham, Alabama

Dakota Courage
Iron Stream Fiction
An imprint of Iron Stream Media
100 Missionary Ridge
Birmingham, AL 35242
IronStreamMedia.com

Library of Congress Control Number: 2022940952

Cover design by Hannah Linder Designs

ISBN: 978-1-64526-358-6 (paperback)
ISBN: 978-1-64526-359-3 (e-book)
1 2 3 4 5—26 25 24 23 22

Emma, Angel, Alicia, and Kylee
God has blessed me by letting me be your mom.
May you each find the courage
to be the hero of your own adventure.

Acknowledgments

First, I want to thank my husband, Kevin. I'm not kidding when I tell you that Iron Stream Media should hire him for their marketing team. He takes my books wherever he travels, selling them on airplanes, at conferences, even on the cruise we took last spring. His love and support have been a lifeline in fulfilling my dreams. I want to thank my four daughters too. They are such a blessing to me, putting up with a stressful mom when deadlines loom. They love to listen to me talk about my stories and write stories of their own. I'm thankful for my parents and all my family and friends who encourage me every day.

I'm thankful for the people in my life who have joined me in this writing adventure. My amazing editor, Karin Beery, who invested just as much blood and sweat, but probably not tears, as me. She's a superstar who pushes me to be the best writer I can be.

I want to thank Hollie Strand, Jeanne Mann, Laurie Parkins, Jake and Angela Mordhorst, Dr. Pam Schmagel, and Beth Picket Pin for answering all my questions and providing great feedback from their professional knowledge so that I don't have to be a forensic examiner, victim's advocate, probation officer, dispatcher, jailer, doctor, vet tech . . . *and* a writer. A huge thank-you to the Adabooktomy Book Club for reading through earlier manuscripts and giving me great feedback.

I want to thank the Iron Stream Media editorial board and staff, Tina Atchenson, Kim McCulla, and many more, who use their gifts and talents to make me look good. I especially want to thank the cover designer, Hannah Linder, as I'm blown away by her talent.

I'd love to thank all you amazing readers too. You have been such a blessing to me as I read your comments, reviews, and emails.

Dakota Courage

Thank you for being amazing! But mostly I'd like to thank Jesus and give Him glory for giving me the desire, the creativity, and the joy of writing. He's the true reason that lives change for the better.

Go to megankinney.net to sign up for my newsletter and hear about upcoming projects and promotions. Thank you and God bless.

CHAPTER 1

Elaine Kent stared at the computer screen so long the numbers blurred. With a deep breath, she closed her laptop. Her sales were depressing. Extra foot traffic from the motorcycle rally would help, but there had to be a way to increase her income on a consistent basis. What could she add to her crowded antique shop to boost business?

As she walked through the former dining room and parlor of the Victorian house—both packed with antique toys, books, and figurines—the Black Forest cuckoo clock tweeted. Three thirty already? Her mail would be there soon.

With nothing else to do in the still-empty store, she walked past the locked cabinets full of valuable antiques back to the foyer. Pushing up onto her tippy-toes, she peered through the door's stained glass to wait for her mail.

A man stood in the rain at the end of the sidewalk talking with her mail carrier. He took something from her, then sprinted toward the shop, his head down and something cradled in his arm like a football. Elaine opened the door as the man looked up.

"Mitch!" She smiled at the familiar face, swinging the door wide for him to run through. "Let me get you a towel."

He stepped up to the waist-high sales counter and set down a bag and her mail. "Looks like you've got jury duty."

She grabbed a towel from under the counter and handed it to him. A white envelope sat on top of the stack. *Seventh Circuit Court Services. Mary Russell.* Her chest tightened. She slid the stack of letters off the counter and under the desk before he saw the name.

Mitch wiped the water from his face and hands. The rain hadn't disturbed his blond, textured highlights. His eyes were the purest of blue, and his rugged stubble darkened his jaw. She'd love to grab her sketch pad and spend the next few hours sketching his lovely face.

He glanced around the shop. "Slow day?"

"You're the first one to come in all afternoon."

"That'll change. The rally starts in a few days. Then you'll be able to retire to Florida for the winter."

Elaine laughed. "I sure hope so. What do you have for me?" She tipped her head at the white bag.

"Wait until you see. This is the best find yet." The bag crinkled as he opened it. He pulled out a tall metal teapot with a long spout and painted glass panels.

Elaine inwardly cringed. "That's sure unique." And ugly. She gently picked it up to inspect it. "I'll have to look up the value of this one. Can you give me a couple of days?"

His lips pushed together. "I was hoping you'd be able to pay me for it now."

For the past few months, ever since Mitch first came into her shop, she'd been able to pay him when he dropped off his treasures, but the odd-looking pot had her stumped. "I've never seen anything like this, so I don't know what a fair price would be." And she couldn't afford to give him more than it might be worth. "You can take it with you if you don't feel comfortable leaving it. I'll understand."

A smile slid across his face. "You keep it. It'll give me an excuse to come back." He leaned on the counter. "You got a boyfriend who'll blacken my eye if I ask you out?"

Her cheeks warmed as she shook her head. "No boyfriend."

"Good to know." He winked. "I'll be back in a couple of days."

Her face blazed. All she could manage was a weak smile as he turned and strode to the door. When it closed behind him, she took the stack of mail from under her desk and fanned her face. The thought of putting herself out there again nearly made her ill, but she missed the security, safety, and companionship she'd had with her husband . . . at the beginning. Mitch had flirted before, but she'd figured it was his way of sweet talking her into giving him a better deal. Could he seriously be interested in her?

Not wanting to overthink it, she put the letters down and picked up the teapot. It resembled an elongated, narrow genie lamp. The glass panels looked to be hand painted. She exchanged the pot for her phone and searched through her favorite antique websites for clues. After coming up empty, she took a picture and posted it online, asking for information about it.

Unable to avoid it any longer, she picked up the mail. She traced the writing on the first letter. *Mary Russell.* If only she could change her past as easily as she had changed her name.

Her hands trembled as she opened the envelope. A meeting with her probation officer. Right in the middle of the Sturgis Motorcycle Rally—her busiest week of the year. She couldn't close the store. She'd lose thousands of dollars in business. But she couldn't skip the meeting either. Her probation officer had been understanding so far, but Elaine didn't want that to change. She still had over four years to work with him. That left only one option, and it wasn't a good one. Elaine grabbed her phone and called her grandma.

"Hi, sweetie." Grandma's soft voice sounded cheerful.

"Hi, Grandma. I have a favor to ask. I have a meeting in Rapid City on August eighth. Do you think you can watch the store for me?"

"Can't you close for just a bit?" Her voice quieted.

"I'd hate to lose business during the rally. That week could give me enough revenue to keep me afloat the rest of the year."

"I can't drive that far."

"I know. I could come get you the night before and we'll spend the night together. I'll have time in the morning to show you how to do things before I have to leave."

"I don't know . . . I don't like staying in strange places. I like to sleep at home."

"It's not a strange place. You used to live here, remember? Aunt Susan turned it into an antique shop."

"Oh, that's right." Grandma giggled. "I forgot she did that. Did you ask Susie to help you?"

Elaine's breath caught. What was going on? "Aunt Susan was killed in a motorcycle crash last spring, Grandma."

Loud breathing followed, then a sigh. "I know. I don't know where my mind goes sometimes."

Elaine didn't know either, and the slip worried her. "Don't worry about next week. I'll find someone else to help or I can close up for a few hours. It'll be OK."

"Are you sure?"

"I'm sure. You have always helped me. I'll figure this out."

A bird squawked and her grandma giggled. "Sally Ann, do you want to talk to your sister?"

It had always amused Grandma to pretend the bird was Elaine's sister, but now she wasn't sure if Grandma realized she and the cockatiel weren't actually related. "Hi, Sally Ann. Are you being a good girl?"

The bird squeaked. Grandma laughed again. Relief and regret poured over Elaine.

The bell above the door jingled and a large, bald man marched in. Without a glance or a hello, he walked past her and headed toward the old dining room.

"I've got a customer. Talk to you later."

"Bye, sweetie."

Elaine ended the call and walked around the sales counter to greet the man. She stepped into the show room, but he'd disappeared. "Hello?"

He appeared beside the shelf of pottery, scowling. A scar ran from the corner of his eye to his chin. "Where is she?"

"Who?" His intense gaze brought goosebumps to her skin as she backed up behind the counter.

He stomped toward her and ripped open the closet door beside her.

Elaine's pulse raced. "Please stop. There's no one here." She tightened her grip on her cell phone.

"I know she's here!" He slammed the door and stormed into the other show room. Vases fell off the shelves as he raged through her store.

When he turned from her, Elaine backed into the corner and dialed 9-1-1.

"9-1-1. What's your emergency?"

"I . . . um."

"What's your emergency?"

The man rounded the corner and charged toward Elaine. "Where is she?"

Elaine held up a finger, surprised at her own courage. "Ma'am, I'm calling about an antique order that I placed weeks ago. It should have been here already. I own The Mother Lode Antique Shop in Sturgis, South Dakota."

"Do you realize that you called emergency dispatch?"

"Yes, I do."

"Are you in danger?"

"Yes. That's correct." Her voice shook so she took a deep breath. The man marched down another aisle, knocking over more antiques.

"What's your address?"

"It's 1409 Junction Ave. I need the items as soon as possible."

"We have officers on their way. Stay on the line with me. Is the other person armed?"

A door slammed. "Where is she?"

Elaine jumped. "I don't know."

A hand grabbed the phone from behind and threw it to the floor. Elaine screamed.

Before she could move, he leaned close, his body odor making her gag, and gripped her arm, dragging her through the old house. Her feet slipped over broken glass.

In the kitchen, he pushed Elaine to the ground. Her head smacked against the cabinet. Pain exploded against her skull. She had to get away from him!

When he opened the broom closet, Elaine scooted across the floor. If she could just reach the back door.

He cursed then took a step closer and grinned. "Maybe I don't need her." He grabbed Elaine's arm and yanked her to her feet. She pulled against him until her shoulder throbbed. "You can take her place."

She whimpered, nausea rolling through her. "Who? Please, let me go."

"Stop! Sturgis Police! Get your hands up!"

A police officer rushed in from the dining room at the same time two burst through the back door. Three guns pointed at the man.

The bald man let go, and Elaine crumpled to the cool tile floor. She tried to stand, but her legs wouldn't hold. Instead, she sat back and closed her eyes. Something crashed then scuffled. She pulled her legs up to her chest and covered her head.

"Ma'am? Are you OK? Do you need an ambulance?"

She took a deep breath and glanced up. Two officers held the bald man against the far wall. They had his arms behind him and his face pushed against the glass of her daisy painting. Relief replaced the fear that had shot through her. The police had saved her this time.

"Do you need me to send for medical?" An officer with brown wavy hair knelt beside her. His dark brows squeezed together. "Are you hurt?"

Elaine rubbed her shoulder. "No, I'm fine."

He smiled. "Do you need help standing?"

She shook her head. Her legs quaked, so she gripped the counter behind her. Despite their recent heroics, law enforcement still made her nervous. When two officers escorted their handcuffed prisoner out the back door, Elaine took a deep breath.

"I'm Officer McGuire," said the brown-haired man. "Let's sit while I ask you some questions." He picked up the two chairs that had been knocked over and set them on either side of her light blue Formica-and-chrome table. She sank onto the vinyl seat while he sat across from her. He pulled out a notebook and pen. "What's your name?"

"Elaine Kent." She sucked in a breath. "Well, that's not my real name. It's Mary Russell. My married name is Russell. My husband died and I've reverted back to my maiden name, but legally it's still Russell." She clamped her mouth shut. She needed to calm down so she didn't appear suspicious.

He finished writing then looked up at her. "So your legal name is Mary Russell, but you go by Elaine Kent?"

She nodded.

"Do you know the assailant?"

She shook her head. A dull ache formed in the back of her head. She reached up and found a large, tender bump.

"Maybe you should start from the beginning," Officer McGuire said.

"The beginning?"

"Yes. Why did the assailant attack you?"

"I don't know. He kept asking me where *she* was, but no woman has been in here all day. Then he grabbed me and said I could take her place. That's when you came in."

"What did he mean you could take her place?"

"I have no idea."

He snapped his notebook shut. "Can we search the house? Maybe someone slipped in while you weren't looking."

She hadn't considered that. Elaine nodded.

McGuire motioned to two other officers. "You check upstairs. Hewitt and I'll check downstairs."

They disappeared, and Elaine squeezed her shaking fingers together. What if someone was lurking around? She raced to the back door and locked it. Hugging herself, she turned around. Her porcelain napkin holder lay broken on the floor. Her fingers shook as she picked up the pieces and threw them away. The daisy painting hung at an unusual angle. When she straightened it, she noticed the oil smudge from the bald man's face. She shuttered as she sat. Who had he been looking for? She hoped he never found her.

Feet stomped throughout the house. With the sound of policemen all around, her adrenaline faded. She laid her head on her hands. Her body slowly relaxed, finally feeling safe.

Minutes later, Officer McGuire returned with a gentle smile. "There's no one in the house. The detectives will question the assailant and hopefully get some answers. In the meantime, I'll leave my business card if you think of any other information."

When the police finally left, she locked the doors after them and flipped the *Open* sign to *Closed*. It was only five o'clock, but she couldn't stay in the shop any longer. Her head throbbed and her nerves were a burnt mess.

A shiver coursed through her. She had always felt safe in the converted Victorian house, but it suddenly seemed too quiet, and there were too many places to hide. She should have searched the house with the police.

All she wanted was to curl up in bed and try to forget the day, but when she walked into the display room from the foyer, her feet crunched on the broken glass. Broken vases covered the floor. She should clean up, but her hands shook when she reached for the broom. The glass would have to wait until morning.

Her phone lay somewhere in the mess, though. She meandered through the room to the foyer searching for it, finally spotting it next to the counter. As she bent to pick it up, Mitch's teapot caught her eye. The ugly thing sat against the wall. She examined it, surprised that it had survived without a scratch. Maybe researching it's worth would distract her. She picked up her phone and relaxed—the screen protector had cracked but it worked.

Elaine headed upstairs to her bedroom and twisted the skeleton key in the lock the behind her. It wouldn't stop an intruder for long, but it made her feel a little safer.

She switched on the small bedside lamp, filling the room with soft light and a sense of comfort. She ran her fingers along the beveled bumps and etched flowers on the crystal lamp shade and down the crystal base.

She'd picked up the lamp at a garage sale. A dirty and stained lamp, with a sticky-note that said *Broken*. Back then, that note could have been glued to her forehead, as broken as she'd felt. That was why she decided that she'd find a way to not only fix the lamp, but hopefully find a way to fix her own brokenness.

She'd grown a lot since the sobbing mess she'd been only three months ago. She wasn't going to let the day's events pull her back into the hole of depression she'd clawed her way out of. If one antique could start her healing, maybe another could keep her on that path.

She slipped into bed and unlocked her phone, anxious to research the teapot. Ugly antiques tended to surprise her with their worth. She opened a forum where she'd posted the picture earlier, scrolling down the page until . . . that horrible man's face popped into her head.

He had been so strong and could have carried her away without much effort. How could she keep herself safe? Better locks, for sure, but that wouldn't help during business hours.

Forgetting the teapot, she searched security systems. There were so many options. Too many price points. Her headache pounded. Once the rally was over, she'd look closer at installing a security system. Until then, she was safe as long as that man was locked up.

After turning off the lamp, she curled on her side and closed her eyes, but with his evil smirk and bruising treatment so fresh, she couldn't settle her mind. Despite her pounding head, she threw the covers off and scurried to the adjacent room.

Within seconds, light filled the space and classical music blasted from her CD player. She squirted oil paint onto her pallet and smeared bright red onto a pure white canvas. Switching brushes, she painted broad strokes of purple then yellow. She didn't care about technique or creating anything beautiful—she just wanted to paint away the anxiety that clawed at her.

By ten thirty, bursts of color that looked like fireworks filled the canvas, her stress and fear had fled, and she stood exhausted in front of her painting. After throwing her brushes into a jar of turpentine, she stumbled back to bed and fell asleep.

CHAPTER 2

The shrill ringing of Elaine's alarm clock made her jump. She turned it off, then slid to the edge of her bed and cradled her aching head. Maybe she should have gotten checked out yesterday.

When her cell phone rang, she reached for it, quickly silencing the noise. "Hello?" she mumbled, fumbling the phone. Who the devil would call this early?

"Good morning, Mary. It's Grandma. I don't mean to bother you, but I can't find my pearl necklace. Do you happen to know where it is?"

"I don't." She sighed. At least it wasn't anything serious. "You probably misplaced it. The next time I'm there, I'll look for it, OK?"

"Thank you, sweetie. It used to be my mom's. Sally Ann is waking up and wants to talk to her sister."

Elaine groaned. That bird wouldn't help her headache at all. "Not today. I've only got a few days until the rally, and I have a ton of work to do in the shop."

"OK. Misty is coming over in a bit anyway."

"Who's Misty?"

"She's my sweet friend."

Elaine sat up straight. "You have a friend? How long have you known her?"

"A couple of months. I met her at the grocery store. I couldn't reach my tea on the top shelf so she helped me. She's so nice. I was sitting on my porch and saw her walk by my house with her dog a couple of times. We started talking. As it turns out, she loves birds."

A sigh of concern escaped. Among everything else going on, now Elaine would have to make time to check this person out. "I think it's nice you have a friend. Maybe when the rally is over, I can meet her, but I'd better go. I need to open the shop."

"OK. Promise you'll be careful with all those motorcyclists."

Elaine smiled. "Most of them are harmless businessmen and weekend riders. I doubt any gang members will be shopping for antiques." But they might stop in looking for some lost girl. "I'll call you later, OK?"

"Sure, sweetie."

An hour later, after downing some pain relievers and eating breakfast, her headache had finally subsided. She swept up the last of the broken glass and dumped it into the trashcan behind the counter.

The front door rattled.

Her heart thumped. She grabbed her phone and typed 9-1-1 while making her way to the door. Her finger shook above the send button as she peeked through the window. The early sun shone on a familiar, handsome face. Exhaling, she cleared her phone and unlocked the door.

"Good morning, Mitch. I didn't expect to see you back so soon."

"And a beautiful morning it is . . . now. I couldn't stay away." He winked and her stomach flipped.

She led him to the counter, where he set down an orange-to-yellow ombre pitcher. A whiff of his spicy cologne weakened her knees—she'd always loved the cardamom, vanilla spice mixture. She swallowed as she picked up the pitcher and tried to refocus her thoughts back to business. "It's stunning. I've been wanting to add to my Amberina collection." She flipped it over. "It's Fenton too. Great find."

He leaned on the counter. "I aim to please. Maybe this will buy me an evening out with a pretty girl."

Elaine's face heated as she opened the cash register. She pulled out a twenty and held it out to him. "Unfortunately, it won't pay for much more than Taco Johns."

"You know that isn't what I meant. Come on, Elly. Go out with me."

Elly? No one had ever given her a nickname before.

His finger caressed her hand when he took the money. "Just one date."

She wasn't ready to say yes, but she didn't want to push too hard either. "I don't have the time with the rally coming up, but I enjoy it when you stop by to talk."

"I'm taking that as a maybe. Did you have time to look up that teapot yet?" He picked it up from the exact place she'd left it yesterday.

"I'm so sorry. I forgot all about it. I had some excitement yesterday."

"What happened?"

Not sure how much she should tell him, she said, "A man came in and I had to call the police."

"Are you OK?" He squeezed her hand then slowly released it, sending warmth through her.

"A little shaken up, but I'm fine. Give me a minute to check on the teapot." She grabbed her phone and pulled up the website. Fifty-two comments. "Looks like your teapot is popular. Wow, someone just offered me a thousand for it. Maybe we should get it appraised before we accept any offers."

"That's a good idea." Mitch checked his watch. "I'd better run. There's an auction in Deadwood this afternoon. I'll keep a look out for you. I have an eye for pretty things." He tipped his head at her and strode toward the door. "I'll see you later."

She waved at his back as the door closed behind him. Elaine squealed, then took a deep breath to calm her excitement. The next time he pressed her for a date she wasn't going to be such a coward.

In the late afternoon, after hours of no customers, she sat on the floor dusting cookie jars. The bell on the front door jingled and she wondered if it might be Mitch. No, he was in Deadwood. She scrambled up to greet her customer.

A small girl, not even as tall as the counter, walked toward the shelf of cut-glass vases. Stray blonde hairs floated around a tangled mess of hair. The girl's navy and pink striped dress barely covered her bottom and the long sleeves stopped halfway down her arms.

Elaine waited for an adult to follow the girl inside. When no one did, she hurried over and knelt to her level. "Hello. Are you here alone?"

The girl blinked several times. "I'm looking for something for my nana. Daddy said she likes this store."

"How old are you?"

She held up four fingers. "Do you have kitties like this?" She pointed to a kitten appliqué on her dress.

"I think so. Did you come with an adult?"

"My daddy. He's outside."

Relief washed over Elaine. "Should we go get him? You really shouldn't be in the store without him. I bet he's worried."

"He's on the phone. I'm not supposed to bother him when he's on the phone." She looked around, then pointed. "That's pretty!" She ran over to a shelf and picked up a rare Hummel figurine of a little girl with two geese.

"And expensive." Elaine took the figurine from her and put it back in its place. Time to move those to the locked cabinet.

"Do you have one with a girl and a kitty?"

"Let's go get your dad first and then I'll show you."

They stepped into the foyer as the door opened. A man with short wavy hair, wearing blue scrubs and a tense expression, stepped inside. He glanced at Elaine before his gaze landed on the child. His face softened. "Clara! Why did you run off like that?" He walked over to them, his hands on his hips.

"You were on the phone." She mimicked his stance. "I'm not supposed to bother you when you're on the phone."

"That doesn't mean you can leave without me."

"I was bored." She rolled her head back and dropped to the floor in a dramatic heap.

Elaine smiled.

The man faced Elaine. "I'm sorry if she was bothering you."

"Not at all. She said she was shopping for her nana."

Clara sat up. "Her birthday is tomorrow, and she wants a kitty cat."

The man sighed. "Get off the floor and we can look for a kitty cat, but don't you think Nana would prefer a pretty vase or lamp?"

Clara stood up straight and lifted her chin. "Daddy! She wants a kitty cat. She told me so. I said, 'Nana, do you want a kitty cat for your birthday?' and she said, 'Goodness no, child. What would I do with a cat?' and I laughed and said, 'Not a real kitty,' and she laughed and said, 'Well, I would love a fake kitty.'" She looked at Elaine. "Do you have any fake kitties?"

Elaine looked from Clara to her dad. "I do have quite the kitty cat section in the other room. I'd be happy to show you."

"Where?" Clara ran down the row of valuable glass vases much like the bald man yesterday. Elaine gripped her chest as she braced herself for the sound of breaking glass.

"Clara! Stop! You're going to break something." Her dad hurried after her.

The girl stopped next to the Sioux Pottery. Elaine held her breath, hoping she wouldn't touch any of it—they were her best-selling items.

When her dad caught Clara, he bent in front of her. "I promised I would help you find a birthday gift for Nana, but you have to listen or we're going home. Now, if you promise to not run away anymore, we'll see if this nice lady will show us her kitty collection."

Clara nodded.

Her dad stood and took his daughter's small hand in his. He nodded at Elaine. "Please lead the way."

Grateful for his quick response and gentle parenting, she started toward the other display room. "The kitties are in the other side of the shop. Follow me." She walked back down the vase aisle, through the foyer, and under an arch to the other display room. Along the back wall, light-wood shelves held her collection of china.

Before reaching the china, she stopped at a case full of Lenox. "See, I have an entire shelf dedicated to kitty cats."

Clara's eyes widened as she put her hands on a shelf and pulled herself onto her toes.

Her dad swung her into his arms. "Now comes the hard part. Which one should we buy?" She reached out to grab one, but he pulled her away. "Don't touch. They're breakable."

She put her chubby hands on his cheeks. "Can I have one too?"

"Maybe. Why don't you pick one out for Nana, then tell me which one you'd like. Maybe you'll get one for your birthday."

Her face scrunched up as she looked back at the cat figurines. "I like them all." There were at least a dozen white cats in different poses.

Unsure how to help her decide, Elaine picked up a cat lying in a flower box. "This one is rimmed in real gold. Quite the collector's items."

"I like the ballerina kitty." Clara pointed to the cat in a pink tutu with a gold crown.

"And which one for Nana?" her dad asked.

"The kitty with the basket of yarn. She loves to make me things with yarn." Clara's smile filled her face.

"Good choice." Elaine picked up that kitty. "I'll make sure to wrap it up really well, so it doesn't break. Is there anything else you'd like to see?"

"Please, can we get the ballerina today?" Clara stuck out her bottom lip.

"Not today, lamb." He kissed her head.

The sweet moment touched Elaine as she walked back to her desk. She wrapped the figurine in tissue paper before putting it in a brown paper sack with a white lily drawn on the front.

"Pretty flower." Clara reached for the bag.

"Careful." Her dad held it out of reach.

Elaine smiled. "I'm glad you like it. I drew it."

His brows rose. "I'm impressed. I think my mother-in-law might like the bag more than the kitty."

"No, Daddy. She loves kitties. But Mommy loves flowers. She likes the orange ones the best, right?"

"Tiger lilies?" Elaine asked.

He smoothed Clara's hair out of her face as he nodded without looking at Elaine.

She reached under the counter, pulled out a stack of bags, and flipped through them until she found the tiger lilies. Her art brought her the most joy when it was shared, so she held it out to Clara's dad. "Here, take her this one."

"That's not necessary."

Clara grabbed the bag. "We can take it to her. She'll love it. Thank you, shop lady."

"It will get ruined outside," he said.

"Why would you leave it outside?" Elaine asked.

"That's where Mommy is. She's outside at the graveyard." Clara hugged the bag to her. "Please, can we keep it?"

Elaine's chest ached. She understood their pain all too well. "Then I insist that you take it. If it gets ruined, you can come back for another one."

His gazed warmed with a grin that caused Elaine's pulse to quicken.

"Let's go to Nana's party." Clara tugged on his hand.

Elaine looked at Clara as heat scorched her cheeks. "Have fun." Then she braved another glance at the little girl's father.

"Thanks," he whispered, taking Clara's hand and turning toward the door. Clara chatted about her nana and kitties as they walked.

He opened the door and shot Elaine one more contemplative look, and with a slight nod they disappeared outside.

Elaine sighed as she cooled her face with the stack of bags. What a day. She'd take embarrassment over two cute, attentive guys instead of one violent thug any day.

CHAPTER 3

Judah held onto Clara's hand as they left the antique store. She clutched the paper bag with the tiger lilies to her chest. How was he going to convince her that they couldn't leave the bag at the cemetery? They had rules about what could be left there, and paper bags weren't allowed. But the kind gesture had waylaid him with such a wave of emotion that he'd barely been able to speak.

"That shop lady was nice." Clara started skipping.

Judah walked faster to keep up. "Yes, she was." And pretty, with red curls in disarray around her shoulders. She'd floated around the store like a fairy. And what a tiny thing. He doubted that she even reached his collarbone and at six feet, he wasn't all that tall.

His chest ached. What was wrong with him, checking out a woman when his life was still turned upside down The only girl he should focus on was the one beside him singing about the birds.

When they reached his SUV, he knelt beside Clara. "Hold Nana's gift carefully so it doesn't break." He handed her the bag then settled Clara in her car seat, kissing her head before shutting the door.

Sweat ran down his neck from the summer heat as he jogged around the truck and climbed in. He blasted the air conditioner. If they didn't leave soon, he'd be late for the birthday dinner, but he dreaded going.

"Daddy, go." Clara kicked his seat.

Judah turned to lecture her about kicking his seat—again—but it slipped away as she grinned her biggest smile. "Patience, lamb. I'm going." He pulled onto the road.

As he drove through town, he thought of the pretty redhead. He hadn't even gotten her name. But thanks to his daughter, he had an excuse to go back and ask.

He pulled up to the curb outside his mother-in-law's split-level home. Cars filled the driveway, but one of them caused anxiety to rise in his gut. A bright red 1990 Camaro. He groaned. Of course his sister-in-law would be at her mother's party.

Judah helped Clara out. As soon as her feet hit the ground, she ran across the lush green lawn to the front door. He trudged after her.

By the time he walked into the foyer, Clara had cleared the top stair, then disappeared from view. Loud voices and bursts of laughter almost drove him back outside. Why did his in-laws have to be so rambunctious? He slowly climbed the stairs and found the living room full of people. His mother-in-law sat in her recliner with her feet up, her swollen ankles peeking out from her flowery dress. She pulled Clara onto her lap with a groan.

"Happy birthday, Nana!"

"What a sweet thing you are!" Her voice rose above the chatter. She pulled out the gift and tore the paper off.

His sister-in-law Zoe stepped up to him. "About time you got here." Her straight, dark hair was pulled into a ponytail, like usual. The only make-up she wore was think, black eyeliner, enhancing her unfriendly look.

"It's barely five."

"Party started at four thirty."

"I had to work. Who hosts a party at four thirty on a Tuesday night?"

"We like to start early. Were you in such a hurry you couldn't brush your daughter's hair?"

Judah sighed and glanced at Clara. Her hands waved all over as she spoke. He heard *shop lady* and *lots of kitties*. Her long hair hung in clumps down her back. He'd taken her to daycare at six that morning. Maybe he had forgotten to brush her hair, but she'd been half asleep.

"And that dress is way too small. It barely covers her bottom. You've got to take better care of her."

He clenched his jaw. "It's her favorite, and she wanted to wear something special for her nana. Whitney bought it for her." The back door opened and the scent of hamburgers filled the air. Judah spotted his escape. "Excuse me, I think the food's done."

As soon as he walked into the kitchen, Whitney's older brother stopped him.

"Hey, Doc. I've got to show you my toe. Hurts like a mother." He took off his shoe and lifted his foot as high as he could.

One of Whitney's uncles smacked Judah on the arm. "When you're done, I have a question about my colitis."

So much for an escape. Laughter pierced his ears before Clara's older cousin plowed into him, followed by three more boys. After eight hours at the hospital, his quiet home beckoned him. He had hoped he could survive the party until cake was served—Clara needed to spend time with her nana—but at the rate the evening was going, he'd be happy to stay through dinner.

****

Elaine held up a brass perfume bottle. "It's from the 1920s and these roses are hand-painted." She squeezed the rubber ball attached to tubing. "The atomizer still works."

The elderly woman took the bottle. "It's gorgeous, but we rode our bikes up here from Denver. I'm afraid it won't make the trip home."

The husband put his hand on the shoulder of his wife's leather jacket. "It has always been my dream to ride to the Sturgis Motorcycle Rally. When my buddy had to get a hip replacement, my sweetheart stepped up."

"That must have been quite a trip." Elaine smiled, familiar with her customer's hesitation and prepared to help. "Would you like me to ship it to you?"

The lady's eyes brightened as she nodded and pulled out her credit card. When they'd finished their transaction, she leaned across the counter. "That's a beautiful necklace you have on. Where did you buy it?"

Elaine fingered the rose quartz pendant wrapped in copper wire hanging from a copper chain. "Thank you. I made it."

"Really? You should be selling those. It's beautiful."

Elaine unclasped the necklace and held it out. "Rose quartz is South Dakota's state mineral."

"It's lovely."

"You can have it. I can make another one. It will remind you of your time in the Black Hills."

"Thank you." She opened her wallet. "How much?"

"It's not for sale. It's my gift to you."

"Nonsense." The lady set fifty dollars on the counter. "I insist."

Before Elaine could argue, the phone rang. "The Mother Lode Antique Shop, Elaine speaking." The couple left with the necklace and the money still on the counter.

"Hello, I'm Bridget Smalls. I work for the sheriff's department. Do you have a minute to talk?"

Her stomach flipped. "Yes, of course." Had she done something wrong? Should she have called her probation officer after the incident yesterday?

"I'm the victims' coordinator. I'm calling as your advocate, to make sure you're aware of your legal rights, the support services available to you, and anything else you might need. Officer McGuire gave me your information. First, I want to make sure you're OK. McGuire said you hit your head."

"It's fine. Only a dull ache now." Her voice quivered. Despite their help yesterday, she hated talking to the police.

"Good. I also want to update you on the case. The perpetrator is Wallace Frank. He pled guilty in court today for an assault charge, but he's already bailed out."

The ache intensified. "Will he come back here?"

"I doubt it. We believe he's involved in a human trafficking operation we've been investigating."

And Elaine had been terrifyingly close to being his victim. Nausea rolled in her stomach. "Trafficking? Why would he come to my shop?"

"I'm guessing it's a wrong time, wrong place kind of thing. Don't hesitate to call the police if you see him again."

"But you don't think he'll come back here, right?"

"We don't know, but the bike rally is a magnet for traffickers. We're close to the interstate, which we call the Midwest Pipeline because it's used to deliver victims to other parts of the country."

"That's awful. I had no idea that was happening."

"Most people don't. Traffickers are good at deception. It wouldn't be a bad idea for you to educate yourself on how to identify traffickers and their victims in case that's why Wallace was in your shop."

"Of course." Elaine picked up a pen. "How do I do that?"

"Check out the website Rally for the Challenge dot com."

Elaine scribbled the name on a sheet of paper.

"Call the police if you see anything suspicious, but do not confront the victims or traffickers. This number is my work cell, but you can also call the Meade County Sheriff's Office and ask for me."

Elaine's mind and emotions swirled. "Anything else?"

"That's all for today. If you have any questions, please call."

"OK. Thanks." Elaine ended the call, then added Bridget's name and number to her contacts. With the shop once again empty, she looked up the website, anxious to learn as much as she could in case anything like yesterday happened again.

Be aware. Stay Safe. At the bottom of the page, she clicked on *Red Flags for Possible Trafficking*. Could she have met a trafficking victim without realizing it?

Sneaks out at night or runs away from home.

Stops attending school.

Has tattoos of gang symbols, bar codes, or dollar signs on their neck or chest.

The list went on. She scanned until she got to the end.

Thirteen years old, the average age a child is first exploited through prostitution.

Horrified, Elaine dropped her phone to the counter, her body trembling. For the first time, she was thankful for an empty store. She needed the business, and the income, but those kids . . . picking up her phone again, she typed away. She hadn't been able to help her foster son, but she had to find a way to help these kids.

CHAPTER 4

Elaine poured her third cup of coffee for the morning, then added lots of cream and three spoonsful of sugar. She took a sip, still hating the taste but needing the caffeine. The bell above the front door rang, so she hurried from the kitchen through the rows of antiques to the foyer.

Clara's dad smiled as he closed the door. "Hello, again."

"Good morning."

"Good morning, uh . . ." He shuffled from one foot to the other, gazing at her until she glanced at the creamer swirling in her coffee much like her emotions. "I didn't catch your name yesterday."

"Elaine." She met his intense stare. Tempted to look away again, she fought the urge and stood straighter.

"It's nice to meet you, Elaine. I'm Judah."

She set her mug on the desk. "Did Clara's nana like her gift?"

"She loved it, all the more because Clara was so excited about it." He gave her a crooked smile.

Her nerves bubbled. "Is there something else I can help you with?"

"I want to purchase the ballerina kitty for Clara's birthday."

"Of course." Elaine scooted around the desk and led the way to the kitten shelves. She picked up the ballerina and handed it to him.

Instead of walking away, he stood there staring at the shelves. "Thanks. Maybe I should get a couple. Which other ones do you think she'd like?"

Elaine glanced back at the shelf. What would a four-year-old like? She never would have considered getting a Lenox figurine for child, but Clara was obviously different. Before she could ask Judah about his daughter, the bell rang again. "Let me think about it for a few minutes. I'll be right back." She hurried to the entrance, excited to have another customer.

A woman with long black hair stood in the foyer. When she turned around, Elaine gasped. The woman—more like a teenager— had blood smeared across her cheek. Her lip was swollen. "I need help," the teen said.

"What happened?" Elaine ran to her.

"Can you hide me?" She glanced behind her, then around the shop. "Please. He's coming."

"Follow me." Elaine pulled the girl toward the kitchen. Adrenalin rushed through her.

She was halfway there when the door crashed open. Elaine spun around to see Wallace filling the doorway.

The girl shrieked.

"Go through there. There's a door in the kitchen that leads to the basement. You can hide there," Elaine whispered in her ear.

The girl ran.

Elaine turned back to her desk. Where was her phone? Wallace stomped toward her. She cleared her tight throat. "The cops are coming. They've been watching the shop."

He kept walking. Not sure what else to do, Elaine stood her ground. When he was close enough, he smacked her across the face. She fell into a shelf, crashing to the floor as pain cracked through her cheek and antiques shattered around her. Wallace hovered over her. She searched the floor for something to use as a weapon. A jagged piece of glass lay only a couple of feet away. She reached for it as a flash of blue tackled Wallace.

Judah twisted one of Wallace's arms behind his back and pulled upward until the bald man cried out. He looked at her as he heaved in deep breaths. "Call the police!"

Elaine nodded, but her feet slipped across broken glass. She braced herself, and a piece of glass sliced through her left hand.

Wallace flipped around and pushed Judah off him. They scrambled to their feet. Elaine tried to push herself up, but she couldn't get traction. She growled in frustration, feeling helpless. Judah crouched low, but Wallace pushed him to the side. He ran for the door. Judah followed him.

She couldn't give up now. Elaine tried to stand again but slipped back down, so she pushed the glass away. She'd crawl to her phone if she had to.

Judah jogged in and knelt in front of her. "He's gone. Are you OK?" He lifted her chin with his finger and studied her face.

Her cheek radiated with pain, but her hand throbbed the most. She turned it over. Blood covered her palm.

Judah took her hand in his. "I need to wrap this. Do you have a first aid kit?"

She shook her head. "We need to call the police."

"I will. Where's a clean towel?"

"In the kitchen in the back."

Judah gently set her hand, palm up, on her bent knee before hurrying away. Elaine closed her eyes. How could this have happened again?

A moment later, Judah returned with a tea towel. "An ambulance and a police officer are on their way." He took her hand and wrapped the towel around it. Blood soaked through the first layer. He wrapped it again and again until the outer layer stayed white, then he tied the corners of the towel together. She trembled as exhaustion claimed her mind and body.

"Who was that guy?"

Elaine shivered. "Wallace. He was after the girl. The girl!" How could she have forgotten?

"What girl?"

"The one hiding in the basement."

Judah's eyes widened. "What are you involved in?"

******

Judah's heart raced as fast as his mind. "Where's the basement?"

"There's a door in the kitchen."

He nodded and stood.

"Police! Hands up!"

Judah turned and a sharp pain sliced his side. Probably bruised his rib when the jerk punched him. Two officers—their guns drawn—glared at him. He slowly raised his hands.

"Officer McGuire," Elaine said, "this man's helping me. He's not the bad guy."

The younger of the two officers lowered his weapon but kept his eyes on Judah. "What's your name?"

"Judah Demski."

"Why are you here?"

"I was buying a present when that man ran in."

The officer holstered his gun and the older one copied him. "You can put your hands down." McGuire walked over to Elaine. "What happened?"

"A girl came in asking for help. She had a fat lip. I told her to hide in the basement, but before I could call the police, Wallace came in and hit me. Thankfully, Judah was here. He saved me." Elaine beamed up at him.

He stood straighter, surprised by the admiration on her pretty face.

"Where's Wallace?"

Judah shook his head. "He got away."

"The girl?"

"In the basement, I hope," Elaine said, pointing toward the back of the house. "I didn't actually see where she went."

"You wait here." Both officers headed back, pulling out their guns.

Judah focused on Elaine. Colored pieces of glass surrounded them. Not wanting her to get hurt again, he kicked the largest pieces away. "I'm going to pull you up, OK?"

She nodded, her curls bouncing around her.

Careful to avoid her cheek and hand, he gripped her by the armpits and pulled her up. She weighed less than he'd imagined. As he wrapped his arm around her, her pale skin turned pink, hiding the splash of freckles on her nose. Her right cheekbone was swollen and tinged purple.

Her whole body shook. "Thank you. If you hadn't tackled him, he might have found her."

He led her to the stool behind the counter and helped her onto the seat, keeping his hand on her waist. "You know that man who attacked you?"

Her blue eyes found his. "Two days ago, he came in looking for some girl. The police arrested him, but he bailed out. I was hoping he'd never come back."

"Who is he?"

"I don't know. The police said his name is Wallace. They think he might be involved in trafficking."

The teenage girl ran into the room and embraced Elaine, almost knocking her off the stool. "Thank you. You saved me."

The police officers followed. Office McGuire's radio squawked. "The ambulance is here," he said. "You both need to be checked out by the paramedics."

Elaine leaned forward to look in the girl's eyes. "Are you OK?"

She nodded. "I am now."

"I'm Elaine. What's your name?"

"Jules." She smiled then winced, lifting her fingers to her lip. "Wally got a good slap in before I escaped."

"Why did he hit you?"

"Teach me a lesson, I suppose. He was spittin' mad when the other girl escaped so he wanted to make sure none of us would try."

Anger coursed through Judah. He wished he'd hit Wallace harder, or at least tried to restrain him better. That man deserved to spend the rest of his life in jail.

"You're so brave." Elaine grabbed Jules's hand. "I'm not sure I'd have had the nerve to escape."

Jules's lips lifted into an uneven smile.

Officer McGuire held the door for the two female paramedics to enter carrying blue duffle bags. He led them over to the counter. "Elaine. Jules. The paramedics need to take a look at your injuries."

The taller paramedic set her bag down as she inspected Jules. "That cut on your lip needs to be looked at. I'm not sure if it's deep enough for stitches."

Jules leaned close to Elaine. She put her arm around the teen. "You can trust them to help."

Jules nodded. "Will you stay with me?"

"Of course." Elaine looked at the paramedic. "You should take care of Jules first. I'm fine."

Unexpected pride filled Judah. Elaine had to be in a lot of pain, but she put the teen first. Wanting to make sure she got the attention she needed too, he pointed at her hand. "Elaine needs stitches in her palm." The paramedics stared at him. "I'm a surgeon at Fort Meade."

The paramedic focused back on Elaine as she opened her bag and pulled out a flashlight. "Let's take a look."

Her partner pulled Jules aside as two male paramedics brought in a gurney. Jules sent Elaine a pleading look.

"I'll be right here where you can see me." Elaine smiled.

Jules nodded. She sat on the gurney as the paramedics took her blood pressure.

Judah focused on Elaine's injuries. Once the gaping wound was unwrapped, the paramedic shone her light on it. Glass sparkled in the cut. Judah winced. "You're going to need the glass plucked out too."

"Your face is swollen and red. What happened?" The paramedic put her light back in the bag.

"Wallace hit me and I fell against the glass shelves."

"Did you hit your head?"

"No."

Officer McGuire stepped over. "She hurt her head two days ago when she was pushed against the cabinets. She refused medical treatment, but while you're here, maybe you can check that out."

Judah's muscles tensed with anger. "Who did that?"

"Same guy. Must have bailed out." Officer McGuire rolled his eyes.

Judah folded his arms in front of his chest. "And now he's on the loose. How can you keep her safe?"

"Our resources are pretty thin right now. Best thing for her would be for her to close for a few days." He glanced from Judah to Elaine.

She shook her head. "I can't close with the rally starting. I need the money."

Judah clamped his mouth shut. He wanted to argue, but it really wasn't any of his business.

Jules ran over to Elaine. "They said I have to go to the hospital. I don't want to go."

"I have to go too." She held up her cut palm. "We can go together."

"Do you know who's working in the ED today?" Judah glanced at the paramedic.

"Saw Conda when we were there earlier. Wilson might be working too."

Judah smiled at Jules. "Both are great doctors. I recommend Dr. Conda. She's kind and gentle. You'll like her. I could meet you there and request her for you."

Jules nodded. He glanced at Elaine, hoping he hadn't overstepped his boundaries. She beamed at him with the same look as before. A sense of protectiveness rose in him. He had no idea what else he could do, but he vowed to himself then and there that he'd do whatever it took to help her feel safe.

CHAPTER 5

Elaine sucked in a deep breath as the emergency department doctor pushed the hooked needle through the skin on her palm. She couldn't feel the pokes thanks to the local anesthesia, but knowing what he was doing turned her stomach.

When he finished, the white-haired doctor wrapped her hand in a sterile bandage. "That should do it. We'll see you back next week to get them removed. Keep it clean and dry in the meantime."

"Thanks." Elaine hopped off the exam table, gathered her purse, and stepped out of the examination room. She looked around for Jules, wishing they had been able to stay together.

Judah stood at the nurses' station chatting with a woman in scrubs. Gratitude rushed over her. What a blessing that he chose today to shop for Clara. Maybe she could draw a few more flowers with kittens for Clara, as a thank you.

He stopped talking when he saw her and walked over. "How are you feeling?"

"My hand is still numb, but my cheek is throbbing. The nurse gave me some pain meds that should kick in soon. You didn't have to stay. I'm sure you have better things to do."

"I got another surgeon to cover my rounds and had my nurse reschedule the only surgery I had this afternoon. I wanted to make sure you have a ride home."

Warmth spread through her at his thoughtfulness. "Have you seen Jules?"

"No!" Someone screamed behind them.

Elaine turned as Jules stormed out of a room. When she saw Elaine, she ran to her, tears streaming down her face.

"What's wrong?" Elaine asked.

"They said I have to go to a foster home."

"That's not so bad, is it?"

"I've already been in a foster home. I hated it. Can I stay with you?"

"Jules. It's time to go." A lady in a brown skirt and coat approached them.

The girl scooted behind Elaine. "I told you, I'm not going. I'm almost seventeen. I can live on my own."

"You don't have a choice."

"Can I please stay with you?" Jules squeezed Elaine's arm.

Shame pricked her. She didn't deserve Jules's trust. "I'm sorry, but I can't take you in. I wish I could."

Jules hung her head. "I get it. No one ever wants me," she whispered.

Sadness filled Elaine's heart as she turned around and hugged the girl. "I want you with me, I just . . . can't."

"Why not?"

The familiar heaviness of regret pressed against Elaine. "I'm not an approved foster mom." Not anymore.

They held onto each until the social worker cleared her throat. Elaine released Jules. Wanting to offer comfort, she brushed the girl's hair behind her shoulders, revealing black marks on her neck. "Is that a tattoo?"

"It's a barcode."

Words from the human trafficking website flashed through Elaine's mine.

"That's an unusual tattoo," Judah said.

Jules shrugged. "It's how the johns know how much I cost."

He gasped. "What?"

Elaine tried not to cry.

"I'm twenty bucks. Some of the girls are worth more." Her words cut through Elaine's heart far deeper than any piece of glass. But it wasn't just what Jules said, it was how she stood—shoulders slumped, gaze on the ground, face hidden behind her hair. She believed what she was saying.

Words escaped Elaine. Her own feelings of worthlessness had too often attacked her, leaving her feeling like garbage. She didn't want Jules feeling that way, not for a second. She couldn't take her home and she couldn't end trafficking, but maybe she could give the girl hope in something else. She looked at the social worker. "Can we have a couple more minutes?"

The woman sighed but nodded.

Elaine pulled Jules away from the nurses' station for a bit of privacy. "A few months ago, I found an old crystal lamp at a garage sale. It was only five dollars because it was broken. But I knew that with a little attention and love it could be beautiful again. That day I had been feeling sorry for myself, but something about that lamp gave me hope, so I bought it, got it fixed, and put it on my nightstand so I could see it every day. After some research, I discovered it was worth almost two hundred dollars. Just because someone doesn't recognize the value of an object doesn't mean it's worthless. You're worth *so* much more than twenty dollars, and you deserve much more than a life of running away."

Jules looked up. "Do you really think so?"

"I do, and I think you should give this foster family a chance."

"I wish I could just go home."

"Why isn't that an option?" Judah asked.

The social worker stepped toward them. "She was removed from her home and her mom's rights were terminated. The rest is confidential information."

"My mom's boyfriend hit me, but it wasn't such a bad place if I stayed out of his way," Jules said. "At least I got to do whatever I wanted most of the time."

Elaine tipped Jules's face up to look her in the eye. "If anyone hit you, it *was* a bad place. And you deserve better than that too."

"You're the only one who thinks so. I don't understand why I can't stay with you."

And Elaine couldn't tell her with Judah, the social worker, and a group of nurses listening in. "Just because you can't stay with me doesn't mean I can't help. I don't know how I can, but I'll find a way."

The social worker touched Jules's shoulder. "It's time to go. You'll be safe at the foster home. I promise."

Jules sagged. "Fine."

Elaine gripped her shoulder. "Promise me you won't run away."

Jules nodded as she followed the social worker out of the emergency department.

Elaine sighed. "I wish I could help her."

Judah stepped beside her. "You already have."

"So have you." She smiled at him. "Thank you for fighting Wallace. I'd hate to think of what would have happened if you hadn't been there."

"Glad I could help." He shook his head as he looked toward the door where Jules had walked away. "I had no idea trafficking took place here."

"Me neither. Not until this week."

"I'm glad Jules escaped."

"I'm glad she had the courage to run." Elaine hugged herself. "It's going to take that kind of courage for her to heal too."

"She's a brave girl." Judah stepped in front of Elaine and motioned toward the door. "Are you ready to go home? My car's out front."

She nodded. They stepped outside as pink and orange streaked along the horizon bringing unexpected beauty to such a dismal day. "Look at that sunset. It's too bad I'm not at my shop. I could set up my easel on the porch and paint this."

"You paint too?"

"Painting is my favorite hobby."

"What kind of painting?"

"I'm proficient in acrylics and watercolor, but I prefer oil because it dries slower. It gives me more time to blend, and blending the paint on the canvas relaxes me."

They got into his car and headed north. Neither of them spoke, which gave her time to watch the sunset fade.

Ten minutes later, they parked in front of her shop. Elaine stared at the front door. Had she locked it before she left? What if Wallace came back? Her fingers shook as she gripped the door handle. The light had faded and darkness clouded her home as fear descended on her. All the peace of the sunset drained away.

"I'll walk in with you and make sure it's safe."

Her gaze snapped to Judah's. The kindness in his eyes moved her beyond her initial relief. It stirred feelings she wasn't ready to explore. "Thank you."

They walked up to the house, standing so close that the occasional brush of his scrubs against her bare arm sent tingles through her. She liked having him that close. She felt safe with him.

"I can't stop thinking of Jules," he said. "How could her mom pick her abusive boyfriend over her child? I'd die protecting Clara."

Elaine nodded. "It's awful but probably more common than we realize." She didn't want to think about her own mom's rejection. "I hope Jules adjusts to her foster family."

"She seemed pretty attached to you."

"I don't know why, but I hope I can find a way to stay in her life."

They stepped onto the porch. Judah stopped and tried the knob. "It's locked."

Her anxiety eased as she handed him the keys.

"Let me go in first."

"Sounds good to me." Elaine stood in the doorway as he entered the house, then reached over and turned on the overhead light. She pulled her phone from her pocket and unlocked it. She'd learned her lesson and was never going to be without it again.

Judah disappeared through the archway then returned. "Nothing is disturbed. Are you going to be OK here tonight?"

Truthfully, she didn't know, but what choice did she have? She hugged herself. "I'll be fine."

"I wish there was more I could do to keep you safe." His brows scrunched together, then his eyes widened. "I've got it. I'll be right back." He ran out of the house. "Lock the door behind me!"

The door slammed shut, leaving Elaine confused. She stood in the foyer listening to the clock ticking. Left alone, uneasiness gripped her like a paint tube squeezer.

The wounded look on Jules's face haunted Elaine. And her pleas to stay with her had echoed a pain she'd tried so hard to forget. Her sweet foster son had clung to her with the same desperation the last time she'd seen him. She rubbed her aching chest, wishing pain meds would numb the deeper hurt of losing her baby.

Dwelling on her loss never solved anything though. She couldn't change things with Marcus, but maybe she could make a difference in Jules's life.

CHAPTER 6

Judah parked in front of The Mother Lode. A tan-and-black head appeared between the front seats. Sheba's tongue hung out of her mouth as she panted, looking out the front window. He stroked her muzzle. "Ready?"

He stepped out into the warm night and let Sheba out of the back. "Heel." She walked beside him up the sidewalk and onto the porch of the yellow Victorian house.

The open sign still hung in the window. Confused, he turned the knob and let himself in. The bell jingled as his pulse sped up.

"In the dining room!"

He flipped the sign to closed, locked the door, then followed her voice. He found her placing old books on the once-broken shelves. A large box filled with broken glass sat next to her. "You've been hard at work."

"I've been wanting to clean up this shelf for weeks. I guess now is as good a time as ever." She stood and wiped her uninjured hand on her jeans. When she turned, her smile fell as she stepped back. "Is that your dog?"

"She is. Her name is Sheba. Sit, Sheba." The German shepherd sat. "Good girl." He glanced back at Elaine. Her eyes were wide and her skin pale. "She won't hurt you. I'd like you to borrow her."

She shook her head. "I can't take your dog. Clara would be upset, I'm sure."

"Clara will understand, especially when I tell her we can come visit her." *And you.*

"I don't know the first thing about taking care of a dog. And I can't have a dog running around with customers."

"She won't run around. She's well trained, so she'll go and do whatever you tell her. But most importantly, she'll protect you if she feels you're threatened. It's only until the police find Wallace or we come up with another solution."

Her cute little nose scrunched. "The thing is, I'm not really a dog person."

He hadn't considered that. "How about a trial run? Let her stay for a few days. See if having her here makes you feel safer. I'd feel better knowing she's here."

Elaine tilted her head. "Why would *you* feel better?"

"Because I want you to be safe." He held his breath, hoping she'd agree. He wouldn't sleep that night if she didn't.

"Are you always this concerned for people you just met?"

"Only the ones who get attacked trying to save young girls from trafficking."

She smiled. "OK. She can stay."

He relaxed. "The first thing we need to do is help you become a dog person. Would you like to pet her?" He stepped toward Elaine, signaling Sheba to go with him.

Elaine's hand shook as she reached toward the dog. She snatched it back before she touched her head. "Are you sure? She's really big."

Judah chuckled. "She won't hurt you. You should see the way Clara climbs all over her." He knelt, and Sheba licked his cheek. "See, she's all sweetness."

Elaine reached out again. She trailed her fingers over Sheba's back. "How will she protect me?"

"My wife trained her from the time she was a puppy. Sheba is great at sensing danger. Once when they were out jogging, my wife turned the corner to our street and Sheba laid down, refusing to move. Whitney couldn't get her to budge and had to take a different route home. Minutes later a gun fight broke out after a drug deal gone bad. Whitney had seen the group but didn't notice anything suspicious. Sheba did. Since Whitney's death, she's been even more sensitive. She wakes me up if a deer tramps through the yard."

"What if she attacks a customer?"

"She won't. If she does, there's a reason. If anything, she'll make that guy think twice before coming back."

"Maybe pepper spray would be a better idea."

"It certainly wouldn't hurt. Do you have any?"

She shook her head.

"Until you can get some, maybe having Sheba would help. How about I stop by in the morning to see how you two are doing?"

"I'd like that."

He would too. "I need to get home to Clara, but before I leave, let me walk you through some basic commands so you and Sheba can get to know each other better."

****

Elaine laid in bed, staring at the huge dog on her doggie pillow beside the bedroom's bow window. Sheba stretched out and rolled over. Then she groaned.

It was going to be a long night. Elaine reached for her phone and Sheba sat up. "It's just me. I'm checking the time," she said, hoping the dog would lie back down. She didn't move.

Elaine looked at her phone. Two in the morning. They had four more hours to try to sleep.

Something crashed downstairs.

Sheba raced to the door, growling. Elaine hurried to the window. A black Lincoln sat under the streetlight. She gripped her phone tighter.

Sheba barked. Another crash. Voices floated up through the wood floors beneath them.

Not again! Elaine fumbled with her phone. This couldn't be happening again.

"9-1-1. What's your emergency?"

"I think someone broke into my store."

"What's your address?"

"1409 Junction Avenue."

"Are you in the store?"

"Yes. I live upstairs."

"Are you upstairs right now?"

"Yes."

"Good. Stay there. I've got two officers responding. Can you lock the door of the room you're in now?"

Elaine glanced at the door. Sheba scratched at it. When Elaine crept closer, the dog growled.

"Ma'am? Are you able to lock the door?"

"Yes. I think so." But did she need to? If the criminals entered, Sheba would protect her. Right?

"Good. The first officer has arrived and is waiting for backup. What's your name?"

"Mary Russell."

"The second has arrived. The door has been forced open. They are entering the store now."

More voices floated up to her. Elaine stopped on her way to the door. Sheba didn't move.

"They have cleared the first floor and basement."

She sagged against the wall, relieved. "What do I do now?"

"You're safe to go down to meet them."

"Thank you."

"You're welcome."

Elaine hung up and crept toward the door, watching Sheba closely. Having Sheba around had eased her fear. Slightly. Maybe this partnership would work. When Elaine put her hand on the doorknob, Sheba sat. "You need to stay, OK?"

The dog put her head on her paws.

That was easier than she'd expected. Elaine opened the door, needing to meet with the police.

Sheba darted through the opening.

Oh, no! "Come back!" Elaine ran after the dog. "Sheba! Stop!" She stumbled down the stairs. What if the dog attacked a police officer?

Lights shone in the dining room, so she ran that way. She rounded the corner in time to see Sheba charging a female officer. "No!"

The officer lowered her gun. "Sheba, sit!" The dog skidded to a halt.

Elaine stopped, heaving in deep breaths. How had the officer done that?

"Where did you get this dog?" the woman asked, kneeling beside Sheba.

"It belongs to a friend."

"*She* belongs to my brother-in-law. How did she end up here?" She glared at Elaine, the dark uniform, dark eye liner, and dark bun enhancing her scowl.

Elaine's heart pounded. "Judah brought her over. He wanted her to protect me."

"It's a good thing I recognized her or she'd be dead. How—"

"About the break-in—" An officer with a buzz cut held up a football-sized rock. "Someone threw this through the picture window."

For the first time, Elaine noticed the breeze. She turned to where the large window had been. Glass covered the ground. She headed toward the broom closet again.

The other officer held up a hand. "Some of the glass has blood on it. I'll need to collect samples for the crime lab."

"Blood?" She shivered. Could it be Wallace's? Her nerves couldn't handle another encounter with him.

The officer pointed from the window to the back of the house. "It looks like two assailants crawled through after they broke the window. They fled when we arrived and managed to get away. Looks like a burglary gone wrong. You'll need to go through the store and see if anything was taken. They probably didn't know anyone was living upstairs." His radio crackled. He raised a finger before stepping into the other room to respond.

"Or maybe they weren't looking to rob the place." The female officer stood and rested her hand on her gun. "Why would Judah think you need protecting on a night someone happens to break in?"

Elaine's stomach tightened. "He was here earlier today when a man came in and assaulted me."

"Why was he here? How long have you known Judah?"

"We met a couple of days ago when he brought his daughter in to buy a gift for her grandmother. He came back today to buy something for his daughter." Why was she being so hostile?

"It's the trafficking case, Zoe." The officer returned and walked to Elaine, holding out his business card. "I'm Officer Holt and this is Officer Charles. We're going to need to see your ID."

"Of course. It's upstairs." Elaine took the card before heading to her room. How could this keep happening to her? When she returned, she gave her ID to Officer Holt. He grabbed his radio and walked to the shattered window. Sheba rubbed against Elaine's leg. She jumped and took a step back, giving the dog plenty of space.

"You don't seem to like Sheba much." Officer Charles narrowed her eyes at Elaine.

"We don't know each other yet. She's only been here a few hours."

She mumbled something about Judah, then crossed her arms. "You don't have any plywood lying around, do you?"

"There's some in the basement." Elaine pointed toward the kitchen.

"You wait here." Officer Charles disappeared around the corner.

Unsure what to do while she waited, Elaine grabbed the broom from the closet and headed toward the glass. The cool night air sent shivers across her skin.

Officer Holt reappeared. "Stop. I need to collect the glass for evidence." She'd already forgotten. He slid latex gloves on his hands then bent down to collect the pieces, placing them in a clear bag. "I've got what I need. Go ahead and clean up the rest." He took the evidence outside.

Once again, Elaine swept broken glass off her shop floor. She should call her insurance company—she still hadn't called for the items broken earlier that day. But even if they paid both of the claims, her payments were sure to skyrocket. Maybe she'd only report the window.

She looked up from a dustpan full of glass in time to see Officer Charles carrying a piece of wood into the room. Elaine rushed back to the closet and grabbed her toolbox. When Officer Holt reappeared, the three of them worked together to cover the gaping hole.

Elaine shivered as scenarios flew through her mind. Was it a robbery gone wrong or something more sinister? And what if the intruders came back? She hoped they'd been scared off for good, but she couldn't be sure.

"That should do the trick for now." Officer Charles handed Elaine the hammer. "We have officers patrolling the area, and we can try to step up a regular patrol in this area, but resources are thin with the rally. Is there anywhere you can go for the rest of the night?"

Elaine shook her head. "I don't have any family nearby."

"Any friends?"

Only Mitch, and she had no idea where he lived. She shook her head again.

The officers exchanged a look.

Officer Charles scowled. "Call 9-1-1 if you suspect anything suspicious. You'll need to make other arrangements in the morning. A dog you can't control isn't the best option. You're putting yourself *and* Sheba in danger."

When the officers left, Elaine locked the door behind them. She turned to see Sheba lying beside the desk. Despite the excitement of the night, the dog snored softly. "What am I going to do about you? You were supposed to keep me safe, not almost get shot." Sheba sat up. "Come on. I might as well try to get some sleep. Not everyone can sleep as easily as you."

CHAPTER 7

Judah buckled Clara into her car seat as Zoe pulled up the driveway with music blaring. If she'd driven across town to confront him in person, it wasn't going to be a quick conversation, so he started his car to keep Clara cool before stepping out of the garage to greet his sister-in-law.

Zoe slammed the car door and marched up to him, her ponytail swishing behind her. "How could you?"

He put his hands up in front of him. "What did I do now?"

"You gave my sister's dog away?"

"She's my dog. I can do whatever I want with her." And how did she know Sheba was gone?

She glared at him. "You had no right. I almost shot her."

Panic surged through him. "Who? Elaine or Sheba?"

"Sheba. Why would I shoot—who did you say? Who's Elaine?"

"The shop owner."

Zoe shook her head. "Her name is Mary."

"Short with red curly hair?"

"And unable to handle a well-trained dog? Yeah, that's Mary Russell."

That didn't make any sense. "Why were you there anyway?"

"A break-in."

"Is she OK?"

"She's fine." She punched her hands onto her hips. "How do you know her and why do you care?"

"I bought your mother's present from her, and the rest of it is none of your business. If you're done interrogating me, I have to go." He jogged back to his SUV, even more eager to see Elaine now.

"If you don't want Sheba, I'll take her!"

"What?" He stopped beside the driver's side door.

"If you don't want her, give her to me. Not Mary."

He didn't have time for Zoe's nonsense today. "I don't know what you're talking about, but I'm not giving up my dog."

"Daddy! Let's go!" Clara bounced in the backseat.

"Hold your horses." He waved at her before looking at his sister-in-law. "Thanks for your concern, but I have to get Clara to daycare before work." He slid behind the wheel.

Clara giggled. "I don't got horses. I just got a doggy and I want to see her."

"Me too." His stomach churned with the need to see for himself that Elaine was OK.

Ten minutes later, he pulled up to The Mother Lode and parked out front. A piece of plywood covered where the picture window used to be. Elaine stood outside painting a hilly landscape dotted with evergreen trees onto the tan wood. He exhaled, relieved to see her, then helped Clara out of her car seat.

She ran to Elaine. "That's pretty!"

She smiled down at his daughter. "Why, thank you, Miss Clara." She turned red-rimmed eyes toward him. A slight tinge of purple stained her make-up covered cheek.

His chest ached. "I heard about the break-in. Are you OK?"

She sighed. "Yes, but my shop's a mess." She placed the paintbrush on a can of green paint, then wiped her hands on her paint-splattered, oversized shirt. "Last night was a disaster."

"Do you know who broke in?"

She shook her head. "They escaped before the police could catch them. Nothing was stolen, but I didn't think there would be." She looked at Clara who stared at them as they talked. "Enough about that for now. Would you like to paint?" Then she glanced at Judah. "If that's OK with your dad?"

"Yes! Daddy, please?"

He looked at Elaine's paint-stained clothes, then at Clara's brand-new dress. "Are you sure? Do you want to show Nana your dress before you get paint on it?"

"She can wear my smock to protect her clothes," Elaine said.

He smiled. He should have known she'd have a solution. "Sure."

Clara cheered. Elaine took off her large shirt, revealing white overalls with even more multi-colored paint splatters. "Let's go inside and you can paint the other side of the board while your daddy and I talk." She gathered up the paint, brushes, and drop cloth before leading them inside. She set everything up again, then draped the smock over Clara. Judah chuckled when it reached the floor.

Elaine held up a thin paintbrush. "Make sure you don't dip the brush in too deep." She demonstrated in the light green paint. "This is the perfect amount. It's OK if it gets on the drop cloth, but you need to try to keep it off the floor."

Clara took the brush and painted broad strokes on the plywood. "Can I paint a smiley face?"

"Paint whatever you want."

Clara dipped the brush back in the paint. As she drew another line, Elaine shuffled toward the counter.

Judah followed. "Are you OK?"

"I almost got your dog shot. You have to take her with you."

"I don't understand. Why would they try to shoot her?"

"She ran out of the bedroom when I went to talk to the police." Elaine wrapped her arm around waist. "I swear, if that cop hadn't known what to say, she would have shot her."

Judah touched Elaine's shoulder, hoping to reassure her. "Sheba did what she was supposed to do. She protected you."

She faced him, her eyes watery. "But I don't want her to die for me. Believe me, I'm not worth it, and it would crush Clara."

Judah squeezed her shoulder. "You're starting to sound like that teenager at the hospital yesterday. You're worth so much more than you think too. Maybe after my shift, Clara and I can stop by and

I'll help you get to know Sheba better. If you're still worried about her after that, I can take her back."

"I usually keep the store open until nine. Is that too late?"

For Clara, yes, but Judah didn't want to leave Elaine scared and uncertain. "How about this? I'm done at six. I'll bring dinner and we'll work in between customers. If you don't mind, Clara can keep painting while you and I work with Sheba."

Elaine nodded. "That could work."

"Where's Sheba now?"

"In the backyard."

He smiled. "I'm not sure she'll be much help out there."

"I know, but I don't know how to control her like that police officer."

"Yeah, I heard you met my sister-in-law last night."

She cringed. "I don't think she likes me very much."

"Welcome to my club." He wanted to ask more about their interaction, but a glance at his watch told him he had fifteen minutes to get Clara to daycare before he had to be at the hospital. Not enough time to discuss everything, but his stomach flopped as Zoe's accusation played in his head. He had to know. "I asked her how you were, and she was confused by your name. She said it's Mary Russell."

She straightened, stepping away from him. "It is, but I go by my middle name now."

"Why?"

"It's a long story. Maybe I'll explain later." She looked past him at Clara. "So, I was thinking about offering art classes this fall."

He blinked, confused at her subject change, but also understanding—he didn't want to explain Zoe so he wouldn't judge her for not wanting to explain her story. Instead, he nodded as he watched Clara paint. "That's a great idea. I think you'd get a ton of kids."

"It would be for adults, not kids. Do you think that's something adults would be interested in?"

"Maybe. Where would you host the class? The community center might work."

"I was hoping in this room or the old parlor. It's bigger."

He glanced around at the packed display room. "What would you do with all the antiques?"

Elaine crinkled her adorable nose. "Sell them?"

He smiled. "That would be ideal."

"It would only be for the winter. If I don't sell them, I could store them in the basement until next tourist season."

Judah pictured the realistic flowers Elaine had drawn on the shop bags. His mother-in-law had loved it as much as Clara did. "I think that's a great idea. I might be your first student."

"You want to learn how to paint?"

"I hear painting is a good stress reliever, and I could certainly use that." Plus, he'd get to spend more time with Elaine. A clock dinged, and Judah checked his watch again. "If you don't mind, I'll go get Sheba so Clara can see her before we leave, then I'd better get Clara to daycare. I'll see you tonight?"

Elaine took a shaky breath. "I can't say I'm looking forward to it, but I appreciate your concern. It's been a long time since anyone's cared about my safety."

It had been a long time since he'd been able to help someone, other than a patient or a four-year-old. It felt good. And as much as he enjoyed sharing a box of mac and cheese with Clara in front of the TV, it was nice to have something else to look forward to at the end of a long day.

****

At six thirty, Judah opened the door to The Mother Load and Clara ran inside. "Lainy!"

Elaine stood behind her desk in a light blue belted dress that flattered her figure, unlike the large overalls from that morning. A tall blond man stood on the other side of the desk leaning toward her.

Clara ran to Elaine and gave her a hug. "We brought dinner. Daddy said Sheba's having a sleepover here. Can I go play with her?"

"Sure. I just let her out. Maybe your dad can show you the way to the backyard." She pointed around the corner. "You can put the food on the table, and I'll slip back when I get a minute."

Judah nodded as he walked past, trying not to stare.

"Who's that?" the guy asked.

"A friend."

"You've turned me down for dinner, but accepted his invite?"

"Come on, Daddy." Clara pulled him past the crystal vases. "I want to see Sheba."

Judah glanced back at the guy who leaned a little too close to Elaine. So what if he did? She was having dinner with *him*. Judah tried not to smile about that as he followed Clara through the old dining room into the kitchen, then set the food on the table.

A dog barked.

"I think Sheba's excited to see you." He opened the back door. Sheba danced around on the weathered deck. Clara ran out and chased her. In the middle of the yard, she fell to her knees and giggled, then put her arms around the big dog.

Judah took some time to examine his surroundings while they played. A tall wooden privacy fence ran down both sides of the long narrow lawn, which ended at a white garage facing the alley. Not a bad place for Sheba and Clara to play. He spotted a dinette set at the end of the deck, so he sat and watched them play.

A few minutes later, the back door opened and Elaine walked out. "If I bring the food outside, will Sheba eat it?"

He shook his head. "She's well trained. She won't sneak food. But will you hear the front bell from here?"

"I will with this." She put a baby monitor on the deck railing.

Judah chuckled. "That's ingenious, but maybe you should look into a higher tech security system."

"I have. Those cost a lot of money. This was five dollars at a garage sale." She smiled. "I'll get the food."

"I'll get the drinks." He followed her into the kitchen. How much did a security system cost? He'd look into it, especially if Elaine didn't warm up to Sheba. Maybe he could make it an anonymous gift.

As he considered that option, he opened the fridge. Two gallons of chocolate milk sat alone on the top shelf. "Looks like there's chocolate milk and chocolate milk."

"I see you've discovered my obsession."

He peeked over his shoulder in time to see her blush. "I haven't had it since I was a kid. Why not?" He poured three glasses before following Elaine outside. Clouds had blown in, covering the sun, while a breeze cooled the evening heat. As he set the glasses on the table, Sheba knocked Clara down and licked her face.

"No!" Elaine lunged toward the steps, but Judah caught her arm.

"Sheba's playing. Listen"

Clara shrieked, then giggled. She jumped up and ran around with Sheba chasing her.

He released Elaine's arm. "See? She's just an old puppy playing with her girl."

Elaine set the food next to the drinks with a disbelieving look. "Sheba is a bit stronger than a puppy."

"Only a bit." He winked at her then turned toward Clara. "Time to eat!"

His daughter ran at him with Sheba galloping after her. Once they were on the deck, Clara faced the dog. "Sheba, sit." The dog sat. Her tongue hung from her mouth and drool dropped to the deck. Clara gave her a tight hug.

"Let's get you washed," he said.

"I'll take her." Elaine stepped around him and held her hand out to Clara. "You can stay here with Sheba." Hand in hand they escaped inside.

Judah bent to pet Sheba's soft fur, the repetitive strokes calming his nerves. "I heard you had quite a night. You were supposed to protect Elaine, not terrify her." Sheba licked his neck and he laughed. "We're going to have to work harder to convince her this will work."

When Clara and Elaine came back out, they carried Sheba's food and water bowls. Clara put the food in front of Sheba but the dog didn't move, exactly as she'd been trained. Elaine put the water down. Sheba lunged for it.

Elaine jumped back with a squeak. Judah laughed, which earned him a scowl. "I thought she'd wait," she said, moving around the table to take the seat farthest from Sheba.

He sat next to her. "I'm so used to Sheba's behaviors that I sometimes forget to explain them. She's trained to eat on command, but she can drink whenever she wants."

Sheba finished gulping her water, then sat next to her food bowl.

"OK, Clara, give her the command."

His daughter pointed at the dog. "Sheba! Eat!"

Sheba dove into her food.

Elaine shook her head. "Our food is going to be cold. We should eat too."

Judah handed Clara her food, then gave Elaine a burger. "Hope you like it with the works."

"I'm not picky. Thanks for bringing dinner. I usually eat alone." As she unwrapped the hamburger, he noticed her bandage was gone.

"Can I see your cut?" He reached for her hand. She took a bite then held it up. Her skin puckered around the stitches, but the redness and swelling had dissipated a bit. "Looks good. Does it hurt?"

"Not anymore." Elaine smiled at him then at Clara. "What did you do today?"

"I went to Miss Mara's house and we colored and we watched TV and we jumped rope. Then Billy pushed Sarah down and made her cry. He had a timeout. Can I paint again? That was fun." Clara took a big bite, smearing ketchup onto her cheek.

Elaine laughed. "You sure can. Maybe when we're done here you can finish your mural."

"What's that?"

"A painting on a wall."

"I like your necklace." Clara pointed to the turquoise beads that wrapped around Elaine's neck three times.

"Thanks. I made it. Maybe sometime I can teach you how to make one."

"Can we do it now?"

"Your daddy is going to show me how to talk to Sheba tonight, but maybe next time."

Clara nodded. "Sarah made me a best friend necklace. I want to make her one. Can I do that?"

"That's a great idea. What's her favorite color?"

"Pink. That's my favorite color too."

Judah had hoped to learn more about Elaine over dinner, but his daughter continued to talk about Sarah, her day, and what she wanted to paint next as she shoved food into her mouth, barely pausing to swallow. When she finished her fries, she took a sip of milk and smiled at him. "Can I go play now?"

Finally. "If you're full, go wash up." Judah grabbed the other half of her burger and took a bite as she ran into the house. "Is she OK in there alone?"

Elaine pointed at the baby monitor. "We'll hear if anyone comes in."

"Will *you* be OK here alone tonight?"

"I survived last night. Well, half a night." She shivered.

Judah covered her hand with his. "I wish I could make this better for you."

"You're a fixer, huh?"

"I'm a doctor. I get paid to fix people."

She tilted her head to the side but didn't pull her hand away from his. "What if people don't want to be fixed?"

Sadness crept in. "It's tough, especially when I know I can help. My wife didn't like help fixing things. She was pretty independent."

"All clean!" Clara ran out of the house and stopped in front of Judah, raising her hands for his inspection. "Can I play now?" Judah nodded and she took off after Sheba.

"That's not a bad thing," Elaine said. "Being independent. I wish I was more independent."

That surprised him. "Who do you depend on?"

She folded the hamburger wrapper into a neat square as she shrugged one shoulder.

"Are your parents around?" he asked.

"I never knew my dad, and my mom lives in Florida. I have a grandma in Rapid City."

"Does someone else own the store and pay the bills?"

"No."

"So you're doing this all by yourself." He shrugged, wondering what he was missing. "Sounds pretty independent to me."

She wrinkled her nose. "I suppose."

Not sure how else to encourage her, or if it was his place, Judah motioned back toward the store. "Do you like selling antiques?"

Her beautiful eyes caught his, causing his stomach to flip. "It's not my first choice. I do love finding and cleaning up old things and making them beautiful though. I just don't like doing it alone."

Judah understood the familiar ache of loneliness all too well, but he didn't want to dwell on it. "How did you get into the antique business then?"

"This is the house my grandma grew up in. She kept it after her parents died, but she lived with my mom and me in Rapid City while I was growing up. My aunt turned it into an antique store. She passed away last fall. She didn't have any kids, so she left the store to me."

"How's business?"

Elaine sighed, slouching into her chair. "It's great during the busy season, but I need to make money all year. That's why I'm thinking about starting the art classes."

"Is that what your aunt did?"

"Her husband's income helped her make ends meet. This was more of a part-time job for her."

"Could you sell the shop and move?" He didn't like the idea, but he wanted to support her.

"I could, but this house has been in our family for eighty years. I couldn't do that to my grandma."

"It sounds like you two are close."

"It's probably silly, but she's my best friend." Elaine smiled. "My grandmother basically raised me. My mom was a teenager when I was born, and she didn't want to be tied down to a kid. She was always off partying, so Grandma took care of me. We played cards a lot—gin was her favorite—and we'd color for hours. I still have all the coloring books we filled. She's the reason I love art."

"That sounds amazing. Do you ever see your mom?"

Elaine shook her head as she tore her napkin into pieces. "She took off with some guy she met on the internet a month before my high school graduation. She used to come home every so often, but I haven't seen her in four years. Last I heard, she was on husband number three." The wind picked up then, blowing the napkin pieces across the table. "I'm sorry to dump that on you. I don't usually talk so much about my mom."

"I didn't mean to stir up bad memories," he said in way of an apology.

"It's OK. I've made peace with it."

"It was nice to hear about your grandma, though. That's why Clara and I moved to Sturgis, so she could spend more time with her nana." Which reminded him . . . "I'd like to hang out all night, but we'd better get started with Sheba so I can get Clara home by bedtime." He collected all the trash and stuffed it into the paper bag.

Elaine sat up straight. "You must think I'm a huge baby. I didn't grow up around animals and haven't had much experience with them."

"There's nothing wrong with being scared of something you don't know. Do you have the bag of doggie toys I left?"

She nodded and hurried inside.

Judah whistled. Sheba and Clara stopped running and starred at him. "Sheba, come!" She galloped over to him. "Sit." She did, just like he knew she would. He ruffled her fur. "Good girl."

When Elaine returned, she handed the canvas bag to Judah. He pulled out a rubber ball with bumps on it. Sheba sat up with her nose in the air, starring at the ball. "Stay!" He threw it as far as he could. She turned toward the ball but didn't move. "Fetch!" Sheba took off after it.

"That's amazing," Elaine whispered.

Sheba ran back to Judah and dropped the slobbery toy at his feet. He ruffled her fur again. "Good girl." When he pulled a thick rope out of the bag, Sheba bit one end and pulled back while Judah pulled on the other. "This one is her favorite toy," he said, smiling at Elaine. "She gets to play with it as a reward for obeying. We always use toys and affection as a reward instead of treats. It's healthier."

"How do you know so much about dog training?"

"Whitney. She was a police officer and wanted to be a K-9 handler. She trained Sheba for practice. She had just been accepted into the program when she was killed." He let go of the rope, ending the tug of war as Elaine took baby steps toward him.

"She sounds like an incredible lady."

Judah's chest tightened. He grabbed the slimy ball and threw it. Sheba ran after it. "She was, at times. She was a high achiever, that's for sure."

"I'm guessing you have that in common. You didn't become a doctor by sitting around."

Judah nodded. "You're right, but Whitney could never relax. If she wasn't working, she was reading leadership books or training Sheba or exercising or cleaning. I hired a cleaning service once, but they only lasted a week before Whitney fired them. She didn't like the way they cleaned the floors. I felt lazy watching football on

Sundays while she ran around the house. I often wondered what she saw in me." He threw the ball again, frustrated at himself for whining. "I'm sorry. I came over to help, not vent." Sheba dropped the ball by Judah's foot. He scooped it up and held it out to Elaine. "Your turn."

"Come on, Lainey!" Clara jumped as she cheered.

Elaine took the ball and her nose scrunched. "It feels so gross."

He laughed. "I should have brought you some surgical gloves. Make sure to tell Sheba to stay before you throw it, or she'll take off right away."

She took a deep breath. "Stay," she said, not as commanding as his voice but louder than he'd ever heard her before. She threw the ball, then smiled when Sheba stayed put. "Fetch!" Sheba took off and Elaine laughed, squeezing his forearm. "She did it!" Her hand fell away leaving doggie spit on his arm.

"Thanks for that." He teased her as he wiped at the spit tickling his skin.

Her cheeks reddened. "Oops." She wiped her hand on her blue dress.

"I've had worse."

Sheba returned and Elaine picked up the ball with two fingers, then repeated the steps he'd taught her. Her squeal of delight when Sheba obeyed warmed him. "I'm going to make a dog lover out of you yet."

"Thanks for this." She grinned up at him.

He swallowed. It had been a long time since a pretty lady had said something that nice to him.

Clara ran over with a stick and threw it above Sheba's head. "Fetch!" Sheba sprinted after her instead and licked her cheek, knocking her to the ground. Clara giggled as she jumped to her feet and ran away. "Come get me, Sheba!"

As Clara played in the yard, Elaine looked up at Judah and tilted her head in an adorable pose. "I know we haven't known each other long, but you shouldn't feel bad about having doubts.

Not that I think you have any reason to doubt yourself. Self-doubt plagues me too. Almost every day. Sometimes all day long."

"How do you get past it?"

"Talking with a friend helps." Her shy smile appeared. "I don't usually tell people so much about my past, but I'm glad I did. The store probably won't make me rich, but it's mine. Maybe I'm more independent than I thought."

A comfortable smile slid across his face. "Maybe I'm not as lazy as I thought." And maybe this relationship could blossom into something more, if he could overcome his doubts. He didn't want his past heartache to hold him back from a great future, especially one that might include a sweet redhead.

CHAPTER 8

On the first Saturday of the Sturgis Motorcycle Rally, it rained. Not a light drizzle, but a heavy pour. It was nearly five o'clock and Elaine hadn't seen a customer all day. With nothing else to do, she sat at her desk and typed *used easels* into the search engine. She cringed. Nearly forty dollars an easel would cut into profits, at least for the first class. If she could get ten people to commit to a six-week class, she'd make enough to help cover expenses, but would that many people be interested?

The front door opened, and Sheba sat up.

Elaine looked up as Mitch walked in holding a two-foot-wide box. "Welcome." She smiled as her stomach flip-flopped.

"Hey, Elly."

"What do you have for me today?"

As he approached, Sheba growled. He stopped.

"I'm so sorry." She looked at the dog while pointing at the bed. "Sheba, lie down." The dog obeyed but kept her attention on Mitch.

"How long are you keeping that?" he asked as he set the box on the counter.

"I'm not sure. You don't like dogs?"

"I love them." He reached out to pet her, but she snapped at him. "She obviously doesn't love me."

Embarrassment heated her cheeks. "I'm sorry. I've never seen her do that, but I'm still getting used to her. Let me move her into the other room. Heel." Elaine patted her leg and stepped toward the dining room. Sheba glanced at Mitch then at Elaine. "Heal, Sheba." The dog whined, then trotted over. What had gotten into her? Elaine would have to ask Judah about it. Until then, she led the dog into the kitchen, then shut the pocket door.

When she returned to her desk, a mahogany clock with a white face and curly black hands sat on the counter beside an empty box. "It's beautiful. Where did you find this?"

"Online. The seller had no idea what it was worth. I hoped you'd be impressed. After that other guy showed up with dinner, I figured I had to step up my game."

Elaine's face heated even more. "It isn't a competition."

"When a pretty lady's involved, it's always a competition." He winked.

Not sure how to respond, she picked up the clock to get a better look. "How much?"

"I paid seventy-five."

If her suspicions were correct, he'd gotten a deal. She could easily make over two hundred dollars selling it online. "Would you take a hundred and twenty-five?"

Mitch nodded. When she handed him the money, he tugged on it, pulling her closer to him. "What would it take to get you to go out with me?"

Since her previous deflections weren't working, she decided to admit the truth. "I think I'm too old for you."

"I doubt it. I have a baby face."

So did she. "I'm twenty-seven."

He smiled wide. "Me too. What if we compromise? I'll bring dinner to you, like your friend did, but it won't be fast food. I could cook for you."

"You cook?"

"Oh, yeah, and I know just the meal to make. Tomorrow night?"

Her stomach bubbled with excitement. Two dinners with two great guys in two days? "Tomorrow night it is."

Mitch leaned in and kissed her unbruised cheek. "Until then."

Her whole face tingled as he let himself out. Mitch was smooth and so like Caleb—sweet-talking her until he got his way. If he had anything else in common with her late husband, she'd have to steer clear of him, but she wouldn't know that unless she spent more time with him. What better way to do that than dinner? Besides, she'd never had a guy cook for her before. The week hadn't gone the way she'd expected, but at least all the surprises weren't bad.

An hour later, after researching art supplies for her class, Elaine finished ringing up her first customer as the door opened. Clara came in followed by Judah. He shook his umbrella outside before stepping into the foyer and holding the door open for the middle-aged customers as they left.

"Lainy!" Clara ran to Elaine and threw her wet arms around her waist.

Elaine laughed as water soaked into her capris. "You're super wet."

The rain had plastered Clara's sleeveless pink shirt and dark pink tutu to her goose-bump-covered skin. Her hair hung in wet clumps, but she smiled up at Elaine. "Daddy said it's raining cats and dogs, but all I see is raindrops. If it does start raining cats, I want to grab one. Daddy said we should come see you and Sheba since he's not working."

"I'm glad you did, but you look cold." Elaine grabbed the yellow sweater from her stool and draped it over Clara's shoulders. "Why don't you dry off first? Then, if your daddy says it's OK, we can work on our mural."

Clara looked at her dad as he approached them. "Can I, Daddy?"

"Sure thing, lamb."

"That's a cute nickname," Elaine said. "Why do you call her lamb?"

"Do you want to tell her?" He kissed Clara's head.

"'Cause when I was born, they put me in a gown with little lambs on it, and since my parents couldn't decide on a name, Daddy called me lamb. And it stuck."

"That's sweet." Their bond warmed Elaine. It was the type of relationship she'd had with Marcus, but that was before . . . Dragging herself out of the past, she smiled at Clara. "If you and your dad will watch the store, I'll go get the supplies. And a towel."

"OK." Clara climbed onto the stool behind her desk. "What do I do?"

"If anyone comes in, tell them I'll be right back."

Elaine walked through the dining room and opened the pocket door to the kitchen. Sheba bounded out and ran through the shop. She turned in time to see the dog jump on Judah's chest and lick his chin. He laughed. Elaine shook her head but smiled. If Sheba did that to her, she'd probably faint.

Not wanting to make Judah wait—or miss a potential customer—Elaine hurried to her apartment and changed into her painting overalls, then pulled her curls into a ponytail. It looked more like a red puff ball than a ponytail, but at least her hair would stay clean. She picked up her canvas bag full of supplies on the way out the door and returned to the store.

When she walked into the dining room, Judah turned from the vase Clara was showing him and smiled. "You look even younger with your hair up." He took the bag from her.

"That's not always good. I already get mistaken for a teenager all the time."

"Wear it down then. It looks good either way."

"I can't. It's a crazy mess most of the time and it gets in the paint. I cut it last fall thinking that would help, but it got curlier. I looked like a clown." She scrunched her nose at Clara. "All I needed was a big, red nose."

The girl giggled.

Elaine tickled her tummy. "Enough about my crazy hair. Let's go paint." She handed Judah the oversized shirt, then led the way to the plywood where Clara had painted a green smiley face sun on the right-hand side and green hills across the bottom. "So, young Monet, what should we add now?"

"I want to paint flowers today." Clara pulled the bag to the floor. She rummaged through it and pulled out a paintbrush.

"That's a great idea. What are your favorite flowers?"

She looked at her dad. "What are my favorite flowers?"

"You picked out yellow roses to take to Mommy's grave this morning. Do you like them the most?"

She nodded. "I'll paint those." She turned to Elaine. "Can you paint the orange flowers for Mommy, like on her bag?"

"Of course, I can." She looked at Judah and pointed at the counter. "Do you want to pull up the stool so you can watch us?"

He shook his head as he sank to the floor next to a shelf of old records across from the window. "I'm good. Sheba can keep me company." Sheba practically sat on him until he wrestled her to the ground, aggressively scratching behind her ears. Sheba crouched low and pounced at him. His laughter soothed Elaine's heart.

This wasn't a bad way to spend a Saturday afternoon. With a smile, she turned back to Clara. "Let me get you started on your roses first. Roses grow on a bush, so let's put a big one right over here." Elaine spread out the drop cloth before pulling out paints and brushes. "You can start on the grass while I paint the bush."

Clara carefully dipped her brush in the green paint then wiped it on the wood with short, thick strokes. Once she was in a groove, Elaine set to work painting the bush.

After several minutes, Clara declared herself done with grass and dropped her brush on the cloth. "Can I paint roses now?"

"We have to let the green paint dry first. In the meantime, we can start on your mommy's flowers. Why don't you paint the stems?" Elaine shifted down the board to a bare spot of wood. "Paint long stems along the base of the board, like this." She painted a thin two-foot green line. "Now it's your turn." She gave Clara the brush and stepped back next to Judah.

"You're a great teacher," he said. "I can see why you want to offer classes here. Have you taught before?"

Her heart pinched. "I was a high school art teacher."

"Why'd you stop?"

She sucked in a deep, nervous breath. "I moved here to take over the shop." *Please don't ask more.* She smiled at Clara's long uneven strokes. She'd already painted a dozen stems and they were all over the place, but Elaine could fix them later.

Judah cleared his throat. "Have you come to any decisions about the classes here?"

"Not yet, but I've done a lot of research. I would need a lot of supplies. After I figure out the profits from the rally, I'll know if I can afford it. And I need to call my tax lady to see if I can run the classes through the shop or if it's best to start a new business."

"Is the class a one-and-done kind of thing or something that takes longer?"

"I'd prefer a six-week class so I can build relationships with my students. When I taught high schoolers, it was fun to introduce a new technique every so often. Also, I like oils, which take time to dry. A week in between classes would be perfect." She was almost giddy just thinking about it.

"I love your enthusiasm."

"Ta-da!" Clara flipped her hand up, Vanna White–style, to show off her stems. "Whatcha think?"

Judah clapped.

"They're magnificent. Are you ready for the flowers?" Elaine asked. After Clara's emphatic nod, Elaine picked up her wooden palette and squirted orange, yellow, and white onto it. Painting with Clara brought a spark of joy she'd missed the past year.

Clara stepped closer to her. "What's your favorite flower, Lainy?"

"I love Gerber daisies."

"What's that?"

"They're big daisies in all different colors. I'll show you." On Clara's first stem, Elaine painted a yellow center surrounded with layers of long orange petals. She darkened different areas to give it a three-dimensional look. Then she copied Clara's earlier Vanna pose. "Ta-da!"

Both Clara and Judah clapped, and Elaine bowed. "Thank you very much. What about your daddy? What's his favorite flower?"

Clara wrinkled her nose. "Flowers are for girls."

Elaine tilted her head. "Are you sure? I think daddies can like flowers too."

Clara turned to her father with her mouth hanging open. "You like flowers?"

Judah chuckled. "I love flowers, and my favorites are the bouquets of dandelions you pick for me."

"Then we'll make sure to dot the hills with dandelions." Elaine winked at him.

Clara smiled before grabbing a paintbrush and swirling yellow paint at her eye level, just above the green horizon. "I'm making fairy swirls."

Warmth spread through Elaine. Not the heat that pinked her cheeks from embarrassment, but the kind that inspired her to create. To show the love between Judah and Clara. In that moment, it felt like yellow highlights on her orange lilies. Maybe later she'd add a little girl to the mural. One bringing a bouquet of dandelions to her daddy who sat against an oak tree.

"How are things with Sheba today?" Judah asked, pulling her attention away from the painting.

"Pretty good, but she growled at Mitch. She even snapped at him when he tried to pet her."

"That's my girl," Judah whispered.

Elaine spun around. Sheba laid her head on his knee. "Did you just reward her bad behavior?"

He shrugged. "She's a good judge of character."

Elaine rolled her eyes. "And how do you know that?"

"Whitney told me. They were inseparable when she wasn't working."

"Mommy was a hero," Clara said. Her tongue stuck out from between her lips as she painted another stem.

"She was?"

"She died saving lots of lives, didn't she, Daddy?

"She sure did, lamb." He looked down at Sheba as he petted her head. Elaine recognized the sadness in his voice. She'd heard it in her own after losing Caleb.

"Do you have any kids, Lainy?"

"No, we weren't as lucky as your mommy and daddy." The memory of a sweet baby boy with dark, silky hair—smelling like baby lotion and giggling at her funny faces—filled her with an intense sorrow she hadn't felt in months. She wanted to run to her room and cry, but she wouldn't run from Clara. Instead, she adjusted her grip on the brush and painted. As the glossy paint glided against the rough wood, sadness flowed out of her.

With each teasing word from Judah, each giggle from Clara, and each stroke of her brush, Elaine relaxed. Her emotions calmed. If painting could help someone like her—a widow, a failed mother, a felon—how much could it help others? Maybe it could even help someone like Jules. She had to find a way to share that healing.

CHAPTER 9

Sunday morning, Elaine dressed in her favorite lime-green sundress splattered with white daisies. She rummaged through the top drawer of her dresser until she found the daisy chain necklace she'd made, then latched the cold metal around her neck. It was a bit early to dress for dinner with Mitch, but she wanted to do as much as she could in the morning so she'd only have to touch herself up before dinner.

In the bathroom, she curled her hair to loosen her curls before adding a touch of make-up. She took a deep breath to calm her nerves, hoping Mitch would appreciate the extra effort she had made. She hadn't had an excuse to dress up since the early years with Caleb. She missed how special she felt on a date, especially at the beginning of a relationship.

Downstairs, she let Sheba out. They'd both barely finished breakfast before the first customers climbed the front porch steps. With clear skies and warm weather, she hoped for a busy day.

The motorcycle rally didn't disappoint, and after hours of a steady stream of customers, Mitch walked in carrying two paper bags. He laid them on the counter then leaned in and kissed her cheek. "How's my girl?"

His girl. Heat climbed up her neck at the endearment Caleb had often used. "I'm not sure about her, but I've had a fantastic day. The weather's great, and the customers have been delightful."

He touched one of her curls as his gaze roamed over her, too much like Caleb. "You look beautiful. Hope you're as excited about our night as I am."

"What are you cooking?" She stood on her tiptoes and tried to look in the bags, but he pulled them toward himself.

"Don't peak. It's a surprise." He nodded toward the dining room. "The kitchen through there?"

"It is. I can show you."

He held up a hand. "You're busy. I'll find it. Cujo isn't back there, is he?"

"*Sheba* is in the backyard. When she comes back in, she'll be up front with me, so she won't bother you."

"I'll get started cooking then. Don't sneak back and ruin the surprise." He grabbed the bags and disappeared through the dining room.

A lady in a Hawaiian shirt put several items on the counter. "Could you wrap them up? I've got limited space."

"Of course." She grabbed the tissue paper. Her mind wandered as she wrapped.

She had to stop comparing Mitch to Caleb. The resemblance was oddly exciting, but shouldn't it repulse her? Caleb had used flattery to manipulate her more often than not. But that didn't mean Mitch would. Did it? Elaine sighed. Mitch wasn't Caleb and she wasn't a naïve teenager anymore. She could enjoy one dinner with Mitch to figure him out before she judged him.

She moved on to the next customer. Loud banging from the kitchen made her jump. She wanted to run back and help him, but he'd have to fumble around without her until the store quieted down. And at least he was trying. Caleb never even attempted to make her dinner. She greeted three more bikers before ringing up two vinyl records for an older man.

Mitch popped his head through the doorway. "Elly, where's the corkscrew?"

"If I have one it's in the drawer under the microwave."

"Thanks." He winked then disappeared.

"He's not bad on the eyes," said a lady in black leathers as she placed a Sioux Pottery vase on the counter.

Elaine smiled and picked up the vase to wrap it. "Did you find everything all right?"

"I was eying those lamps in the window, but they're too big for the bike. Do you have anything smaller?"

There was always the crystal lamp beside her bed. Normally she wouldn't hesitate to sell items from her personal collection, but something held her back from offering it. "I'm sorry. That's all I have right now, but my inventory is always changing. I might have something later in the week."

"I might stop back in then."

Elaine ran the woman's credit card. "Thanks. Have a safe vacation."

As the woman left, Elaine drummed her fingers on the counter as she thought about that lamp and how Jules's eyes had lit up when Elaine told her its story. If anyone deserved to own that lamp, it was Jules. Would a teenager think it was a lame gift? Probably, but Elaine didn't care. She scrolled through her phone until she got to Bridget's number. She had no idea if they'd even let her give Jules the lamp, but it didn't hurt to ask.

* * * * * * *

The scent of Italian spices filled the house. Elaine's stomach growled as she sat on the floor in her now-empty store rearranging the carnival glass. The yellow bird in the cuckoo clock sang eight times. No wonder she was so hungry—she'd been too busy to break for lunch.

Mitch poked his head out of the kitchen. "Dinner's ready."

"Perfect. There's still an hour before closing, but I doubt I'll see many customers this late. My Aunt Susan was right when she said once the bars filled up her shop emptied." Elaine stood, grabbed the baby monitor, then hurried to the kitchen.

The lights were off, but two candles on the table lit the room. Mitch had served large pieces of lasagna and long stems of asparagus. A perfect triangular piece of chocolate cheesecake and an empty wineglass sat above each plate.

Her stomach growled. "This looks delicious."

He draped a tea towel over one arm. "Ciao! Welcome to La Mother Lode," he said with an Italian accent as he pulled out her chair.

She laughed as she sat.

He pushed her chair in. "For today's special we have triple cheese lasagna with Italian sausage sprinkled with freshly grated parmesan cheese, bacon glazed asparagus, and triple delight cheesecake." He turned toward the counter, grabbed a wine bottle, and placed in front of the towel. "This meal pairs well with Black Hill's finest merlot." He filled both glasses halfway.

Elaine shivered. She'd hated it when Caleb drank too much, and she hadn't touched alcohol since Marcus left. "Could I get a glass of water?"

"But of course. It's my pleasure to serve you." He put the bottle down and filled a glass with water for her, then placed it in front of her with a bow. "If you'll excuse me, I'm sure your date will be here soon." He backed away, put the towel on the counter, and returned. "Elly, you look beautiful," he said without the accent. Before she could respond, he kissed her cheek.

The scent of alcohol on his breath tightened her stomach.

"This looks great." He sat across from her. "I did some research and this place got five stars on Yelp!"

Elaine smiled, but the wine bothered her. A drink with dinner didn't mean Mitch would indulge like Caleb used to. She was being paranoid. Mitch deserved the benefit of the doubt.

Determined to enjoy the evening, she took a deep breath before digging into the lasagna. The perfect blend of Italian spices, chewy noodles, and gooey cheese tasted familiar. "This is delicious."

"Only the best for you." Mitch smiled and picked up his wine glass. "A toast?"

Elaine froze. Drinking wine would violate her probation, but she didn't want to explain that to Mitch. She put her fork down and picked up her glass.

"To the most beautiful lady in the Black Hills."

They clinked glasses.

While he drank, she tipped the glass enough that she hoped it convinced him, then set the glass down. "I don't know much about you," she said, needing a distraction from the wine. "Where did you grow up?"

He cut into the lasagna and took a bite. "St. Paul."

"Any siblings?"

"A sister. She's married with a couple of kids."

"Do you like kids?"

He shrugged. "Kids are fine. I'd rather talk about you, though." He grabbed her left hand.

Pain sliced through her palm. She yanked it back, stroking the tender flesh. "Sorry. It's still sore."

"What happened?"

She flipped her hand over to show him the stitches. "I cut it on a piece of glass."

"The broken window?"

She shook her head. "A teenager ran into the store. She was running from this guy. When I tried to help, he pushed me and I landed on some broken glass."

He pointed his knife at her. "You shouldn't get into the middle of other people's problems."

"She came into the store for help. What else could I do?" She took another small bite, but the lasagna lost its flavor. Did he really think she should ignore someone in need?

Mitch sighed. "I'm sorry. I just don't like the thought of you putting yourself in harm's way." He gently pulled her hand toward him and kissed her palm next to the healing cut. "If you haven't noticed, I kind of like you."

Elaine tugged her hand away and tucked it into her lap, forcing herself to eat other bite. Caleb had tried to protect her too, but in the end, he'd hurt her the worst.

"I hope the guy didn't break anything too valuable."

"It was a shelf of carnival glass. I keep the rare pieces in another area, so the broken ones weren't too expensive."

"You know so much about this stuff. I'm amazed by you every time I come in."

"You're not a collector?"

He shook his head.

"How did you get into the antique business?"

Mitch smiled. "My grandmother has a house full of them. One day I broke a vase and she had a fit. Apparently, it was worth hundreds of dollars. I started paying more attention to the other things around there, researching their value. I was shocked at how much you could get. That's when I started going to estate sales, garage sales, and auctions. Most people have no idea how much their old stuff is worth."

"Is it all about the money, then?" This side of him shocked her.

"And meeting cute shop girls."

Surely he had higher ambitions than that. "Besides reselling antiques, what else do you do?"

He shrugged. "I've got quite a few ideas brewing. I just need the capital to start."

"I understand that. I'm thinking of starting art classes, but, like you, I need the money first."

"I bet you'd be brilliant at teaching. What kind of art will you teach?" He picked up his wine glass and leaned back in his chair.

She enjoyed his undivided attention as she tried to ignore the wine. Reminding herself that he wasn't Caleb, she told him about her teaching days and the art she loved to create. With each of his smiles and questions, she relaxed a bit more. Despite his similarities to her husband, there was a lot about Mitch to like. Maybe dinner hadn't been a bad idea after all.

CHAPTER 10

L eaning against the headboard of Clara's twin bed, Judah cuddled her close as he closed her favorite princess book. "Time to go to sleep, lamb."

She blinked her long lashes at him. "One more?"

"We've read it three times. You need your sleep." He slid out from under her and gently laid her on the pillow. She closed her eyes, and he smoothed the silky hair away from her face.

"I love you, Daddy."

Those words melted his heart. "I love you too." He kissed her forehead before sneaking out of the room. As he closed her door, the doorbell rang. Annoyed, he checked the time. It was almost nine. Who could be bothering him now?

After a quick look through the peephole, he clenched his teeth. He opened the door and stepped aside, allowing Zoe to march in. Anger flashed across her face. She held up a manila envelope. "I knew there was something wrong with that woman. How could you let her around Clara?"

"Who are you talking about?"

"Mary Russell."

"Who?"

"Elaine."

That again? He folded his arms in front of him. "What's this about?"

She pulled papers out of the envelope and shoved them at him. "She kidnapped a child. You need to keep Clara far away from her."

The breath rushed out of Judah as he reached for the papers. On the top left corner was a grainy mug shot of Elaine. Her curly hair hung past her shoulders, her eyes were puffy and her nose was red. *Russell, Mary Elaine. Second degree kidnapping.* His heart pounded as he squeezed the paper in his fist. Was this a joke? Zoe wouldn't stoop so low, would she? But had he really allowed his precious daughter to be around a kidnapper?

"I knew you wouldn't believe me if I didn't bring proof. I suggest you go get Sheba and stay away from this woman."

How could sweet, shy Elaine be a kidnapper? She'd risked her life to save a teenager. She never tried to get Clara alone. It didn't make sense.

Zoe stepped closer to him. "I want your word on this, Judah. Keep that woman away from Clara."

He tossed the papers onto the couch. He understood Zoe's fears, but there had to be more to the story. "You can't tell me what to do with my daughter. You're her aunt, not her mom."

She glared at him. "You're putting Clara in danger."

"I would never do anything to hurt Clara and you know it. Thank you for your concern, but I'll handle this. It's none of your business who I let around Clara."

"This *is* my business. I'll be watching your kidnapping friend." She slammed the door on her way out.

Judah squeezed his eyes closed not wanting to believe any of it. Had he put Clara in danger? Was there more to the story—more to Elaine—than what the file showed, or was she so talented that she'd fooled him?

He needed answers, and they couldn't wait until tomorrow. He could call Elaine, but what if she was the talented con artist Zoe said she was? Instead, he dialed the babysitter. He needed to confront Elaine face to face.

CHAPTER 11

Elaine drank the last of her water, then set the cup down next to her full wine glass. "Do you play any sports?"

"Played soccer in high school. I wasn't very good at it. Tell me more about your childhood. Do your parents live close to you?"

"My mom wasn't around much when I was a kid. My grandmother raised me. I'm not sure who my dad is."

His eyebrows lowered. "I'm sorry. That must have been hard."

"It's all I knew and my grandmother is wonderful, so I don't feel like I missed out on much. What about you? What are your parents like?"

"Disappointed," he mumbled.

"In what?"

His charming smile reappeared. "Forget I said anything. I want to know more about you."

And she was dying to know more about him. Was their disappointment because they had unreasonable expectation or because he hadn't reached his potential? Every time she tried to ask about him, he'd change the subject back to her. She was tired of hearing her own voice—it felt more like an interview than a conversation. "There's not much more to tell."

"I don't believe it. A girl like you deserves to be spoiled. There's a concert at the Full Throttle tomorrow night. Say you'll come with me."

"Sorry I can't. I have to work the shop."

"Don't you close at nine? We can go after."

Butterflies fluttered through her, but she wasn't so sure it was from anticipation or something else. Loud music, crushing crowds, more drinking. "Concerts aren't really my thing."

He winked. "I know you'll love it. Don't say no. Just think about it."

She nodded as she watched him eat. She had no intention of going with him, but she didn't want to spoil their evening either, so she kept quiet.

After Mitch ate the last bite of his food, Elaine stood and took his plate. "Since you cooked, I'll clean up." As she set the dishes in the sink, Mitch's arm circled her. She jumped, spinning around.

"What's the hurry?" He rubbed her back, sending shivers through her. His face inched closer.

Elaine held her hands up even as she leaned forward. A nervous giggle escaped moments before he touched his lips hers. His free hand cradled her cheek. Her skin tingled as his fingers traveled down her neck then her back to her waist. As he pulled her to his chest, he planted kisses along her jaw before returning to her lips.

Excitement flashed through her. She hadn't kissed anyone since Caleb. But this was a first date and she still had questions. She leaned her head back. "Wait. This is too fast."

"But it feels right." He kissed her again. "We've got chemistry."

She wanted to resist, but she froze as he continued to kiss and touch her. She didn't want this. Why wouldn't he listen to her? Caleb had done this their whole relationship—ignored her, manipulated her, and pushed her into things she didn't want. Her sweet boy's cuddles, ripped from her because of Caleb's idiotic plan to kidnap him. Maybe things could have been different. She could have made the transition easier for Marcus. She could have stayed in his life, visited him at his new home. She'd been a puppet with Caleb, but not anymore.

Anger simmered and she shoved against his shoulders. "Please, Mitch. I asked you to stop."

He continued pawing at her.

Panic tightened her throat. "Please stop."

"What's going on here?"

Mitch groaned.

Elaine turned her head to the side. "Judah." She exhaled the pent-up tension and took deep, thankful breaths.

Judah stood in the doorway, fists tight and biceps bulging, before he stomped over and yanked Mitch away from her. Her knees buckled, both from relief and fear, as she grabbed the counter to support herself.

"Hey!" Mitch swore. "What's your problem, man? You're interrupting our date."

Judah's nostrils flared. "I think your date is over."

"That's none of your business."

"It's everyone's business when a woman says no and her attacker ignores her."

"I wasn't attacking her. We were just fooling around." Mitch smirked. "Jealous that she didn't put out for you?"

Elaine gasped.

Judah scowled. "You need to leave."

Mitch turned to Elaine. "Catch you later." He moved past Judah, bumping him in the shoulder. Judah didn't budge but Mitch stumbled. Elaine sagged against the counter as he disappeared through the kitchen door.

How had she let this happen? And what if Judah hadn't shown up when he did? She trembled at the possibilities. Heat infused her face.

Judah stepped toward her. "Are you OK?"

She nodded, pressing her hands to her cheeks to hide her embarrassment.

"Did he hurt you?" His gentle voice offered comfort, but it made her feel guilty for putting herself in that position.

"No. It's my fault." She dropped her gaze to the floor, her terrible judgment wreaking havoc once again.

"You should sit." He led her to a kitchen chair. "Would you like something to drink? Chocolate milk, maybe?" She lifted her head and gazed into his sympathetic eyes. She nodded. When he returned with her drink, he sat in Mitch's seat across from her. "What happened?"

The heat in her cheeks intensified. She squeezed her eyes shut as humiliation washed over her. "I didn't know he was going to kiss me. I feel like such an idiot for leading him on."

"Even if you did somehow lead him on, it didn't look like you were willing. That's not your fault."

"It all happened so fast. One minute I was clearing the table, and the next we were kissing. Or he was kissing me. I don't know." Shame kept her gaze on the brown milk in front of her.

"Maybe I overstepped, but I heard you tell him to stop. Too often Whitney came home telling me that victims blame themselves, but it's never the victim's fault. No means no. If Mitch can't respect that, then he's the one who should feel ashamed."

Elaine met his gaze. Not feel ashamed? Caleb had never accepted responsibility for anything. She wasn't sure how to process Judah's words. "I'm glad you came in when you did."

"Me too."

"The sad thing is that I saw the signs, but I ignored them. I didn't want to believe Mitch was like my husband. Why do I fall for guys who want to control me?"

"Your husband was controlling?"

She nodded. "And manipulative. Most of the time I didn't know what was happening until it was too late. I didn't see how Mitch was doing the same thing until tonight." She rubbed her forehead. "I can't believe I let it happen."

"You didn't let anything happen. Something happened *to* you. It's not your fault any more than it's Jules's that she was assaulted." Judah covered her hand with his. "And you wouldn't blame Jules, would you?"

Elaine shook her head so hard her curls blocked her view of Judah. "Of course not. Those thugs are entirely to blame."

"Exactly. I'm glad you're finally seeing it my way." He caressed her hand.

Unlike Mitch's touch, she enjoyed the tingles he created. "Thank you. Even though we've just met, I feel safe with you. I've never felt safe around a man before."

His brows crinkled. "Not even Caleb? Why?"

"His behavior was erratic. I always thought he could hurt me if I angered him bad enough. I'm not trying to make excuses or gossip about my husband. I just want you to know that your kindness hasn't gone unnoticed." Although, how he could be so kind to her confused her. If he knew what she had done, things might be different. Even when Caleb had manipulated her, Elaine couldn't blame everything on him. She gave a quick prayer of thanks that Judah didn't know the truth, otherwise he might not think so highly of her. "I don't know why you stopped by, but I'm glad you did."

Judah straightened, pulling his hand away with him. "I had something to discuss with you but maybe now's not the time. I can come back tomorrow."

"I'd like you to stay. To be honest, I don't want to be alone right now, but you can go if you need to. I'm sure Clara's wondering where you are."

"Clara's asleep. The neighbor girl is babysitting." He stared down at his hands. "I don't want to upset you anymore than you are."

Anxiety twisted her stomach. Her emotions tumbled like they were in a washing machine—spin, soak, spin. "I think you have to tell me now. I won't get a bit of sleep wondering about it if you don't."

Judah took a deep breath. "My sister-in-law came over tonight. I didn't ask her to, but she ran a background check on you."

He knew! Elaine jumped to her feet. "I should never have let you come by so often. Take Sheba home. You and Clara need to stay far away from me."

Judah stood. "I came to get your side of the story. I know there's more to it."

"My side doesn't matter. I did the crime, I went to jail, and I'm trying to salvage my life. I don't want to drag you and Clara into this."

"I want to hear your story. I need to know what happened because I can't imagine you doing this." He pulled her chair out. "Please, tell me."

How could she tell him about the worst day of her life? But he deserved to hear the truth. Maybe then he'd leave before she hurt him and Clara.

Elaine steadied her breathing and sat. "I married Caleb right out of high school. He was the only boy interested in me, and I craved his attention. I thought he was the smartest guy ever and I was lucky to have him. My grandmother tried to warn me, but I agreed to everything he suggested no matter how crazy.

"I wanted kids so bad. I wanted to be a better mom than I had, but after years of trying, I learned I couldn't have kids." A familiar ache pulsed in her chest. "It devastated me. Caleb kept trying to make it better, but he couldn't. It was the one part of me that he couldn't control."

"How did that lead to kidnapping?"

How indeed. "One day he suggested we become foster parents. We did all the training, then got a call that a four-month-old baby boy needed a home. I instantly fell in love with my sweet, little Marcus." Love welled up in her, and she blinked to keep the tears away.

"How long was the baby with you?"

"Three years. For three years, I raised him. I got up with him every night for the first six months, I taught him to walk and talk. I held him when he hurt himself. He was mine." She smiled, but reality crashed into her just like it had back then. "But he wasn't really. The state terminated his parents' rights, but the law wouldn't allow us to adopt him because he was Native American and we weren't."

"That must have crushed you." Judah's voice softened.

"It did. I tried to be strong around Marcus, but as soon as he went to sleep, I cried for hours. I tried to stop, but I couldn't. And Caleb couldn't handle it. He started drinking more and using drugs. One day, he told me to pack. He wanted to take Marcus and get out of South Dakota."

"Did he honestly think that would work?"

She nodded. "He thought keeping Marcus would make me happy, and I wanted to keep him so badly that I didn't care what it took. But we got caught. We made bail, but . . . the loss was too much. The depression crippled me." Tears slid down her cheeks. "Caleb only wanted to help me, to get our family back."

Judah ran a hand through his hair and took a deep breath. "What happened?"

"He told me he had a plan to kidnap Marcus again. I tried to talk him out of it, but he wouldn't listen." Her throat tightened. "He had this crazy look. I'd never seen him like that and it scared me. I did the only thing I could think of. I called the police." Her voice cracked. "The last thing I did for my husband was betray him."

Judah squeezed her hand. "You did the right thing. You looked after Marcus."

Tears clouded her vision. "I didn't do enough. Caleb shot the foster mom, then ran off with Marcus. His foster mom recovered, but my baby"—she took a shaky breath—"a rattlesnake bit my baby and he lost his leg."

"I'm so sorry, but that's not your fault."

She shook her head. "I should have done more."

"You did everything you could."

Maybe.

"What happened to Caleb?"

A sob rose in her throat. "He wouldn't surrender." The tears fell. "He died in a shootout." And she lived every day knowing that she'd put him there. The crushing guilt she'd buried slammed into her.

A warm arm wrapped around her shoulder. "I'm sorry."

Sobs shook Elaine as the old familiar ache consumed her. She missed Marcus so much she could barely breathe, and Judah's kindness only made it worse. She'd betrayed Caleb. She'd crippled Marcus. She hurt everyone she loved.

Taking a shuddering breath, she dried her eyes and pulled away from him. Hoping the truth would scare Judah into staying far away from her, Elaine asked, "What else do you want to know?"

With a napkin from the table, he wiped her tears. "You turned your husband in. They still charged you with kidnapping?"

"Accessory to kidnapping. They offered me a plea. I served nine months work release, which is ironic since I was fired from my teaching job because of the felony. I got a job at a fast-food place until my sentence was served, then I moved here to run the store."

He rubbed his eyes. "I don't know what to say."

"You don't have to say anything. I knew taking Marcus was wrong, but I didn't care. In my heart, he was my child, and a mother would do whatever she could to keep her child."

He looked her in the eye. "Do you regret it?"

"I do, because it hurt Marcus. I thought I was helping him, but in the end, I hurt him the most."

"What happened to him?"

Her eyes welled up with fresh tears. "I don't know. I don't deserve to know. And now you know the whole ugly truth. I think it would be best if you and Clara stayed away from me."

He nodded. "There's a part of me that thinks you're right."

Disappointment slashed through her, but it was for the best. She couldn't bear it if she hurt Clara or Judah.

"But the louder my sister-in-law protests, the more I want to defy her." He chuckled.

Elaine sighed. "This isn't funny."

He leaned forward and grabbed her hand. "You know what you did was wrong, and you've taken responsibility for the crime. Paid your debt to society. Don't you deserve a second chance?"

"People won't see it that way."

"People don't know you like I do."

"*You* don't know me. We only met last week."

He sat back and folded his hands together. "You're great with Clara, and she requires supernatural patience at times. You were sweet and kind with Jules. Your creativity amazes me. I love your humble heart and the way you blush when you're embarrassed. And even your insistence that I stay away from you to protect Clara has me wanting to do just the opposite." His gaze locked with hers. "I care for you, and I would like to spend more time getting to know you."

Her stomach flipped. "You'll be sorry."

"What if I'm not?"

"What about Clara?"

"She adores you. Spending more time with you would be good for her. She doesn't have to know that we are anything but friends, but I won't pressure you."

Elaine took a deep breath. She didn't know what to say. He seemed too normal, too grounded, too stable, but those were the same reasons she wanted to say yes. It wouldn't last, she knew that. She only hoped he didn't hate her when it ended. "If we take it slowly, then I guess."

Judah smiled. "For the record, I haven't dated in years so I'm a bit out of shape socially."

She rolled her eyes. "If you're out of shape, I'm a couch potato. Tonight's fiasco is proof of that."

"Speaking of that, can I help you clean up?"

"You don't have to. You should get home to Clara."

He stood. "She's sleeping, the babysitter would love the extra cash, and I'm not ready to leave yet."

A different heat crept up her face at his sweet words. "If you wash, I'll dry."

"Deal." Judah stepped over to the sink.

Now that was nothing like Caleb.

CHAPTER 12

A t her desk, Elaine wrapped the crystal lamp in paper, tucked it into a square box, and tied a red ribbon around it. With her Copic markers, she wrote *To Jules* in swirly letters on the top, then drew a large crown with sparkling jewels.

A customer approached with several knickknacks, so she set it aside.

After a few more customers, a woman entered wearing a black leather jacket, a black polo shirt, and a red plaid skirt. Her long copper hair blended into light tips like the ombre vases that lined the shelf next to her. Sheba sat up in her bed beside the counter, sniffed the woman, then laid back down.

Elaine finished ringing up a customer, then turned to the newcomer. "Can I help you?"

"Are you Elaine? I'm Bridget Smalls. You asked me to stop by."

That was Bridget? Elaine had expected someone older and less trendy. After recovering from her surprise, she grabbed the package from the floor. "Thanks for coming. I'm glued to the store until the rally is over. If Jules doesn't want it, would you bring it back?"

"Sure. I love the art." Bridget ran a black fingernail over the crown. "Did you draw that?"

"I did."

"You're very talented. Maybe you could teach art to the kids at our group home. They're always looking for teachers to lead the girls in fun activities. I think art could build their confidence."

A familiar sadness filled Elaine at the reminder of her lost dreams. "I'm actually thinking of starting art classes here, but they would be for adults." She cleared her throat, hoping Bridget wouldn't ask any more questions. "Any updates on the case?"

"With Jules's testimony, we can link Wallace to a trafficking group we've had our eye on for a while. There's a BOLO out for his arrest. Unfortunately, police resources are overwhelmed because of the rally. Our human trafficking task force is working overtime, though, so hopefully we'll catch them soon."

The bell chimed and a group of bikers entered.

Bridget tilted her head toward the door. "Looks like you're busy now, but before I go, I wanted to see how you're doing. Are you sleeping and eating OK? Do you have more anxiety than before?"

"I'm not sure it's possible to have more anxiety than before, but I'm sleeping and eating fine." She patted Sheba's head. "My friend brought over his dog for protection. We had a rough start, but it's comforting to know she's here to protect me."

"Not a bad idea. You sound like you're doing OK, but make sure to drink plenty of water."

"Water?" People had suggested a lot of things to Elaine over the years, but she'd never gotten that recommendation before.

"Believe it or not, it flushes out stress hormones, reduces anxiety, and improves depression."

Elaine smiled, feeling better already. "Thanks. I will."

"You have my number if you need anything." Bridget picked up the box. "I'm available day and night, even if you only want to chat."

Would she dare call just to chat? What would they talk about? "I'll think about it, and thanks again for taking this to Jules. Tell her I'm thinking of her."

"Sure thing."

As Bridget walked out of the store, someone carried in a large vase of red roses and daisies. The delivery man set them on the counter and smiled. "Enjoy."

Elaine breathed in the floral scent. The deep red blooms contrasted with the bright white petals and yellow centers, bringing brightness to her oak desk. Excitement surged through her as she pulled out the card and tore open the envelope.

Elly, I had fun last night. Hopefully we can have dinner again. Mitch

Her heart fluttered. How sweet.

Wait . . . what was she doing? Her stomach dropped. This was the sort of thing Caleb would do. Here she was falling for the wrong guy again. Judah, on the other hand, reminded her of the daisies. Strong, steady, dependable. But could she trust her own judgment? What if choosing the wrong man was hereditary?

What if she was just like her mom?

She sank onto the stool behind her as the truth washed over her. There was no way she was going to end up like her mom, swept off her feet by any guy who showed up with roses and ignoring the way he treated her. She had to break this cycle.

CHAPTER 13

Judah walked into the doctor's lounge and sank onto the couch. After back-to-back surgeries, he needed a break. He unlocked his phone and found The Mother Lode's website. He scrolled past pictures of vases, a picture of the cuckoo clock, and an old desk polished to a shine. His finger hovered over the phone number. He wanted to see Elaine again, but he didn't want to push her. Maybe a casual dinner, no expectations.

He pushed the number and nervously tapped his foot on the floor as it rang.

"The Mother Lode Antique Shop, Elaine speaking."

"Hi, it's Judah. I'm between patients so I thought I'd see how you're doing."

"It's been busy, but I'm good."

"That's good." He took a deep breath. "Clara's spending the night at her grandmother's tonight. Would you like me to bring dinner over later?"

"I'd like that." Her voice softened at the end, setting his stomach aflutter.

"Then I'll see you tonight." He leaned back as he ended the call. He should have asked her what she liked to eat. When he brought burgers, she said she wasn't picky. Maybe Italian? No, the house had smelled like Italian spices last night, and he didn't want to remind her of Mitch. He could brave the crowds and get something from a food truck. She was stuck in the store all day and probably hadn't had any of the amazing food the rally attracted.

Energized by the thought, he hopped up from the couch. Only a few more hours until he would see her pretty face again. He hurried to his office, not even caring that a mound of paperwork waited for him.

****

Judah strode up the walkway to The Mother Lode. His mouth watered from the aroma that floated from the bag of food he held.

Elaine stood on the front porch with two glasses of water. Her hair brightened against the yellow sleeveless shirt. "It's such a nice night, I thought we could sit out here." She pointed to the swing that hung from the ceiling. Matching wrought iron tables sat on either side.

A group of motorcyclists revved by. The street bustled with people, but he didn't care as long as he got to sit on the swing with Elaine. "It's certainly not a peaceful night. But I'll take time with you any way I can get it." Judah set the bag down, then pulled out a Styrofoam container and handed it to her.

She sat and opened the lid. "I love Indian tacos."

He smiled, delighted that he'd guessed right. He took out his taco and joined her. "Any new ideas on the art classes?"

She shook her head and took a bite.

"Where's Sheba?"

Elaine wiped her mouth with a napkin before pointing at the house. "I put her out back just before you got here." She started to say something, but the rumble of Harley engines drowned out her voice. She frowned. "I thought we could keep an eye on the store out here, but now I'm not so sure."

Judah closed his container, then reached for hers. "Do you still have the baby monitor? We could join Sheba out back. Enjoy the fresh air without the noise."

"That's probably wise." She picked up their glasses and walked inside.

When they reached the back door, she gifted him a small smile as he held it open for her. Sheba was lying on the deck. She jumped to her feet and brought him a tennis ball. "We'll play later," he said, rubbing her head as the house muted the roaring motorcycle engines. Once they were seated, he shifted his chair so he could see Elaine. "This is much better. How's your taco?"

"Very good." She looked down at her container and took small bites, not once looking at him.

"Elaine?"

"Yes?"

When she still didn't look up, he set his taco down. "What's going on?"

Finally, she tilted her chin up, her eyes wide. "What do you mean?"

"You seem distant."

"I'm sorry."

"Did something happen today?"

She shook her head.

"Are you still upset about last night?"

"No. I mean, I am, but that's not bothering me now."

"Then what's bothering you?" He stilled as he waited for her answer.

"I'm scared."

He tensed, his senses on alert. "What happened? Did someone threaten you?"

"Nothing like that." She looked off into the yard. "I'm scared of you."

Judah sat back, shocked and hurt. "I would never hurt you."

"I know."

"Then why? Is it because of Caleb?"

She touched his hand, calming his anxiety. "No, I'm not scared of you hurting me or anything. I'm scared of the unknown."

The tension eased from his body. "This is scary for me too," he said. "But that's why I'm here, so we can get to know each other."

"I know that. But I don't want to make the same mistakes my mom made. I grew up watching her float from one bad relationship to another. I always wondered why she kept dating scumbags. But I get it now."

"You do?"

"Yeah. It's what she was comfortable with, what she knew. I've been thinking and rethinking through my date with Mitch. I was flattered by him, but that's no reason to let things get that far. It's just that he's so much like Caleb that I was comfortable being around him. I know what to expect with him. You"—her eyebrows lifted— "are a mystery, and that scares me."

The last of his anxieties began to calm. Having dinner with Elaine was a big step for him, but he was realizing it was an even bigger step for her. "I want to keep spending time with you, but I don't want to scare you. How do we move past this?"

She scraped through her taco toppings with her fork. "I don't know. I'm trying to be brave for once, but it's not easy."

For once? That didn't make sense. "Elaine."

She looked at him.

He grabbed her free hand. "You've proven yourself pretty brave already. This is new territory for us both. Let's start with small steps, like sharing a taco on the deck and talking."

"I'm also really nervous being around Clara."

"So far, your every action around her has been for her wellbeing. I'm not worried that you're going to hurt her."

"I would never hurt her on purpose, but I never wanted to hurt Marcus either. I hurt the kids in my class by abandoning them. Some of them had really opened up to me about their lives. I can't imagine how they felt when they heard about me in the news. I'm another person who hurt and disappointed them."

Judah understood Elaine's fears more than she probably realized. "I want to shelter Clara and protect her from every bad thing too, but I couldn't protect her from losing her mom. I can do my best to protect her and teach her how to protect herself when I'm not there, but she's going to get hurt. That's the way life is. When that happens, I'll be there to comfort her, and I'll try to teach her how to cope with the hurt. I know some day I'll hurt Clara too, even though I don't mean to. All I can promise her and myself is that I'll never do it on purpose. That's all I'd ever ask of you too." He locked his gaze onto hers. "If you can promise to always try to protect Clara, then I trust you."

"I'd protect her with my life." Her lips slowly curved into a smile. "Have you ever felt like you don't deserve the blessings in your life?"

"Every day."

She squeezed his hand. "You're a blessing to me. One that I don't deserve, but I think I'll keep you anyway."

He grinned. "Good, because I'm kind of stubborn. I don't want to give this up until we've given it a fair try."

"Thank you."

With that out of the way, he finished his taco with gusto. The food tasted better without the tension between them. As they talked about the small details of their day, he loved her new comfort level with him. She told him of the crazy outfits she'd seen that day and even laughed so hard she snorted. Laughing with Elaine was becoming a new favorite activity.

When they'd finished eating, she took his empty container and stood. "How about some ice cream? I have chocolate."

"I'd like that."

"You can play with Sheba while I dish it up. The poor thing must get bored sitting by me all day." She slipped inside.

"Sheba, come." The German Shepherd ran over and dropped her ball. Judah tossed it a few times before Elaine returned with ice cream smothered in chocolate fudge. "You sure like chocolate."

"Is it too much for you?" She handed him a bowl.

"Not at all." He took a bite of the rich thick chocolate topping with a hint of vanilla. "That fudge is amazing."

"It's an old family recipe." She moved past the table and sat on the steps so he joined her. "We've been talking a lot about me. How about you? Did you always want to be a doctor?"

"Kind of. I grew up on a ranch in the eastern part of the state. I helped my dad and older brother with the cows and horses every chance I got. I went to college to become a veterinarian, but I took a human anatomy class and loved it."

"Do you still love it?"

"I do. I like to help people and I love being challenged. Working at the VA hospital, I feel like I'm still serving my country by taking care of our soldiers."

"You're fascinating." Her adorable head tilt as she studied him. *Fascinating* wasn't a word he'd use to describe himself. And if she didn't stop looking at him like he'd just pulled a puppy from a burning car, he'd end up doing something foolish, like kissing her. It was too soon for that.

"And now you've made me blush," he said.

Elaine laughed. "Good. You know how I feel all the time." She took a bite of ice cream before asking quietly, "How did you meet your wife?"

"I joined the air force to pay for medical school and was stationed at Ellsworth Air Force Base, east of Rapid City. I joined a local softball league to meet people. Whitney was the star pitcher."

Elaine sighed. "Love at first sight?"

He laughed. "Not at all. She was always giving me a hard time. I was the only one on the team who wasn't a first responder. She called me *softy* for the first few weeks because I told her I had to be careful not to get calluses. I was shocked when she asked me out."

"She asked you out? I would never have the nerve."

"That was Whitney. When she knew what she wanted, she went after it."

"How did she die?" Elaine tilted her head and a curl fell across her cheek. "You don't have to tell me if you don't want to. It's none of my business."

Judah ate another bite of ice cream as he considered what to share. The story never got easier to tell, but he wanted to know Elaine better and he wanted her to know him too. Setting down the bowl, he focused on the back fence. "She was shot by a drug runner. Her Kevlar vest protected her from the shots to the chest, but a bullet nicked her neck. She died before help could get there."

"I'm so sorry."

"Thank you."

"Did you have family around to help?"

He shook his head. "Not right away. After we got married, I was transferred to Randolph Air Force Base in San Antonio. Whitney was hired with the San Antonio Police Department and promoted to the narcotics division." As if she knew what they were talking about, Sheba leaned against him. Judah petted her behind her ears. "That's why Zoe blames me for Whitney's death. I'm the reason Whitney moved to San Antonio, so I'm the reason she's dead."

"I don't think anyone can blame you for that, but grief sometimes twists things in our minds."

Sheba stood and growled into the dark yard. Alarm rushed through Judah as he moved in front of Elaine. His gaze bounced around the yard as he tried to see what Sheba sensed. "Who's there? Show yourself." He pulled his phone from his pocket, just in case.

A light above the garage turned on and Jules stepped into the yard. "It's me."

His body relaxed. She dragged another girl behind her, blonde hair falling over her face.

"Jules!" Elaine stepped around him and ran to them. "What are you doing here?"

The girl hugged Elaine. "I promised Ginny I'd go back for her. Will you help us?"

CHAPTER 14

Elaine's heart hammered against her chest. She searched the yard. "Did anyone see you come here?"

"I don't think so."

"This is the first place they'll look for you." She ushered the girls inside. Shocked that Jules had taken such a risk, Elaine's insides shook.

Judah followed them in and leaned toward Elaine. "I'm staying until these girls are gone," he whispered.

"They won't hurt me."

"I know, but we don't know who's following them."

She hadn't thought of that. "Thank you." She touched his arm, then turned to the girls. "We've got to call the police. They need to know you're here."

"No!" Jules pulled Ginny closer to her side. "They'll make me go back to that foster home. I hate it there. They treat me like a baby."

Elaine sighed. "There's no way I can keep you safe."

Judah stepped forward. "You'll all be in danger if you stay here. Including Elaine."

"How about we call Bridget?" Elaine pulled out her phone. "She mentioned something about a group home. She can help us with the police, then make sure you're both safe."

"What if I say no?" Jules clenched her jaw.

Elaine tried to understand the girl's perspective. "I know it seems like you don't have a say in your own life, and maybe you haven't for a long time, but we're trying to keep you safe. Let's give Bridget a chance. I think she'll surprise you. What do you say?" She held her breath.

Jules sagged. "OK, fine. You can call her."

Relieved, Elaine locked the back door and pulled the shades. She would have had to call someone regardless of whether or not Jules wanted her to, but it was good to know the girls would cooperate. She motioned to the kitchen chairs. "Why don't you sit?"

Jules pulled Ginny over and practically pushed her into a chair before putting her backpack on the floor and sitting next to her. Ginny pushed her long blonde hair away from her face. Even with her heavy make-up, she looked younger than Jules.

Elaine's stomach sank. What must they have been through? "Judah, will you get them each a glass of water while I call?" He nodded, so Elaine stepped into the dining room to call Bridget.

Loud music blared through the phone. "Elaine. How's it going?"

"I'm sorry to call so late, but I have a situation."

"Hold on. I'm at a concert. Let me find a quieter place to talk." The music faded. Elaine peeked into the kitchen. Jules and Ginny sat at the table whispering to each other. Judah stood at the sink washing their ice cream bowls. "Sorry about that. What's up?"

"Jules is here with another girl. She doesn't want us to call the police, but I'm afraid those men will show up. You're the only person Jules will let me call."

"I'm at the Buffalo Chip. I can be there in ten minutes. Make sure the doors are locked and don't let anyone in."

"Thank you." Relieved, she took a deep breath, then joined the girls in the kitchen. Jules and Ginny stared at their water glasses.

Elaine sat across from them. "I bet your foster parents are going crazy looking for you."

Jules's shoulders slumped. "They don't care."

"I would be frantic."

Jules put her backpack on the table. She unzipped it and pulled out a familiar box. "This is the lamp you paid two hundred dollars for, isn't it?"

"I didn't pay two hundred. It's *worth* two hundred. I hoped it would remind you of your worth."

"When Bridget gave it to me, I thought you might care what happens to me."

"I *do* care, which is why I called Bridget. And I'm glad you're safe. Are you two hungry? I can make you sandwiches while we wait."

They both nodded, so she pulled out some bread, sandwich meat, and cheese. Judah silently helped. By the time the girls finished eating, the doorbell chimed. Elaine glanced at Judah. "That's probably Bridget."

"I'm on it." He hurried out of the kitchen with Sheba following him.

Elaine smiled at Jules then Ginny. "I'm glad you came here. I'll do all I can to help you."

Jules grinned. "See, Ginny. I told you she'd help."

Ginny nodded.

"What do we have here?" Bridget stepped in wearing the same clothes as earlier, but the skirt seemed shorter and the eye make-up darker.

"Thanks for coming." Elaine stood and offered Bridget her chair before joining Judah at the counter.

"I'm glad you called." Bridget looked at Jules. "Who's your friend?"

"Ginny. I told her if I got out that I'd come back for her."

"That was a dangerous risk you took. Are you planning on going back for more girls?"

"No. I gave Ginny a place and time to meet before I left. Figured if she wasn't there, I'd never be able to find her, but I had to try."

Bridget raised her eyebrows. "You should have told me so we could have helped you."

Jules shrugged again. "I did OK."

Bridget shook her head as she looked at the younger girl. "Ginny, I'm Bridget Smalls. I work for the sheriff's department as a victim's advocate. I'm here to help you."

Ginny nodded.

"How old are you?"

"Fourteen," she whispered.

"Where are you from?"

"St. Paul."

"Do you have any family there?"

Jules sat up straight and squared her shoulders. "She ain't got no one, just like me."

Bridget sighed. "Jules, let her answer. Ginny?"

"I got a mother."

Jules scowled. "She can't go back to her. She's the one who sold her."

Elaine pressed her injured hand to her chest. Judah wrapped a hand around her free one.

Bridget turned toward them. "I called the police on my way over. Would you guys mind watching the door for them?"

"You called the police?" Jules stood so fast her chair thumped on the ground.

"I had to. I need to make sure we're all safe. I also called your social worker so she could let the Joneses know that you're here. She's on her way too, but I promise we'll work this out together."

Jules glared at Bridget then at Elaine.

Elaine gave the girls what she hoped was a confident smile. "Trust Bridget. She knows what she's doing, and she wants to help. We'll be in the other room if you need anything, OK?"

Jules grabbed her chair and slammed it down before sitting. "I'll hear you out, but I'm leaving if I want to."

Elaine's chest ached as Judah led her into the foyer. He stood in front of her desk and leaned back so he faced the door with Sheba at his side. Caleb would have told her what to do and where to go, but Judah simply stood with her. His respect and distance drew her to him. Standing next to him, she leaned her head against his shoulder, and he draped his arm around her. Instead of feeling trapped, Elaine felt protected.

Had Ginny ever felt protected? "I can't believe a mother would sell her child into prostitution." She looked into Judah's face. "It's not fair. How could anyone sell their child? I would do everything I could to protect my child if I had the chance."

"I don't understand it either. I would sacrifice everything to keep Clara safe."

"I wish there was more I could do." She wished she could keep Jules and Ginny there. She could keep Jules and Ginny there. She had plenty of space for them, but she knew the court would never agree.

Blue and red lights flashed outside. Elaine took a step back and Judah grabbed Sheba's collar. He strode to the door and opened it as two officers in dark blue uniforms climbed the steps.

Officer Holt entered first. "Ma'am."

Elaine pointed to the dining room. "Bridget and the girls are in the kitchen through there."

He nodded and walked that way. Then Zoe stepped into the shop, glaring. Elaine's stomach clenched.

Zoe faced Judah, her hands on her duty belt. "What are you doing here?"

"None of your business."

Her steely gaze landed on Elaine. "You have some nerve getting involved with Judah. Is it Clara you're after?"

Elaine stepped back as if slapped.

"That's out of line." Judah crossed his arms.

Zoe stepped close to Elaine. "You may have him fooled, but I'm watching you. One wrong move and I'll personally haul you back to jail. You'll serve the rest of your four-year sentence." She followed her partner into the other room.

Terror raced through Elaine. Could Zoe really find a reason to send her back to jail?

"Are you OK?" Judah asked, leaning close and lowering his voice.

Elaine shook her head. "Can she do that? What kind of wrong move is she looking for?"

"I don't know. Do you know someone who you can ask?"

"I'm meeting with my probation officer in a couple of days. I could ask him."

"That's a good idea. I might know someone who could help. I'll make some calls."

She touched her chest. "You'd do that for me?"

"Of course. I'd do far more to protect you." He wrapped his arm around her again.

Elaine leaned into him as she tried to process her ever-changing life. For a girl who had never gotten in trouble before her arrest, she sure was seeing a lot of the police lately, but the more she saw them, the more comfortable she felt. Safe even. Not counting Zoe, they seemed like they wanted to help her. Even if they did, Elaine hoped she wouldn't need to call them again.

CHAPTER 15

Elaine handed a bill of sale to the customer as her sons carried a long, hundred-and-fifty-year-old dresser out the front door. "Thank you for your business."

"I'm the one who should be thanking you. This will be perfect for our bed-and-breakfast." The woman smiled brightly before following her sons out the door.

Elaine walked into the front room where she had displayed the dresser. With it gone, she had room to rearrange the display cases. With one of the larger cases in the middle of the room nearly empty, she could move it to the back of the room and use it for storing painting supplies. The extra space should be enough to set up six easels. It should be enough space for an art class.

Eager to see what it would look like, she gathered the retro lunch boxes and put them with the antique toys near the boarded-up window. Once the shelves were empty, she grabbed both sides of the case, stretching to reach both ends. Pulling it toward her, she managed to slide one side a few inches. Her muscles shook as her injured hand lost its grip. The case tipped toward her. As she steadied it with her shoulder, the bell rang. Great.

"I'll be with you in a second!" She needed to tip the case back without pushing it over. Her knees ached as gravity pushed the case against her.

"Whoa. What are you going?" Bridget peeked her head around the case.

"I was trying to move it."

Bridget grabbed the other side and helped her tip it back.

"Thanks. It didn't look that heavy when I started."

"Where are you moving it?"

"To the back. My aunt was right. The rally has been great for business. I've sold so much inventory this week that I thought I'd do some rearranging. Make it easier to walk through the store. What are you up to?"

"I was on my morning walk and thought I'd stop in and see how you were doing."

That's when Elaine noticed Bridget's workout clothes and high ponytail. "I should join you sometime. I never make the time to exercise."

Bridget grinned. "You should. I only live half a mile away. I could walk over before you open the store. It's always more fun to exercise with a friend."

Happiness spread through Elaine. *A friend.* She'd never had a close friend before.

"Do you want some help moving this monstrosity?"

"I'd love some. If you take that end, I'll take this one." They lifted together, then took small steps through the store until they reached the open spot on the south wall.

Bridget stepped back and looked at their work. "Is this where you want it?"

"It's perfect. Thanks."

"Glad I came when I did. What else do you need help with?"

"I need to restock the shelves."

"Then let's go."

Elaine walked over to the stack of boxes sitting on her desk, handed one to Bridget, then grabbed another one.

Bridget opened a box and took out a bag of paintbrushes. "Are you selling painting supplies now?"

Elaine took a deep breath, nervous about telling anyone else about the class. If she told too many people, they'd hold her to it. But if she wanted to make friends, she needed to start trusting people. "No, but I'm thinking about turning this room into a studio and offering art classes."

"I thought you weren't interested in teaching art."

"For kids, but this would be for adults. There are a lot of logistics I need to work through before I invest too much money, but I found those brushes at a great price and couldn't resist." Elaine pulled out plastic paint pallets.

"What kind of logistics?"

"Where to have the class. I'd prefer to have it here and save some money."

Bridget looked to the ceiling then around the room. "I think it would be perfect here. This is a great house. Do you know how old it is?"

"At least a hundred years."

"That's epic. My house is nearly that old. Would you care if I sent my contractor over to scope out the place? I'm in the middle of a remodel, and I'd love to duplicate all this woodwork. I love the crown molding and arched doorways."

"Send him over." Knowing that Bridget appreciated the artistic touches of the house, Elaine liked her even more. She hoped Jules and Ginny could learn to like and trust her too. The thought of the young runaways touched something in her heart. "Why do you think Jules came here last night? This should have been the last place she went."

"Jules trusts you. I'm shocked at how quickly she's connected with you. With her history of adults hurting her, I'd expect her trust to be hard-earned."

"I'm confused too but honored just the same."

"It's shocking, but not that confusing. You saved her, you listened to her without condescension, and you gave her a meaningful gift, probably the nicest gift she's ever received." She put the last bag of brushes on the shelf. "In a world like Jules's, you're probably the only nonthreatening adult she knows."

That reality broke Elaine's heart. "I only did what any decent person should do. I can't imagine the abuse she's suffered. I had no idea girls were trapped in such a horrible life here. I'd do anything to protect them." She got up to grab the last box.

When she returned, Bridget was watching her with narrowed eyes. "Do you mean that?"

"Of course."

"Good. After our first call, I did some research on you."

Panic seized her. "Oh?" Her hands shook as she opened the final box.

Bridget laughed. "Don't look so scared. You're not the only one with a past. When I say I did my research that means I dug deeper than the criminal records and news articles. I've learned there's usually more to a story if you're willing to listen, so I talked with the child's social worker and the lead detective on your case. I'd love to hear your side."

Elaine froze, too confused to keep working. "If you knew about my record, why did you ask me to teach art to kids? You know why I can't."

Bridget shrugged. "I believe in second chances. I'm a second chance."

"You?"

"I work with trafficking victims because I escaped that world ten years ago."

Ten years? She either looked young or she had been a child when she was trafficked. "I'm sorry."

"It's not your fault."

"Can I ask what happened? You don't have to tell me if you don't want to."

"I don't mind telling you." Bridget set down the last of the brushes. "When I was twelve, I went to a party with an older girl. I thought I was so cool going to a rager. After drinking too much, I passed out. When I woke up, I was in a strange house. My 'friend' was long gone, but half a dozen men and at least ten other girls, mostly in their teens, were there."

How could something so awful happen to someone so young? "Your parents let you go to a party like that when you were twelve?"

"They didn't know. I snuck out after my mom went to bed. They had just gotten a divorce, and my dad bought me a smart phone to talk to him. I disabled the parental controls and found a chat room. Now I know they were targeting young girls, but back then I thought I was so cool. That's where I met Shadow."

"Your friend?"

Bridget nodded. "She said she was sixteen and had divorced parents too. None of my friends' parents were divorced, so it felt good to connect with someone who understood my pain. By the time she invited me to the party, I trusted her completely."

"You must have been terrified."

Bridget's eyelids drooped. "I had never been so scared."

"How did you get out?"

"My parents hired a private detective. He worked with the sheriff's department. They had been investigating the group for a while. Thankfully, they were busted a month later."

Tears welled up in Elaine's eyes. "How do you heal from that?"

Bridget set more pallets on the shelf. "Lots of amazing counseling and tons of hard work. Working as a victim's advocate is my way of giving back and moving forward. If my experiences can help other victims, that's one more way for me to take back the power my captors took from me."

Elaine couldn't imagine the strength it took to move on. She'd never experienced anything so vile, and she still struggled with her mother's abandonment and Caleb's control. She wiped the tears from her face. Could she ever get to the point where she could help other women like herself?

"Where should I put this?" Bridget held up a stack of plastic drop cloths and faced Elaine. "Hey, don't cry for me."

"I can't help it. You survived something horrible."

"I did, but I'm not *just* a survivor. I'm a warrior. I'll never say I'm thankful for the evil that was done to me, but I'm thankful for the chance to take that experience and help other girls. Our pasts don't need to dictate our futures."

"How?" Maybe if she could learn how Bridget did it, Elaine could move on too.

"I own up to the mistakes I've made, and I live in the freedom of forgiveness."

"How, after what they did to you?"

"Because forgiveness takes away their power over my feelings and thoughts and gives it back to me."

Elaine leaned back on her hands in shock. What would it feel like to have that kind of power? "I wish I could take control over my life like that."

"You can. It starts with forgiveness." Bridget squeezed Elaine's shoulder. "And sometimes the person we need to forgive the most is ourselves."

Her mom's abandonment whirled through her mind. Elaine's chest ached just thinking about how unwanted she'd felt each time she left. And Caleb, who'd promised to always love her but ended up manipulating her. He'd abandoned her in a way too. Then there was her sweet Marcus and his new family and the pain she had caused them.

If only she could ask them for forgiveness. Maybe she could write an apology to Marcus and his new family. She'd caused just as much heartache for them as her mom and Caleb had for her. But Bridget was proof that people could heal. Maybe Elaine and Marcus could heal too.

Bridget grabbed two empty boxes. "Where do these go?"

"Downstairs." Elaine took the remaining boxes and led Bridget to the kitchen. She opened the door and they threw the boxes down. "I'll break them down later. I appreciate the help today."

"That's kind of what I do these days. And if you're still interested in helping girls like Jules, I have a few ideas."

"My record . . ." She reminded Bridget, not wanting to get too excited.

"Let me worry about that. I have to talk to my boss, but I'm sure we can figure something out."

Hope surged through Elaine as more light cut through the fog of her past.

After Bridget left, Elaine pulled out a notebook and jotted down some ideas for the art class. She'd never taught adults before. Could she do the same thing with them as she would with Jules? The phone rang. "The Mother Lode Antique Shop, Elaine speaking."

"Hello, sweetie," her grandma said in a soft voice.

"Hi, Grandma. How are you?"

"I'm fine. I was wondering if you have my emerald broach. I can't seem to find it anywhere, and I wanted to show it to Misty. It's been in the family for generations, you know."

"I know, but I don't have it. Did you look in the jewelry box on your dresser?"

"That's the first place I looked."

"Maybe it fell behind the dresser. I'm coming to Rapid City tomorrow for a meeting. I can stop by and look."

"OK, dear. Maybe you can meet Misty then."

"I won't have a lot of time, but if she stops by, I'd love to meet her. Have you been shopping yet this week?"

"No. I don't have to go."

Elaine sighed. "You do if you want to eat. Do you have food in the house?"

"Of course. Misty brought me food yesterday."

"She did?"

"She's very nice. She asked if there was anything she could do for me, and I told her I don't like shopping. She offered to do it for me."

"Did you get a receipt?" Elaine appreciated Misty's help, but until she had a chance to meet this lady, she was still responsible to help her grandma with her needs.

"Of course. She brings my groceries and gives me the receipt, then I give her money. She never asks for more."

Relieved but still curious, Elaine wondered if she should make extra time to stay in Rapid City and meet this woman. "She does sound nice. I hope I get to meet her. Would you like me to bring you and Misty some lunch when I come tomorrow?"

"That would be wonderful."

As Elaine hung up, the front door opened. A group of bikers walked in and nodded at her. Before she could greet them, Mitch stepped in spinning an old globe.

Her stomach turned. "Mitch."

He smiled. "Elly. You're looking pretty today."

"What can I help you with?"

"Did you get my flowers?"

She pointed to the still radiant roses and daisies on the counter.

"Not as pretty as you, but they're nice. How about dinner tonight? There's this great place—"

"The thing is"—she squared her shoulders and held her head high, hoping the extra height would steady her voice—"Judah and I are kind of seeing each other."

He blew out a breath. "I lost to the dog guy?"

"No, it's not like that." She wasn't quite sure what to say that wouldn't be rude. "There's no winner or loser. There's just a . . . connection with him that I'd like to explore."

"A connection." His shoulders hunched. "I don't know how to compete with that."

"It's not a competition."

"I get it, I think. Can we still be friends?"

"Just friends? No asking for dates or flirting with me?"

His cocky grin reappeared. "Depends on your definition of flirting. Telling you you're beautiful when you wear pink isn't flirting. It's the truth."

Heat singed her cheeks. "If you say so." She pointed at the globe. "Is that for me?"

"If you want it. I'm not sure how old it is, but it has USSR instead of Russia, so it's at least a few decades." He set it on the counter. "Do you have any idea what it's worth?"

It was about the size of a smaller beach ball with a thin metal base. "I saw one on eBay going for close to eighty-five dollars, but I'll have to wait to research it. What little free time I've had this week has filled up, and I need to print off some flyers for tomorrow so people know the store's closed."

"Why would you close during the rally?"

"I have an appointment in Rapid City tomorrow at ten and I can't get out of it." She sighed as more customers walked in. "I don't have a choice."

"I'll help."

She laughed. "You have a good eye for antiques, but running the store is different."

"I'm sure it is, but I spent ten years working the concession stand at my dad's movie theater. I might not be able to answer any questions about this globe, but I can run a credit card machine."

Hope sprung up in her. Maybe it could work. "Are you sure? This is a lot to ask."

"Of course I'll help, especially if it proves I'm the best friend you've ever had."

Feeling lighter than she had when he walked in, she breathed in a full breath. "If you have an hour or so now, I'll show you how to run the register. Maybe these people will buy something, and you can ring them up."

He saluted her. "I'm at your service, babe."

She laughed and led him to the back of the counter. "All the merchandise is marked." She showed him how to ring up and track purchases on her iPad, then explained her shipping policy.

Mitch nodded, then patted the large antique cash register. "If you can do all of that on there, what's this big thing for?"

"It's a glorified money holder." She pushed the top button and cranked the lever on the right. The drawer popped open. "Tada!" She smiled. "Any questions?"

"I should be able to remember all this."

"I'll write down the password and directions in case you forget, and I'm only a phone call away if you need anything. If it gets too overwhelming, you can always close. I'll print off those flyers and leave them for you, just in case."

He squeezed her shoulder. "I won't let you down."

A chill ran through her as she shifted away from him. Sheba growled and sat in between them. "She's a good chaperone."

"Will she be here tomorrow?"

"If you're not comfortable with her, I can leave her in the backyard. The weather's supposed to be nice." Elaine bent down and pulled out the bags and tissue paper. "Make sure to wrap the breakable items really well before putting them in a bag."

"Got it."

A customer approached the counter, and Mitch turned on the charm. Elaine relaxed against the wall as he handled the transaction like he'd been doing it for years. First Bridget, now Mitch. Maybe her luck with friends was finally changing.

CHAPTER 16

At exactly ten o'clock, Elaine walked into her probation officer's office. Mr. Hughes looked up from his papers when she entered. Her stomach tightened. His military hairstyle always intimidated her.

"Ah, Mary Russell. On time as usual. Have a seat." He motioned to the chair opposite his desk.

She sat and laced her fingers together, trying to calm her nerves.

"How have you been this last month?" He opened his laptop and started typing.

"Working hard at my antique shop."

"Have you been busy with the rally?"

She nodded. "When the weather is nice."

"It looks like you've had a busy week. The police were called four times to your residency."

Zoe's threats ran through her mind. "That's correct."

"It also looks like you were the victim three times and the last call was to help a minor. Seems you've landed yourself in the middle of several trafficking escapes. They weren't able to tie the vandalism to the traffickers though."

Elaine shook her head.

"Your random drug tests have come back negative. Unless you have something to discuss with me, I think we're done here."

She wanted to be done, but first, "I do have a question. I was told by a police officer that if I made one wrong move, I'd be forced to finish out my sentence in jail. Is that true?"

"It depends on what you do. Most misdemeanors won't send you back to jail. If you kidnap another child, of course, you'll go back." He raised an eyebrow.

She shook her head so hard that a red curl brushed her nose. "I don't plan on repeating that again. Ever."

He nodded. "I believe you. You seem like you've learned your lesson, and I understand the unique circumstances surrounding the crime you committed. If you find yourself in a situation that you're unsure of, just call and ask me." He handed her a business card. "In case you lost the last one."

"Thank you." Elaine opened her purse and pulled out an envelope. "I wrote an apology letter to Marcus and his family. Is it possible for you to get it to them?" Even if it never reached them, it had been therapeutic to write it. Thanks to Bridget, she was finally on the path to self-forgiveness.

"I'll get it to the victim's advocate on the case and she'll pass it on." He took the letter. "I'll see you next month."

That was it? Even with all of the calls to the police? Relieved, she tucked the card into her purse and walked out of the office. "Thank you." No one stopped her in the hallway or on her way to her car. With each step, her stomach relaxed.

Zoe hadn't given a bad report and Mr. Hughes believe Elaine. By the time she slid into her car, she'd relaxed so much that her stomach growled.

As promised, she picked up take out, then drove to her grandma's house. A newer residential area turned into rows of older, split-level and ranch homes with large oak trees dotting the boulevard. She pulled into the single-car driveway of her grandmother's light blue ranch house.

Elaine grabbed her things and made her way to the front door. She pushed the doorbell with her elbow as the greasy smell of fried food drifted up to her. Her stomach growled again. She had skipped breakfast because of her meeting, but now that hope had replaced stress, her appetite roared to life.

Her grandma answered the door wearing her usual cotton floral dress. Her formerly chin-length hair curled tightly around her head. "Hi, sweetie."

"Hi, Grandma." Elaine kissed her grandma's cheek before stepping inside. "Did you get your hair cut recently?"

"Misty cut it. She did such a beautiful job. I'd rather pay her than go all the way to the beauty parlor."

"Is Misty a cosmetologist?" Not that it would be hard to trim her grandma's curls.

"She says she cuts her own hair, so I thought why not? I love it." Her grandma smiled.

Elaine walked through the living room to the dining area. Like the outside, the inside reflected the seventies—worn, light brown carpet, an orange-and-brown floral couch, and an orange recliner. Sally Ann perched on the music rack.

"What's Sally Ann doing at the piano?"

"She likes to sing when I play." Grandma scurried to the piano bench, sat, and pounded out a lively tune. Sure enough, Sally Ann sang along.

Elaine laughed at the crazy duo. It felt good to laugh again. It felt like she could finally hope for a better future, for herself and for her grandma. They had always had each other and it used to be enough. Maybe it could be again.

As the song ended, Grandma petted Sally Ann's head. "That's a good girl." She looked at Elaine. "Tell your sister she did a good job."

Elaine sighed. "Good job, Sally Ann."

The yellow and gray cockatiel whistled.

Grandma held her finger out and Sally Ann hopped on it. "Let's get you tucked away in your room while your sister and I eat our lunch." The bird whistled again. "I'll wash my hands, then we'd better eat. Misty will be coming home soon."

After they'd both cleaned up and sat down, Elaine handed Grandma her food. "I picked up gyros from The Gyro Hub because

I know you like it. I didn't know what to get Misty, so I got her the same thing."

"She loves everything at the Gyro Hub. We eat there about once a week."

"You do?" Her stomach clenched. "You spend a lot of time together. Wasn't she just here yesterday?"

"She's here every day. She lives here."

"What?" Panic rose in her throat. "You're letting a stranger live with you?" Elaine hadn't made a big deal when Grandma's memory slipped now and then, but this was going too far.

"She's not a stranger. She's my friend. Sally Ann and I get lonely sometimes, and Misty said she could protect me if someone tried to break in."

"How? You met her at the grocery store. What do you know about her?"

"I know that she's nice."

Elaine gently grabbed her grandma's hand. "She sounds very nice, but we don't know anything else about her. It would break my heart if something happened to you."

"I know, sweetie. Once you meet Misty, you'll love her too."

"I hope so." She kept an eye on her grandma as they bit into their lunches. When grandma picked up a fry, Elaine noticed that her finger was bare. "Where's your wedding ring?"

She looked down at her hand. "I misplaced it. I took if off before bed because my fingers swell something awful at night. I must have knocked it off. Maybe you can look behind my nightstand before you leave."

First her necklace, then her broach, and now her ring. Uneasiness slithered over Elaine's skin. "I'll look now." She nearly sprinted to her grandmother's room and around the quilt-covered bed, then to the white-washed nightstand. She pulled it back so quickly the alarm clock fell to the floor. Ignoring it, she sank to her knees beside the nightstand, running her fingers through the shag carpet. Nothing. She rummaged through the drawers. Untucked the sheets and blankets to look in the bed. Checked inside each pair of shoes in the closet.

Her stomach tightened as she ran to the dresser. Dropping to her knees, she checked under and behind it. Then she searched the jewelry box and drawers. Nothing but an empty space where her granddad's watch had been.

"Mary!"

She looked at the doorway as her grandma stepped in.

"What are you doing? You've wrecked my room."

She sat back on her knees and examined the mess. "I'll fix everything. I'm just looking for your jewelry. Did you put Granddad's watch somewhere? It's always on the dresser and now it's gone."

With her brows bunched together, Grandma shuffled over to the dresser and looked at the doily next to the silver-handled brush. "No. It's been there since he last put it there the night he died."

Elaine stood, her skin crawling. "Where does Misty sleep?"

"In your old room."

Elaine hurried to the next room. The scent of cat urine filled the air. She knew that smell. Caleb had smelled like that. Other than smelling bad, the room looked mostly the same. Elaine's early attempts at oil painting covered the pink walls. Her old pink comforter even covered the bed.

A duffle bag sat on the comforter. Was Misty planning a trip she hadn't told Grandma about? Hopefully the jewelry wasn't in there. It would break her grandma's heart if it was.

Elaine stepped over to the bed and opened the bag. Crumpled clothing filled it. She rifled through it but only found more clothes. A sliver of relief eased in. Maybe Misty was harmless and Elaine was overreacting.

She backed up, but her foot caught on something. Glancing down, she noticed a black strap sticking out from under the bed. She crouched down and pulled on it. Another duffle bag. Elaine opened it. More dirty laundry. Relieved, she dumped the contents onto the bed.

As she sorted through the clothes, a clear bag filled with white powder fell from the pocket of some jeans. Nausea rolled through her. She searched through the pockets of another pair of jeans and pulled out her grandma's wedding ring. Her stomach cramped.

Elaine should have expected something bad to happen. Everything was going too well for her. She'd allowed herself a moment of joy and reality stole it from her as easily as Misty had stolen Grandma's ring.

Elaine dreaded calling the police once again. How many times could she call them before they started to think *she* was the problem? Would they believe the drugs weren't hers? She remembered Mr. Hughes's business card in her purse. He said to call if she was unsure about what to do—she was definitely unsure.

CHAPTER 17

At lunch, Judah slipped away from the hospital and headed to Main Street. He parked on a side street, walked around the rows of thousands of gleaming motorcycles, and weaved through the crowds to the food trucks. The scent of corn dogs and funnel cakes—accompanied by loud mufflers and blaring rock music—made braving the crowds worth it.

His insides fluttered, but he couldn't tell if it was excitement or nerves. He hoped Elaine would be happy about his surprise date. With another surgery in a couple of hours, he'd have to make it quick, but he really wanted to see her.

With a sack full of artery-hardening food, he walked into The Mother Lode, bumping into someone as he opened the door. "Excuse me," he said, moving aside to let the women step out. Inside the shop, customers filled the rows. He had to move around the line before he could even see the counter. Instead of a head of red curls, Mitch stood next to the register smiling at two women in bike leathers.

Judah seethed as he marched over to him. "Why are you here?"

Mitch turned and smirked. "I'm helping Elly." He handed the women two hand-decorated bags. "You ladies enjoy your afternoon."

"Where's Elaine?"

He shrugged. "She had an appointment and asked me to run the store for her."

Judah glanced at the empty pet bed. "Where's Sheba?"

"In the backyard. She kept growling and scaring the customers."

The unease Judah usually felt around Mitch grew. Sheba wouldn't growl at him for no reason. Judah hadn't trusted the man before. Now he really didn't trust him.

He pulled his phone from the pocket of his scrubs and called the hospital. "Nancy, it's Dr. Demski. How's Mr. Weber looking for his three o'clock hernia surgery?"

"I was just about to call you. I found an irregular pulse when I took his vitals in pre-op."

Judah sighed. He hated that Mr. Weber had to wait for the surgery, but he couldn't put him at further risk. "Then we'll have to reschedule. Have his primary care doctor order a cardiac work-up. I'll be out of the office the rest of the day." After finalizing a few more details with the nurse, he hung up and stared at Mitch. Elaine might trust him to run the store, but Judah trusted Sheba and his gut. He didn't know what it was about the guy, but it wouldn't hurt to watch him. "My schedule just opened up. I can stay and help."

"I don't need help."

Judah pointed at the line. "It looks like you do. I'll wrap up the merchandise while you ring it up."

Mitch shrugged then took a purple vase from a lady dressed in a crop top and jean shorts. "Will that be all?"

"Depends." She leaned on the counter toward Judah. "Maybe we can meet down at the Full Throttle Saloon tonight. I'll buy you a beer."

He grabbed a bag from below the counter. "No, thanks. Did you find everything you were looking for?"

"I sure did, Doc."

Mitch snorted as he put the vase in front of Judah. "You should go with her. I've got everything here under control."

Judah wrapped the vase while Mitch rang it up. When he passed the rose-drawn bag to the woman, he forced a smile. "Enjoy your time. Drink plenty of water."

"You're such a nerd," Mitch said under his breath.

Judah wanted to snap back, but another customer stepped up to the counter and Mitch started his spiel again. Judah lost track of the time as a steady stream of bikers kept them busy. As much as he didn't like the situation, he silently thanked Mitch for keeping Elaine's store open for her. When the customers thinned out, Judah stretched his back.

"Can't handle an hour on your feet, Doc?"

"I perform multiple-hour surgeries every week."

Mitch snorted. "Sure." His phone rang and he checked the display. "I've got to take this. You can man the register."

"I don't know how."

"I'll be right back," he said over his shoulder as he stepped outside.

A middle-aged man put an engraved wooden box on the counter. Judah swallowed. He turned it overlooking for the price. "That will be thirty-five dollars."

"Even? What about tax?"

"Oh, yeah. How much is tax? Six percent, so thirty-seven?"

"Got me. I'm from Ohio." He pulled out a credit card.

Judah stared at the card, then looked around for a card reader. All he could find was an iPad and the giant cash register. "Do you have cash?"

The man laughed as he put the card back and pulled out a fifty. Judah's fingers stiffened as he turned to the register and pushed a few buttons. Nothing. He turned the crank. Nothing. He pulled out his wallet and handed the man a twenty.

The man laughed again. "It's going to be a long day if you can't figure out how to open that thing. Maybe you should run after that kid. I think he's taking off."

What? Judah scooted around the man and out the door. Mitch was sinking into the driver's seat of a car when Judah reached him. "Where are you going?"

"Sorry, dude. I've got to go. My granny's sick. There are directions under the counter, but Elly said to close up if you couldn't handle the heat." He winked then closed the door.

Judah ran a hand over his face. Closing the shop might be the smart idea, but as he watched Mitch desert Elaine, he knew he couldn't too.

* * * * * * *

Elaine paced her grandma's living room, hugging her stomach as she waited for the police to arrive. Mr. Hughes had assured her she'd done the right thing, but Zoe's threats replayed in her mind.

The front door opened. A woman not much older than Elaine walked in wearing a tan scarf over long brown hair. She froze when she saw Elaine. "I'm sorry. Is Wanda here?"

Misty. Elaine wanted to call the cops and tell them to hurry, but she couldn't let Misty know she'd called. "She's not feeling good so she's lying down. How can I help you?"

"Who are you?"

"I'm her granddaughter."

The woman's eyes narrowed. "She doesn't have any family."

"Yes, she does. Me and my mom."

"What's your name?"

"My grandma calls me Mary."

The woman took a step back, her mouth hanging open. "I thought Mary was a bird. Sally Ann's sister?"

Elaine groaned. "As you can see, I'm not a bird."

"I don't mean to bother you. I'll just go to my room." Misty ducked her head as she hurried past Elaine, her fringed purse swaying by her hip.

Elaine followed her but stopped in the doorway. "I know who you are. My grandmother talks about you all the time. She told me you've been staying here."

"Yeah, she invited me." Misty scowled at her over her shoulder. "Did you go through my stuff? You had no right." She stuffed her belongings into the duffels—including the bag of drugs—then swung them over her shoulder.

"I was looking for my grandma's lost jewelry." Elaine pulled the wedding ring from her front pocket. "I found this in your jeans pocket. Where's the rest of her jewelry?" Her voice shook, but she blocked the doorway.

"I didn't take them. She wanted me to get the ring cleaned, so that's why I had it. I wouldn't do nothing to hurt Wanda." With her head held high, she pushed past Elaine into the hallway.

Elaine grabbed her arm. "You can't leave until you talk to my grandma. She won't understand why you left."

"I come and go all the time."

Panic rose in Elaine's throat. She had to keep Misty there. "You're taking your stuff. Does that mean you're not coming back?"

"Why do you care?" Misty stilled. "You called the cops, didn't you? After all I've done to help your grandma." She yanked her arm free. "Thanks a lot."

Elaine ran around Misty and blocked her path. "Please, I just want her stuff back. I don't care about anything else in there." She pointed at the bags.

"I didn't take nothing. She probably lost it."

Grandma's bedroom door opened and she stepped into the hall. "Misty? When did you get home?"

Misty took advantage of the distraction and shoved past Elaine, stopping halfway through the living room before turning around to face them. "Sorry, I've got to go. Thanks for letting me stay. Peace." In a few strides, she was out the door.

Elaine had to do something! She jogged outside as Misty hopped into an old brown pickup. As she drove away, Elaine pulled out her phone and snapped as many pictures as she could until the truck disappeared around the corner. She glanced at the photos. Each one was blurry. Great.

She was searching for one useable picture when a patrol car pulled up to the house and a uniformed officer got out. Her nerves sparked as she hurried to him. "Misty drove away in a light brown pickup. She has drugs in her bag and maybe some of my grandma's stolen jewelry."

"Which way did she go?"

Elaine pointed down the street. "Left onto Arizona Street."

"Did you get a plate number?"

She shook her head.

"Stay here." He ran to his car and pulled away with his lights on.

Adrenaline coursed through her. If they didn't catch Misty, would her grandma be OK staying alone? Elaine didn't like the idea, even if they managed to arrest Misty. Who knew if she'd made copies of the house key? And what was to stop someone else from doing the same thing? Grandma had sacrificed so much to care for Elaine. Now it was her turn to take care of Grandma.

CHAPTER 18

At nine, Judah locked the front door of The Mother Lode, turned off the lights, then emptied the coffee pot into his mug and drank the weak-but-warm coffee. Exhaustion weighed heavily on him, but he desperately wanted to see Elaine before he left. He let Sheba out back and followed her onto the deck. As he stepped outside, a car pulled into the driveway and the garage door opened.

He sucked in a worried breath. She'd be expecting Mitch at the store, not him. Would she be upset when she saw him? He'd only run off a few customers with his ineptitude. Hopefully, he hadn't hurt sales too much.

Elaine parked in the garage, then hopped out and walked around the back of the car to the passenger side. Judah strode over to meet her, finding her standing in front of the open front door. A bare bulb hung above her car, barely illuminating the packed space.

"Let's get you and Sally Ann inside first, then I'll come back for your luggage."

"I want to go home." An elderly voice cracked.

"You can't. I'm sorry, but the police don't think it's safe for you to stay at your house right now."

"You said Misty wasn't coming back."

"She probably isn't, but she could have made keys and given them to other people. You can stay here until we get the locks changed."

"Susan turned my parents' home into a store. I don't want to live in a store."

Judah stepped into the garage. "Do you need some help?"

Elaine screamed as she spun toward him clutching the neckline of her shirt. "Judah! What are you doing here?"

He held up his hands. "Sorry. I didn't mean to scare you. I was here helping out today and saw you pull up."

"Where's Mitch?"

"He took off shortly after I arrived. Said something about a sick grandma."

Elaine sighed. "I was afraid something would happen. Thanks for sticking around."

"Of course." He leaned toward the lady in the front seat. "Hi. I'm Judah." He held his hand out.

She smiled and put her hand in his.

"This is my grandma, Wanda. She's coming to stay with me for a little bit."

"It's a pleasure to meet you. Can I escort you inside?"

Wanda looked at Elaine. "Are you sure I can't go home?"

"I'm sure. Let Judah help you while I grab Sally Ann's cage." Elaine shot him a grateful look, then scooted past him to the other side of the car.

He led Wanda through the gate, and Sheba galloped over to them.

"It's a puppy." Wanda's face lit up. "I didn't know Mary got a puppy."

"She's actually my dog, but we're going to leave her outside for now." He led Wanda into the kitchen.

"This is my parents' house," she said, pulling the kitchen curtains closed. "I grew up here, but now it's a store, not a home."

Elaine burst through the back door holding a bird cage in one hand and a suitcase in the other.

Judah was dying to ask about the bird, her grandma, and Misty, but he could tell by the look on Elaine's face that it wasn't the time. Instead, he reached for the bird cage and suitcase. "You get your grandma settled and I'll carry her stuff up."

"Thanks." She passed everything to him, then took her grandma's hand and guided her up the stairs. He followed two steps behind.

Elaine led them to a pale pink room with a painted vine of roses along the top. A pink-and-yellow quilt covered the full-sized bed, and a Tiffany lamp sat on a long, white dresser.

"It's beautiful," Wanda said, pointing to the roses. "Did you paint this?"

Elaine smiled. "I did. Do you remember where the bathroom is?"

Wanda nodded.

"Should I put the bird here?" Judah pointed to the dresser.

"That's perfect."

He set the cage next to a framed photograph.

Wanda walked over to the picture and picked it up. "That's me and my sister. I'm the little girl and she's the baby."

Judah snuck a peek over her shoulder. Wanda looked to be a little younger than Clara in the photo. She sat on the steps of this very house holding a smiling baby. "Looks like Elaine got her red curls from you."

"Both my daughters were redheads too." Grandma smiled.

Elaine leaned near him, making his pulse jump. "It's a family legacy. Grandma, I'll help you find your toothbrush so you can get ready for bed."

Judah put the suitcase on the bed before looking at Elaine. "I'll wait for you in the kitchen."

She touched his forearm when he passed her. "Thanks."

He smiled, then headed to the kitchen and poured two glasses of chocolate milk. He set them on the table as he waited. All things considered, that had gone well. Elaine didn't seem to be mad, but maybe that would wear off after she got her grandmother settled.

The light pattering of footsteps sounded moments before Elaine stepped into the kitchen. Her curls frizzed around her shoulders and her eyes drooped. He pulled her toward a chair, but she leaned into him and laid her head on his shoulder. He happily wrapped his arms around her and held her. "You look exhausted."

"It was a long day." She shivered.

He tightened his arms. "Do you want to talk about it?"

"I do, but it's quite the story. Do you need to get home to Clara?"

"I had the neighbor girl pick her up from daycare. I told her I wasn't sure when I'd be home, so I'm good for at least another hour." He led her to the table and pulled out a chair.

Elaine sat. It wasn't until she scooted her chair in that she smiled, reaching for a glass of chocolate milk. "I'm going to need this tonight. Have I told you about Misty?"

Thirty minutes later, Judah drained the last of his chocolate milk as Elaine finished her story. It hit him in the core, reminding him of some of his elderly patients who had been easily swindled. "Do the police think they could get the jewelry back?"

"The officer said they'd try. I need to find pictures of each item so they can check with the local pawn shops. They said it happens more often than we'd think." Elaine slouched back in her chair. "If I'd paid more attention to my grandmother, this wouldn't have happened. I've been so wrapped up in my own problems that I've neglected her."

"You run a business in a different town, are trying to add onto it, and have gotten caught in the middle of a trafficking investigation. You're doing the best you can."

"Thanks, but I'm not sure if that makes me feel better about myself." She rubbed her temples. "I'll get to make up for lost time now. I'm not sure she can go back home even after we get the locks changed. She's too gullible. I'm in no position to judge anyone on their criminal behavior, but it breaks my heart that someone would do this." Her cinnamon lashes blinked back tears. "How are you not running away from me as fast as you can?"

"I have no plans to run from you." He scooted his chair closer to her and draped his arm around her shoulders, hugging her close. "See."

"Maybe you should." But even as she suggested it, she laid her head on his shoulder.

"Let me be the judge of that."

He couldn't imagine how he'd respond if he'd had half of her circumstances dropped on him, yet despite everything, she kept putting everyone's needs in front of hers. Her compassion attracted him. A desire to show her how much she attracted him overwhelmed him.

Dipping his head, he tilted her chin up and touched his lips to hers. Warmth swept over him in waves as he deepened the kiss. He wanted to hold her tighter, to crush her to him and prove to her how irresistible she was, but not tonight. Not when she was tired and doubting herself. Instead, he lightly ran his fingers down her arms as he inhaled her sweetness, then broke the kiss.

He pulled away from her before he kissed her again.

"You read my mind." She smiled up at him. "I was just thinking that I needed a distraction. Of course, I was thinking of a subject change, but your distraction was much better."

He brushed a peck across her lips. "A subject change is probably a safer option." But his brain was struggling to focus. He latched onto the first topic that came to mind. "You said you were in Rapid City to see your probation officer. How was that?"

"Good, actually. Mr. Hughes knows about my calls to the police and about the traffickers."

"Do you have to see him again?"

She nodded. "I'll meet with him every month for the next four years. But I'll only have random drug tests for the next year, as long as they remain clean."

"Why the drug tests?"

"It was a condition of my probation. They found drugs when they searched our home, and Caleb was high on meth when they shot him. They didn't believe me when I said I didn't know he was using, and they definitely didn't believe that I wasn't using too."

"And now?"

She smiled at him. "For the first time in a year, I'm glad I had a test this week. If they do find Misty and her stash, the test proves that I wasn't using."

Footsteps pitter-pattered down the stairs before Wanda appeared. "Mary. Can you take me home? I don't want to stay here. I want to take a bath, and you don't have a bathtub."

"There's a tub in my bathroom. Give me a minute and I'll help you."

"Will you take me home tomorrow? I'll need my piano so Sally Ann and I can sing." Wanda's scrunched eyebrows and sad eyes stoked sympathy in Judah.

"Not so soon, but maybe I can find some songs on my phone that you and Sally Ann can sing to." Elaine left Judah to hug her grandma, then led her to the stairs. "Let me walk Judah out, then I'll be right up. OK?"

With drooping shoulders, Wanda nodded before trudging up the stairs.

Elaine returned to him. "I hope she can adjust to staying here. I have no idea when or even if she'll be able to go home. It might be selfish of me, because I know she hates change, but I've been thinking about it all day, and I want her to stay here."

Judah laced his fingers through hers, enjoying the warmth their connection created. "I don't think it's selfish, especially since you only want to protect her." His watch dinged with a message. "It's my babysitter. I'd better go."

Without breaking contact, he led her through the darkened store to the front door. "Don't forget that Sheba's out back. Clara and I will stop by after work tomorrow."

Elaine wrapped her arms around him. "I don't know how to thank you for all your help today."

He kissed the tip of her nose. "It was my pleasure." He let himself out and waited for the lock to slide before heading to his car. The warmth of her hug still surrounded him. It would be another long day tomorrow, but knowing he'd see Elaine at the end of it, he couldn't wait for morning to arrive.

CHAPTER 19

Elaine snuggled into her pillow, eager to enjoy another hour of rest.

A bird twittered. Then a dog barked, making her ears ring. She popped up as Sheba ran to the door and barked again. Sally Ann squawked. Sheba barked. Elaine's head pounded.

"Quiet, girl." She slid out of bed. Sheba ran over to her and licked her hand. The soft light that filtered in around the closed curtains wasn't enough to brighten her room, so she pattered over to the door and flipped on the overhead light switch. Sheba followed.

Someone tapped on her door. When Elaine opened it, her grandma held out a yellow mug. "I made you some tea."

Elaine took the cup and silently willed it to contain caffeine. After the emotionally draining events of the day before, she could have slept all day. "Thanks. What time is it?"

"Six o'clock. When the dog barked, I knew you'd be up. Can I meet her?"

"Who?"

"The puppy."

"Sure, come in." She stepped back as her grandma shuffled in and went straight for Sheba. The German Shepherd sat quietly, but her tail blurred across the carpet as Grandma petted her head. When she sat in the wicker chair, Sheba put her front paws on her legs and laid her head down. Sheba looked as harmless as a poodle as she soaked up her grandma's attention. Elaine felt silly for ever being afraid of her.

"She's beautiful. What's her name?"

"Sheba."

Her grandma looked around as she stroked the dog's head. "This room is beautiful too. All of these rooms were plain white when I was little. Did you paint them?"

Elaine nodded. "It gave me something to do when I first moved here."

"You've always been so talented. You should paint for a living."

"I'm thinking about teaching art again. What do you think?"

"You'll do great at whatever you do."

Of course she'd say that. Grandma always supported Elaine's dreams. Always putting Elaine's needs first to make sure she could strive for her goals. It was time for Elaine to give Grandma what she needed, even if she didn't know she needed it.

Elaine kneeled beside Sheba but looked at her grandma. "Are you settling in OK?"

"I miss my house."

"I know you do. I have to open the store in a couple of hours, but maybe tonight we can move some things to help you feel more at home. Will you be OK while I'm working?"

Her grandma's face scrunched up into the familiar look of anxiety. "I have to watch *Live* at nine o'clock, then *Judge's Court*, and *The Doctors* after that."

Elaine smiled. "That's perfect because the only TV in the house is in your room. Maybe I can find a recliner to put in there for you."

"Don't go to too much trouble. I won't be here long. I plan on calling the locksmith today so he can change the locks, then I can go back to my house."

"It's a good idea to call a locksmith, but I've been thinking . . ." Elaine took her grandma's hand. "I want you to live with me here."

"But why?"

"You've done so much for me, and I want to do the same for you. You shouldn't have to wait for me to visit you to go clothes shopping or hire someone to buy groceries." Elaine squeezed

Grandma's hand. "And I miss seeing you. I can't visit as much as I'd like because I have to run the store. If you're here, we can see each other every day."

Grandma smiled as she patted Elaine's hand. "That's sweet, but you don't need me in your way."

"You wouldn't be in the way. We'd look out for each other."

"I don't know if I'd be a very good lookout."

"But I could look out for you and make sure no one takes advantage of you again."

Grandma stiffened. "Misty didn't take advantage of me. She's my friend."

"She stole your jewelry."

"She said she didn't. I'm sure I misplaced it. I'll look when I get home."

Elaine sighed. "I found your ring in her stuff. If you move back to Rapid City, I'll worry about you."

Grandma lowered her chin. "There's no reason to worry. I managed to take care of myself and two young girls when your granddad died."

"I know, but now it's time for someone to care for you. I want to do this."

She shook her head. "I don't want to live here."

"Why not?"

"I don't like what Susan did. She turned it into a flea market full of strangers and vagrants."

"I didn't know you disliked it so much." Regret beat in Elaine's chest. "I don't want to force you to stay here, but maybe if you could see the house the way I do, you might learn to like it again."

"I don't know." As she said it, Grandma looked around the lavender room again. "I do like this room though."

"Susan left most of the walls bare, so I spent the last year adding color." Elaine pointed to the chain of daisies crowning the walls. "I painted those because they reminded me of your wedding bouquet. In the foyer is Granddad's counter that he made for his hardware shop. Remember when it was in your living room and I'd pretend to be a cook with my toy food? You always said I was your favorite chef."

Grandma smiled. "I always wished he could have known you. He had such a fun, silly personality. You two would have been good friends."

"I wish that too, but I was blessed with the best grandma." And Elaine would do whatever she could to protect her. Standing, she extended a hand toward her grandma. "The store doesn't open until eight. Why don't I show you around? Then I can cook you some real food. I've heard my food used to taste a little like plastic."

"Can we bring Sheba?"

"Of course. You can even feed her if you'd like."

Grandma took her hand and stood. "Come on, girl, let's go get some breakfast." She patted her leg, and Sheba obeyed, walking next to her and panting happily. Elaine followed, hoping the tour would convince her grandma that the house wasn't that bad.

In the kitchen, Elaine linked her arm through her grandma's and motioned to the light-blue and chrome dining set. "Do you know where the table came from? It was here when I moved in."

"That was my mom's. It was an anniversary present from my dad. She always had a spotless kitchen." Grandma smiled. "My mom taught me how to make lemon shortbread tarts at that table. Remember when I taught you?"

"They're my favorite. Should we look around some more?" Elaine pulled her into the dining room. "When I first moved here, there were shelves and antiques shoved everywhere. I moved the bigger display cases to the outer walls and have tried to group things together." They walked into the foyer. "There's Granddad's old counter."

Grandma walked over and ran her hand along the smooth wood. "He would have loved knowing you were using it as a sales counter again." She looked around with her eyebrows scrunched. "What else is different here?"

Elaine was clueless. "Other than the old cash register, I haven't made any changes in here."

Her eyes widened. "The stairs are gone. There used to be a staircase right there." She motioned to the door behind the counter.

"They're still there." Elaine opened the door. "Aunt Susan had it converted into a closet, but you can still go upstairs. It's used for storage now."

"I used to run up those stairs and slide back down on my belly. Once I even tried to slide down the banister, but I fell and broke my pinky toe."

Elaine hugged her. "I didn't know you were such a daredevil."

Grandma smiled and lifted her chin. "There's a lot you don't know about your old grandma." But then she looked at the closet. "I don't like all of these changes."

Not wanting to dwell on that one change, Elaine pulled Grandma away from the offending closet and under the archway into the parlor. "This is where I'd like to hold the art classes. Sales have been great this week. If I start moving antiques to other display cases, I'll eventually be able to empty this room. What do you think?"

"I like the idea of an art studio better than an antique store."

"Why is that?"

"Because I love to watch you paint and I don't like all the strangers coming and going through my parents' house. When will they start coming?" Her voice wobbled.

Elaine checked the cuckoo clock. "Not for almost two hours."

"And they go anywhere they want?"

"Only in here and the old dining room. No one goes to the kitchen or upstairs."

Grandma fiddled with her ring. "It doesn't bother you?"

"It used to, but it can be nice too. I'm never late to work and I can go right to bed after the store closes when I'm tired. And I never get hungry because the kitchen is so close. Which reminds me that I need to make breakfast. What would you like?"

"Eggs and toast are fine."

"Come with me. I'll show you how to feed Sheba and that can be your job while you're here. She eats every morning and evening."

Grandma grinned brightly as she shuffled into the kitchen without waiting for Elaine. When Elaine caught up, she was already filling Sheba's water bowl.

"I had no idea you loved dogs so much. How come we never had one growing up?"

"Your mom is allergic. I even tried the non-shedding kind, but she sneezed and wheezed so much we had to find her another home. Since your mom was always coming and going, I didn't think it was fair to have a dog only to rehome her whenever she moved back."

An idea popped into Elaine's head. Before she could talk herself out of it, she said, "I never thought of myself as a dog person, but Sheba's grown on me. I think I'll miss her when Judah takes her back. Maybe I should get a dog. You can help me pick one out."

Grandma clapped. "Oh, I would love that."

Elaine hugged her then pulled out the dog food from the pantry. "You've got a deal."

After Sheba was fed and running out back, Elaine pulled out the eggs and bread. "I'll cook if you make the coffee."

Grandma patted her hand. "Tell me more about this art class you want to teach? Misty always talked about going to one of those canvas painting places. Is that what you're doing?"

Elaine's skin crawled at the mention of Misty, but she forced a smile. "Nothing like that. I'd like it to be more like adult education classes. Kind of like what I taught at the high school. We'd start with acrylics, since they're the easiest to work with, then move on to oils or watercolors. Each medium would be a different class."

"That sounds wonderful. Sheba and I can walk around the neighborhood and put-up flyers." Grandma measured out the coffee, putting in more than Elaine usually did, but she didn't care.

Love for her grandma burst inside her—she was so lucky to have someone so supportive in her life. "That's a great idea, but first I have to get through tourism season so I have enough money to get started."

"Whatever you need, dear. I'm glad you want to teach again." She patted Elaine's cheek. "You were born to be a great teacher. So patient and kind."

Elaine blinked back the sudden moisture that filled her eyes as she cut butter into the hot frying pan. As the eggs popped and sizzled, joy flowed through her. Being around Grandma was like having her own personal cheerleader. She'd missed that support, and she wanted to give it back. Somehow, whether at the store or in Rapid City, she'd figure out a way for her and Grandma to be together again.

CHAPTER 20

When the store emptied for the afternoon lull, Elaine wandered outside into the August heat and sat on the swing, needing to rest her feet. A breeze blew through the porch, making the high temperature bearable. A group of motorcycles roared by. Only four more days of tourists before Sturgis shrank back down to seven thousand people. Then she'd have to start advertising her art classes. If sales continued the way they had been, she'd have enough for ads *and* supplies.

A silver Charger pulled up to the curb and Mitch stepped out of the car. He waved. She sighed.

He strode up the walk and onto the porch. "Hey, pretty lady. Sitting down on the job?"

"Finally. We had a busy morning so I'm taking advantage of the lull. Thanks for filling in for me yesterday."

"Anytime."

"How's your grandma?"

"She'll live. How'd your friend do?" He smirked. "Did he botch everything up?"

She clenched her teeth at his lack of concern for his grandma *and* her shop. Despite that, he'd helped her more than she expected so she managed a civil tone. "He rose to the occasion. I could tell by the sales that it was a busy morning for you. It means a lot to me that you helped."

He leaned forward. "How much?"

But his usual smile had lost its charm. Before she could respond, a couple in matching red Sturgis Motorcycle Rally shirts walked up the cement path.

Elaine stood. "Welcome. Go on in and look around. I'll be there in a minute." They smiled as they entered the shop. "I'd better get in there."

"Sure, but I wanted to let you know that I won't be around for a couple of days. With my granny being sick, my parents think I should visit her. Honestly, we don't know how much longer she'll be around. She's a collector, though, and her house is full of stuff. I thought I'd see if there's anything you'd like to have at the shop."

Elaine cringed. "You want to sell me your dying grandmother's trinkets?"

He waved her off. "It's not like that. She's been saving stuff for decades, but no one in the family's really interested in any of it. I figured I could help my parents *and* you by prearranging someone to sort through her stuff. You know, take some of the stress out of things for them while giving you first crack at a collection."

"Would I need to travel to her home?" She'd have to close the store and get permission from her probation officer if it was out of state. "Where does she live?"

"Just outside of Minneapolis. I could take you. A road trip would be a blast, and she has a huge house, so there'd be a room for you."

"I wouldn't feel comfortable cataloging her stuff without permission from her and all her family."

"We'll talk about it when I get back. I'll miss you." He pulled her close and kissed the corner of her mouth, as if he'd missed her cheek. "See you in two days."

She wiped her cheek with her hand as he walked away. Unease crawled over her. It was probably all the death talk. She knew people made arrangements for their estates all the time, but something about Mitch's grandmother didn't feel right to her.

****

That evening, Elaine stood at the counter polishing silver spoons when the door opened and Clara ran in with a bouquet of wild flowers. "These are for you."

Clara's sweet offering brightened Elaine's mood. She set down the spoons and pulled Clara into a hug. "Thank you. They're gorgeous. Would you help me pick out a vase?"

Judah walked in and closed the door as Clara took Elaine's hand. "Looks like you've finally found your Lainy." He smiled at Elaine. "You're all she could talk about after she chose the flowers."

"They're beautiful. We're going to pick out a vase for them. Would you like to help?"

He smiled as he shook his head. "You go ahead. I can cover the counter."

Clara tugged on Elaine's arm. "Where are the vases?"

"This way." Together they browsed the shelf of crystal vases.

Clara first picked a pink-tinged one, then set it back when she saw a long crystal one. "I like them both." She stuck her tongue out in concentration as she pushed a plain one out of the way.

While she decided, Elaine snuck a glance at Judah. Instead of watching the door, he was watching them. His gaze locked with hers. He looked cuter than usual in his blue scrubs. Her cheeks heated and her heartbeat sped as she turned back to Clara, who reached for a vase with tulips engraved in it. "This one."

Elaine took it. "That's perfect. Should we get some water?"

Clara nodded.

"Let's tell your dad where we're going."

"Daddy! We've got to put the flowers in water!" Clara pulled Elaine toward the kitchen.

She laughed. "She's a born leader."

"That's one way to put it." He smiled. "I usually call it bossy."

"Come with us, Daddy."

He motioned to the door. "Shouldn't someone watch the store?"

Elaine shrugged. "We'll hear the bell if anyone comes in."

He nodded as he joined them. They made their way to the kitchen, where Grandma sat at the table talking to Sally Ann, who was perched on her finger.

"A birdy!" Clara ran to the table and stood next to Grandma.

"Her name is Sally Ann." Grandma smiled at Clara. "What's your name?"

"I'm Clara. I like birdies. Can I hold her?"

"Sally Ann loves little girls. Put your finger out and she'll hop on it."

Clara stuck her finger out. The bird stepped on it and Clara giggled. "Look, Daddy!"

"You're a natural, lamb."

"I want a bird too. Can I have one?" The wide-eyed, pleading look she gave him would have sent Elaine running to the nearest pet store.

He cringed. "I don't think Sheba would appreciate having a bird around. I notice she's not inside." He glanced at Elaine.

"I just put her outside for a potty break. Once Grandma puts Sally Ann back in her room, I'll let her back in."

Clara petted Sally Ann's chest. "Does she talk?"

"She can't talk, but she loves to sing. If I had my piano, we could show you. Maybe you can come visit me in Rapid City and we'll put on a performance."

"Can I go to her house, Daddy? She said I could."

"I think Elaine's grandma is staying here for a bit. Maybe you could sing your favorite song to her."

Clara leaned on the table and started singing "Twinkle, Twinkle Little Star." Sally Ann twittered, and Clara and Grandma laughed before continuing the song together.

Elaine had just enough time to set the flowers and vase on the counter before Judah took her hand and tugged her toward the doorway, out of Clara's and Grandma's direct sightline. "How are you today?" he whispered.

"We had a good morning together, but I still haven't convinced her to move here."

"How long do you have to figure this out?"

She shrugged. "Grandma called the locksmith, and he can't make it to her house for two weeks. That buys me a little time."

"Would she consider moving into assisted living?"

"I'm not sure she can afford to, and it would break her heart to move without Sally Ann."

"What about your mom? Have you asked her about it?"

Elaine snorted. "My mom only cares about herself. Even if she agreed to help, I wouldn't trust her to stay. Besides, it was Grandma and me for so long that her staying with me feels right."

He took her hand in his. "You're sure you're not taking on too much with the store and worrying for your grandma?"

"I worry about her anyway. If she's here, at least I don't have to worry about anyone else taking advantage of her. It would also be nice to have her around. After I got married, I didn't see her that often, then after my arrest I moved here. This morning felt like the old days. I even told her I'd get a dog."

Judah laughed. "Did Sheba work her charms on you?"

"She's growing on me, and she's made Grandma so happy. I haven't seen her that happy in years. Or maybe I was so focused on my own problems that I didn't notice her feelings."

"Don't be too hard on yourself." He laced his fingers through hers. "I'm here if you need anything."

Her insides melted.

After taking her other hand, he pulled her closer to him. "There's one thing that's been distracting me all day, and I wanted to talk to you about it."

"What's that?"

"You."

"Me?" She grew nervous. What now? She'd been as open about her past as she could. Had Zoe made up stories about her?

"Specifically, your kisses."

Relief and embarrassment replaced her nerves. Her face ignited.

A feather-light kiss tickled her lips. "I missed you today." He kissed her again, long enough to send tingles down her spine.

Sally Ann whistled.

Elaine laughed.

Judah leaned into the dining room's archway and glared at the bird, then turned his smiling gaze at her. "Insolent bird."

"Don't talk about my sister like that." She laced her fingers through his and pulled him into the kitchen, then released him before her grandmother or Clara noticed.

Clara giggled as she held up her finger. "Look, Daddy! I'm holding Sally Ann again."

"You're doing great, lamb."

Elaine put the flowers in the vase and filled it with water, dipping her fingers in the cool stream and patting them to her hot face. Judah had the power to turn her into a fiery kiln. She should be scared, but instead she felt . . . happy. Giddy almost.

She smelled Judah's spicy cologne moments before he stepped next to her. "Do you need any help?"

Her face heated again. "I'm trying to cool my face and you're not helping."

"I love it when you blush. You look very pretty with pink cheeks." He kissed her cheek then leaned against the counter.

"That's good because it happens all the time. It's embarrassing."

"It's adorable."

"You're impossible." But amazing at the same time.

Before she picked up the flowers, he pulled her injured hand toward him and inspected her stitches. "It looks like your hand has healed. When do you get your stitches out?"

She sighed. "I'd completely forgotten. After the rally, I guess. I can't take another day off."

"I can take them out. Let me get the first aid kit out of my truck."

"You can do that with the things in your first aid kit?"

"I'm a surgeon. I have a custom-stocked first aid kit." He kissed her palm. "I'll be right back."

As he jogged away, Clara and Grandma started their version of "Rockin' Robin" with Sally Ann.

Leaning against the counter, contentment washed over Elaine. She could get used to seeing all the people she cared for in one room together. And if that care grew?

Falling in love again meant risking deep heartache again. She didn't know yet if Judah was worth that risk, but the sight before her did a lot to convince her he was.

CHAPTER 21

The next afternoon, Judah sat beside Elaine on her porch swing. He wrapped an arm around her as she tucked her long blue-and-purple tie-dyed skirt under her legs. He felt scruffy in his scrubs, but the trip home for a change of clothes wasted valuable time he could spend with Elaine.

Laughter came from inside the house where Wanda and Clara played with Sally Ann. "How's your grandma doing today?"

"She's fine in the house, but she's still not comfortable with the store. I can't get her to go past the kitchen even if the store's closed."

More laughter. "Sounds like she's happy."

"She acts like it too, but she keeps talking about going home and getting out of the store." Elaine laid her head against his arm. "Thanks for bringing Clara over. I don't remember Grandma ever laughing this much."

"Of course. Clara is having fun too. Maybe if we create new memories here, Wanda will want to stay."

"I hope so. Sometimes I wish I had a cousin or sibling who could help out."

"Share the burden?"

Elaine shook her head. "Give her the time she deserves. Even if she moves in with me, I'll still have to run the store so she'll be alone most of the day. If I had a sister, she could take Grandma to the movies or to Bingo." She glanced up at him. "You said you grew up on a farm with an older brother. What was that like?"

Judah held out his left hand. "See that scar along my thumb? Asher, my older brother, threw a knife at me."

"Did you deserve it?"

"What makes you think I deserved it?"

Elaine tilted her head to the side.

"OK, I probably did. I caught him kissing his girlfriend behind the barn and wouldn't stop teasing him. In his defense, I don't think he meant to actually hit me, but his aim has always been awful. I had to get five stitches and he had to do my chores for a month. It was an even trade."

"Did your other brother throw knives at you too?"

"Not knives, no." Judah chuckled. "But once my little brother threw a screwdriver at me. I ducked and it stuck into my hollow door. I can't remember what I did to deserve that one."

"Did you fight a lot?"

"Actually, no. Mostly we'd make up games about being Old West cowboys riding our horses all over the farm or swimming in the stock dams and fishing in the creek. We played games in the fields until Mom called us in for bed."

"Your childhood sounds magical." She held his hand in her dainty, smooth one and lifted it to her lips, kissing the puckered scar. "I bet it's worth it to have someone who loves you no matter what."

"I'm not sure sibling love is unconditional, but I wouldn't trade my brothers for anything."

"And what do your brothers do now?"

"Simeon is a mechanical engineer in Waterloo, Iowa. Asher farms the family land. His wife is a lawyer who tries to work from home most days, but I can't imagine that's easy with their four kids running around. Actually, it was my sister-in-law I called after Zoe threatened you."

She faced him. "What did she say?"

"She said that in order to go back to jail, you'd have to commit another felony or specifically violate your probation. Basically, Zoe's threats are harmless unless you break the law."

She leaned back against him. "That's pretty much what my probation officer said too. That's reassuring. The next time you talk to her, tell her thanks from me."

"I didn't tell her why I needed the information. Usually she would have pressed me, but her youngest was demanding her attention. I'm not quite ready for all the questions from my family yet. They tend to *lovingly* butt into my business."

"Do you see each other often?"

"The last time we were all together was last September. I try to go home for Clara's birthday each year, but last year it was only a couple of months after Whitney's death, so it was kind of a blur."

"Is Clara close in age to her cousins?"

"Ezra is the closest. He's six weeks younger than her. He has two older sisters and a baby brother."

"That sounds fun." Judah could hear the smile in Elaine's voice. "Do they get along?"

"Clara loves being around them. I'm planning on heading over for a vacation in a few weeks to celebrate Clara's birthday. My parents are bringing their RV from Florida, so we'll all be together."

She sighed. "Your family sounds amazing. Why didn't you move closer to them after you left Texas?"

"Guilt." His gut tightened. "I felt like I should let Whitney's family see Clara grow up since it was my fault she moved to Texas."

"You were the reason she moved there, but it's not your fault Whitney was killed."

"Technically I know that, but it doesn't make the guilt go away. It hasn't been all bad, though. Despite my problems with Zoe, Whitney's family loves Clara and she adores them. And if I had moved closer to home instead of here, I would never have met you, and that would have been a real tragedy." He cradled her cheek in his hand and kissed her. Her arms wrapped around his neck, her fingers stroking the hair at the base of his head.

Feet stomped onto the wooden porch and a throat cleared. Elaine squealed and jumped to her feet.

An older man stood on the porch holding a large bouquet of yellow roses. "Flower delivery for Elaine Kent."

"That's me." She took the flowers. "Thanks."

"Looks like my timing was perfect." The man chuckled as he left.

Judah's passion instantly cooled. Elaine searched through the flowers, pulled out a small envelope, and tore it open. His gut twisted as she read it. Her eyes widened. She put the flowers on the wide railing before sitting on the swing, bending the card in half.

Jealousy picked at him. He didn't have to ask who sent them. "Why do you keep encouraging him?"

"I didn't know I was. He stopped by on his way out of town to ask about picking up antiques for the store. Nothing about it was flirtatious. I can't understand why he sent flowers."

"I've never met a guy who's so pushy."

"I'm not sure what else I can do," she whispered, glancing up at him. Her heavy eyelids and frown stole the anger from him. It wasn't her fault. He had no right to be angry at her.

He took her hand, flipping it over so her healing cut faced up. "I'm sorry. I'm not usually the jealous type."

"You're jealous?" She pulled her hand back. "Don't you trust me?"

"I trust you, but I don't trust Mitch. I'm afraid he's going to hurt you, and I couldn't handle that." He reached for her hand again and laced his fingers through hers. "You honestly don't get how amazing you are." He squeezed her fingers.

She sighed. "I don't deserve you."

"I will take pleasure in proving you wrong." Before he could start, she leaned in and kissed him. Her boldness sparked something in his chest that pulsed through him.

Elaine smiled against him. "Your belief in me encourages me to be braver. When Mitch gets back, I'll talk to him. I'll tell him he needs to respect my boundaries."

"You don't have to do it alone. I could go with you. I'll make sure he knows you're not interested."

She shook her head. "The old me would have jumped at your offer, but I need to start defending myself. If I can stand up to a trafficking thug and a petty thief, I can stand up to Mitch."

Judah laughed and his attraction for her grew. "I know you can. You're stronger than you think you are. Clara could learn a lot from you."

"Maybe, but it's not all good."

"My past isn't all good either. Sometimes those are the best lessons."

"I guess."

Judah didn't want to argue, but he also didn't want to let Elaine fall too far into her fears. Despite the warm summer air, he tucked her next to him and pushed them back in the swing. "If Clara could learn one thing from you, what would you want it to be?"

They rocked in silence several times before Elaine said, "You don't always have to be polite. Sometimes you have to be rude to protect yourself, and that's OK."

He weighed the advice in his mind. "I'm not sure I want her to grow up to be rude."

"I don't want her to either, but there were too many times in my past that I went along with someone because I didn't want to hurt their feelings. I let my mom walk over me my whole childhood. I should have stood up to Caleb when he wanted to kidnap Marcus. And now Mitch thinks he can keep flirting with me after I asked him to stop. When I stood up to Misty, it felt good. I wish I had learned that earlier. It's much harder to learn as an adult."

He kissed her temple. "You're doing an awful job convincing me that you're a bad example for Clara." As they swung, cuddling together, Judah began planning more opportunities for Clara to learn from Elaine.

CHAPTER 22

Elaine sat at the kitchen table twisting copper wire around a raw amethyst rock with needle-nose pliers. The scent of bacon hung in the air as Grandma sat beside her cutting an obituary from the paper. The baby monitor sat on the table. Sheba snored softly on the floor.

"What day is it, sweetie?"

"Saturday."

"Herb Hanson's funeral is on Wednesday. I'd like to go."

"The rally will be over by then. I can take you." Elaine glanced up at her, still in her floral robe. "Did you remember that the lady from the sheriff's office is coming any minute?"

"Why are the police coming again?"

"She's not a police officer. She's a victim's advocate, and she has some information on a case I'm involved in."

The bell chimed through the monitor. Before Elaine could put all the beads away, Bridget walked into the kitchen.

Elaine blushed. "Good morning. I'm sorry there's such a mess in here. I lost track of the time."

"Don't worry about it. What are you doing?" she asked as she approached the table.

"Making jewelry." Elaine held up the pendant. "I'm going to start selling them in the shop."

"That's pretty dope. I'd wear it."

"Are you the police woman?" Grandma asked.

"The victim's advocate," Elaine said. "Her name's Bridget. Bridget, this is my grandma, Wanda."

"Good morning, Wanda."

Grandma ducked her head and stood. "I'll go up and see how Sally Ann is doing. Can I take Sheba with me? I want them to become friends."

"I don't know if that's a good idea. What if Sheba attacks the bird before you can stop her?"

"I'll keep Sally Ann in her cage."

Elaine didn't want Sheba to be too far away in case anything else happened at the store, but she couldn't tell Grandma that without alarming her. "Maybe you can keep her while Bridget and I talk to see how they get along."

Grandma rewarded her with a bright smile. "Come on, Sheba. Let's go meet your new friend." She patted her leg and led the dog from the kitchen.

Elaine gathered up the rest of her supplies, sweeping them into a box. "Have a seat. Would you like a drink?"

"I'm good." Bridget sat in the newly vacated chair. She pointed at the box. "Are you going to teach jewelry-making classes too?"

"I hadn't thought about that. Maybe."

"How are your plans for the art classes coming?"

"Good. I've found a lot of supplies at a great price."

"I mentioned your idea to a deputy I work with, and she said she'd be interested in taking a class. She paints to relieve stress but has never had training. She said she'd love to learn more advanced techniques."

Giddiness danced through Elaine. "Really? I paint for stress relief too. Maybe I should do some research and market my classes that way."

"If you do, make sure you send me the info. I'll share it at the office."

"I'd love that, thank you. So, what's the information you said you had for me?" As excited as she was about her art classes, not knowing Bridget's news was making her nervous.

"The meeting with the state's attorney was a bit frustrating. Wallace failed to appear at his hearing—no surprise there—so the police are looking for him."

"Why is he out?" More importantly, would he come back? Elaine glanced at the stairs to her grandma's room.

"He was able to post bond. Once they find him, I'll be fighting for them to charge him with a lot more than assault. With Jules's testimony, we should be able to link him to a trafficking gang that the task force has been investigating for a while. I'm hoping we can move in soon, but if we can't get the leader when we do, he'll move the operation somewhere else."

"Who's the leader?"

"We still don't know."

"Can't Jules help you?"

Bridget shook her head. "She's never seen him. She's heard him talking, but she was locked in another room. There's another guy too—one who lures the girls in—but Jules and Ginny said they were drugged and can't remember what he looks like." She blew out a long breath. "I want to catch these guys so bad I can barely sleep at night."

Even though Elaine was impressed with Bridget's dedication, she couldn't stop feeling anxious for her new friends. "I bet Jules and Ginny would certainly sleep better too."

"So would the rest of their victims."

So would Elaine. "Thanks for the information. You didn't have to deliver it face to face though. I'm sure you have other things to do."

"Actually, I come bearing gifts." She held out a clear bag with a pearl necklace inside. "The detective found this at a pawn shop. He thinks it might be your grandma's. When I called about the status of her case, he asked if I'd have you take a look at it."

Elaine opened the bag and let the necklace fall into her hands. She flipped over the clasp and ran her finger over the *WK* engraved on it. "It's definitely hers. Maybe now she'll believe that Misty is bad news." Elaine slid the necklace back into the bag.

"I hope so. She'll need to sign some paperwork claiming the necklace, then I can release it to her."

"If you don't mind, I can take you to her." Elaine led Bridget to her grandma's room and knocked. After Grandma's quiet "come in," she opened the door. Grandma sat against the headboard watching *I Love Lucy,* with Sheba lying on the bed beside her. Sally Ann sat in her cage on the dresser swinging on the wooden swing.

Elaine hated to disturb the tranquil scene, but Grandma needed to hear the truth. "Grandma, Bridget brought your pearl necklace."

"How did *you* find my necklace?"

Elaine took a steadying breath. "Misty pawned it." The tears in Grandma's eyes crushed her.

Bridget sat on the edge of the bed and held out a piece of paper. "The police will keep looking for the other items. I'll need your signature proving the necklace is yours, then you can keep it."

Grandma nodded as she took the paper and scribbled her name on the line. She handed it back to Bridget without looking up.

"I'm sorry someone you thought was a friend turned out to be an enemy. You deserve better. Elaine's told me how much you've done for her. I'm glad you have each other."

Grandma glanced up with a slight smile, loosening Elaine's chest. "Thank you."

Bridget patted Grandma's hand then stood. Elaine led her silently out of the room. When she closed the door, she gave Bridget a small smile. "Thank you for that. You have a gift at setting people at ease."

"It's easy to redirect her thoughts from Misty to you. She's still struggling with the betrayal, but hopefully she'll look to you for comfort." Bridget checked the time on her phone. "I need to head out for another meeting. I'll let you know if I hear anything else about Wallace or the jewelry."

As Elaine walked Bridget to the front door, they passed a newly emptied display case in the parlor. With her jewelry-making supplies put away, she might as well rearrange the room now.

After seeing Bridget out, Elaine grabbed a screwdriver from the front closet and turned her attention to the case. One of the legs needed attention before she moved it. She'd just tightened and tested the leg when the bell chimed, startling Elaine. She tried to stand, but her legs wobbled as pin pricks ran up her shin. She started to say something but paused. She didn't want a customer to find her crawling around the floor. The last thing she needed was word to get back to Zoe that she was stumbling around the store—she'd assume the worst and probably accuse her of being drunk. Instead, she stretched her neck to peek around the shelves.

A bald man stood in the doorway.

Her pulse pounded in her ears.

Wallace stomped through the store. With her legs still tingling, she scrambled around the other side of the shelf. Grandma was safely upstairs, but so was Sheba. Elaine groaned.

She pulled her phone from her pocket and put it on silent. Then she opened her text box and typed 9-1-1.

Need help. Mother Lode, 1409 Junction Ave. Dangerous intruder. Can't talk, hiding. Elaine Kent.

"Hello-o," Wallace said. "You have a valuable customer."

Shivers ran over her skin. Her phone lit up.

Sending help. Is anyone hurt?

Her fingers trembled. *No. He doesn't know where I am.*

Are you in a safe spot?

He whistled as he stomped through the store. *No.*

Can you get to somewhere safe?

I'll try.

The whistling faded. Why hadn't she kept Sheba with her? If she could get to Grandma, maybe they could hide until the police came. No matter what happened, she had to protect Grandma.

Elaine crouched behind a shelf. The stairs in the closet. Wallace didn't know about them.

Something crashed in the kitchen.

Sucking in a breath, Elaine ran into the foyer, sliding into the closet behind her desk. Using the light from her cell phone, she ran up the stairs on her tip toes and stopped at the top. She needed to calm down. But she needed to hurry.

Quieting her breaths, she gripped the antique knob and turned it slowly. Cracked open the door. Stuck her head into the hallway. Empty. Elaine stepped out of the stairway.

A floorboard creaked.

She spun around.

"Found you."

Her lungs seized.

Wallace stood at the top of the kitchen stairs. "You owe me some money. Those girls you stole would have brought in hundreds of dollars a night."

Nausea rolled in her stomach. She could make it to Grandma's room—she had to.

Elaine turned and sprinted. Feet stomped behind her. She reached for the knob as a hand grabbed her arm.

"You're coming with me."

"Grandma!"

He pulled her toward the stairs.

"Let Sheba out!"

Sheba barked as Wallace dragged Elaine down the stairs. She had to slow him down. At the bottom, she relaxed her legs, forcing him to drag her dead weight behind him.

"Get up!" He grabbed both arms.

Her phone slipped out of her hand. Scratches and thumps sounded above them before a snarl and a snap. A brown and black blob flew at Wallace. He screamed. Elaine scrambled away in time to see Sheba sink her teeth into his leg.

Elaine backed under the kitchen table as she looked for a weapon. Her scissors! She reached up and gripped the cool metal.

Sheba snarled, her weight shifting forward and her teeth bared. Wallace turned his back to Elaine. Her heart pounded. A flash of silver moved through the air, and Sheba howled.

"No!" Elaine charged, but her feet slipped on the tile. While she struggled, Wallace limped out the back door.

Ignoring him, Elaine crawled to Sheba. A knife protruded from her side. Blood oozed from the site. Elaine grabbed a towel from the counter and pressed it to the wound as tears ran down her face. "Stay with me, girl."

The front bells rattled as the door banged. "Police!"

Footsteps. Shouts. Sheba panting.

Officer Holt knelt in front of Elaine. "Are you OK?"

She nodded. "Sheba . . ."

"Where is he?"

"He went out the back. It was Wallace. He's bleeding."

Officer Holt ran out the back door. Another officer ran out after him. Zoe holstered her gun, then scooped up Sheba.

"What can I do to help?" Elaine scrambled to her feet.

"Call the Black Hills Animal Hospital. Tell them I'm coming."

Someone touched Elaine's arm. She jumped.

Grandma stood there in a blue muumuu, her skin as pale as the pearls around her neck. "Are you OK?"

Elaine exhaled a pent-up breath as she pulled Grandma into a tight hug. "I'm fine." But her body shook and a lump formed in her throat.

"What happened? Why were the police here? Where's Sheba?"

The vet! Elaine grabbed her phone, her purse, and her grandma's hand. "Come on. We'll call Judah and the vet from the car."

CHAPTER 23

Elaine sat on the hard metal folding chair beside her grandma. Shelves of pet food filled the far wall of the small waiting room and a poster of dog breeds hung between two windows on the wall next to them. She looked from one to the other and back again while they waited for news. Zoe stood at the desk talking to the receptionist, ignoring Elaine.

The front door opened, and Judah rushed in. Worry lined his face as he searched the room.

Elaine stood, her heart hammering against her ribs. Would he blame her? As soon as he saw her, he stepped toward her, the tension melting from his face. She launched herself into his arms, breathing in his antiseptic scent and snuggling in closer to him, soaking up his comfort.

"Are you hurt?" he whispered, stroking her back.

"No," she said, not minding his question, even though she'd already told him when she called.

"You're trembling. You should sit." He led her back to the chair and sat next to her, lacing his fingers through hers. "Has there been an update?"

Elaine shook her head. "She's in surgery. They were able to give her blood. I didn't even think that was possible with dogs." As the adrenaline wore off, she leaned her head against his shoulder. "You should have seen her. She was so brave. She doesn't deserve this."

Judah laid his head against hers. "She's a tough dog. She's been hurt before. Do you need anything?"

Elaine shook her head. "I'm just glad you're here."

He sat forward to look at Grandma. "Wanda, what about you? Is there anything you need? Water or a snack?"

"No, thank you," Grandma whispered. Elaine reached for her hand, and wrapped her fingers around Grandma's, hoping to give her comfort.

Zoe's footsteps echoed on the faded tiles as she marched up to Elaine and stopped in front of her. "The officers have terminated their search for the intruder and are back at your house wondering where you are."

"Can you tell them I'm here?"

Zoe stared at Elaine for so long that her stomach bubbled with nerves. Had she messed up by not waiting for the police to come back? "Fine." She turned and walked outside.

Confused, Elaine exhaled and looked up at Judah. "Why does she hate me so much?"

"It's not you she hates. It's me. You're just getting caught in the crosshairs."

"I don't blame her. I wouldn't trust me around Clara if I was Zoe."

"For the record, I trust you with Clara, and that's all that matters. I wish I could tell you to give it time, but I've known Zoe for seven years and she's never liked me." Judah kissed the top of Elaine's head. "I'm sorry. We don't need to talk about this now."

The office doors opened, and Officer Holt walked in.

Elaine stood. "I'm sorry I left the shop. I wanted to be here in case something happened to Sheba."

He nodded. "I understand. I'd be here too if someone stabbed my dog. Any word yet on how she's doing?"

"Not yet." Judah stepped beside her. "Did you find Wallace?"

The officer shook his head. "We searched a ten-mile radius of your place, but he disappeared. That's not hard to do with thousands of people wandering around. There's a BOLO for him, but extra people equal extra crime. There's a good chance he'll come back, but we can't spare the manpower to watch your place. Is it possible to leave town for a few days?"

"What? Why?"

"We're pretty sure Wallace isn't local, so he'll probably head out when everyone else does. If he doesn't, he won't be able to hide as easily after the rally. We'll have more resources to keep you safe then."

Nausea rolled around inside her. There was only one day of the rally left, but it could be her busiest day.

"Elaine." Judah squeezed her hand. "It's for your safety."

She clenched her fists in frustration. "I understand, but how safe will I be if I'm unemployed and homeless because I can't pay my bills?" She shook her head. "You know there isn't a hotel room available within a hundred miles and I can't close my business." And now—thanks to Misty—she couldn't even go to her grandma's house.

"Why don't you and your grandma come to my house?"

Her pulse quickened, but she couldn't sort out her emotions at the moment. "No. I won't put you and Clara in danger like that."

"I doubt Wallace knows who I am or where I live. Besides, with Sheba in surgery, Clara and I might need a distraction."

"That's a good idea," Officer Holt said. "At the very least, you need to get out of your home until after the rally. We can't tell you what to do with your business, but we advise shutting down the store."

Elaine nodded. "Thank you. I'll consider it."

His radio squawked. "I've got to go. Call us if you need anything."

She rubbed her temples to ward off the growing headache. What should she do? The rally had brought in more than expected, but one lost day could impact her for months. She had no way of predicting how successful the art classes might be. She couldn't risk closing.

Judah squeezed her hand. "What are you thinking?"

Stepping away from him, she crossed her arms in front of her chest. "I have to open the store. If I don't, I might as well close it for good."

Judah ran a hand through his hair. "It's not safe."

"I know, but I don't have a choice. I'm holding some items for customers who wanted to wait until they were ready to leave town to pick them up. They're already paid for. There's only one more day of the rally and then I can close for the rest of the week."

He moaned. "You're right. You can't close the shop, but that doesn't mean you have to be there alone. I have the day off tomorrow. I'll stay with you at the store."

"What about Clara?" Elaine shook her head. "You should spend your day off with her."

"Clara loves it when our neighbor babysits. And when this is over, we can make it up to her and take her on an adventure. She'd love it if you stayed with us."

"I can't stay the night. What about my grandma?"

"There's room for her. And Sally Ann too."

His blue eyes and crooked smile were hard to say no to, but she couldn't back down. There was too much at stake.

He lifted his hands in surrender. "I'm not making a pass at you. This isn't about our relationship. It's about keeping you safe while a madman—who has attacked you three times already—is on the loose. The spare rooms are in the basement, and there's a bathroom and a living room down there too. You wouldn't even have to see me."

Elaine hugged herself as Judah studied her. She glanced at Grandma, who sat watching the exchange with wide eyes. She couldn't put Grandma at risk.

Judah sighed. "I'm not going to pressure you, but if you choose to stay at the store tonight, I'll be sleeping on your porch. It's the only way I'll get any sleep."

"What about Clara?"

"She can stay at her grandma's, but she'd rather have a sleep-over with you."

Elaine knew he was serious about sleeping on her porch just as much as she knew he was right about it being unsafe. "OK, you win. We'll stay with you tonight." She stepped into his arms and relaxed against him.

"Thank you." He kissed her head. "I'm not sure how much longer we'll be, so I'll call the neighbor and see if she can pick Clara up from daycare." He pulled his phone out and stepped to the corner.

Elaine sat next to Grandma and took her hand. "We're going to stay at Judah's house tonight."

Her brow scrunched together. "But why?"

"The police don't think it's safe to stay at my house. Judah says we can bring Sally Ann too. Hopefully, it won't be for too long." She laid her head on Grandma's shoulder, like she had when she was a child. It offered just as much comfort now as it did then.

Zoe walked back in and sat on the furthest chair from them. She pulled out her phone as she continued to ignore them. Two hours later, Elaine stood to stretch her legs as the vet stepped into the waiting room. Zoe and Judah both rushed the doctor.

"Judah Demski?"

"That's me," he said. "How's Sheba?"

"The knife missed all vital organs, but it broke a rib and she's lost a lot of blood. If she survives the night, her quality of her life will diminish significantly. Is it still your desire to spare no expense to save her life?"

"Yes!" Zoe banged her fist on the counter. "I'll pay the bills myself."

Judah touched his sister-in-law's shoulder. "That's not necessary. Do whatever it takes to save her."

Zoe blinked at him, then nodded.

Elaine slid her hand around his arm and hugged it.

"There's nothing you can do waiting here," the vet said. "Sheba's sedated and should sleep through the night. We'll know more in the morning."

Judah nodded. "Please call me if anything changes." Zoe opened her mouth, but he held up a hand, silencing her. "I'll call you as soon as I hear anything."

Zoe lifted her chin. "Thank you, Judah." With slumped shoulders, she left.

Judah sighed as he handed the receptionist his credit card.

"That was kind of you," Elaine said. "Why did you promise to call her?"

"As much as I'd love for Zoe to leave me alone, I know she's reacting out of fear. Clara and Sheba are her only connections to her sister."

"Do you think this will improve her opinion of you?"

He shrugged. "That is something entirely out of my control, but I didn't do it to get on her good side. I don't want her to worry unnecessarily. I know she doesn't believe it, but I never wanted to hurt her."

His concern for Zoe undid Elaine. Despite everything Zoe had said and done, Judah's character didn't waiver. Maybe Elaine had finally found someone she could have a healthy relationship with— if Judah could overlook his sister-in-law's faults, maybe he could love a convicted felon, mistakes and all.

CHAPTER 24

Elaine followed Judah down a private driveway to a stone home with tan trim and green siding nestled among pine-tree-covered hills. On one side of the roof, two peaks poked into the sky with three on the other. A covered porch wrapped around the house with tan shutters guarding the large windows.

Her throat tightened. She could picture Judah living on the childhood farm he described, but she couldn't see him living here. She'd never been in such a big house. Saying yes to Judah was the right thing, but she wished she could drive back home and crawl into her cozy bedroom. She glanced at Grandma. "What do you think of Judah's home?"

Grandma's mouth hung open. "This house is huge. Are you sure this is the right place?"

"I'm sure. I know we're not ones for adventure, but at least we're together."

Judah pulled around the house and into the second stall of a three-car garage. He jumped out and motioned for her to take the first one.

Elaine hesitated, but when he wouldn't stop, she parked inside and stepped out. "I think I should park in the driveway. What if my car leaks oil all over your nice garage?"

He chuckled. "It's a garage. It's meant to get dirty. I'll get your bags if you want to get Sally Ann."

Elaine hurried to her grandma's door and opened it. She sat straight and stiff, holding tight to her purse. "You can get out now, Grandma."

"Will I have to move again? I was just starting to like my new room."

"I'm sorry we had to come here, but it's not safe at the store tonight."

"Can we go back tomorrow?"

Elaine crouched down, hoping her brave facade would help. "I hope so."

"And this house is safe?"

Judah stopped next to Elaine, a suitcase in each hand. "It is. I even have an alarm system and cameras around the perimeter. I can show you if you come inside."

"OK." She got out of the car still gripping her purse.

Elaine grabbed Sally Ann's cage and bag of supplies as Judah led her grandma into the house. She followed them through the mudroom and into a kitchen straight from *Better Homes and Gardens*—marble countertops, stainless steel appliances, and even a bowl of fake fruit on the huge island.

Sally Ann whistled and Elaine giggled. "I'm impressed too," she whispered.

Judah dropped the bags onto the floor, then took the cage from her and put it on the pristine counters.

Elaine reached for the cage. "She'll make a mess there."

"We can clean it up. She won't hurt anything." He took her hand and led her to the great room where her grandma sat, straight as the pillars outside, on a cream leather couch.

He sat next to her and pulled out his phone. "Wanda, let me show you what my security cameras see." He held his phone in front of her. "Here's the front view." He swiped over. "And here's the garage side." Swipe. "The back." Swipe. "And the other side. I get a notice every time activity is detected. Does that make you feel safer?"

Grandma nodded. "I think Sally Ann and I would like to go to our room. I'm quite tired."

"It's downstairs. I'll show you."

Grandma's hands tightened on her purse. "In the basement?"

Elaine cringed. "I forgot. She hates basements. She won't go down there."

"OK." He stood and offered Grandma his hand. "You can stay in my room."

Was there no end to his kindness? Elaine had no idea men like Judah existed until now. She knew she was feeling especially vulnerable after the day she'd had, but she was on a cliff about to fall for him. Hard.

A door slammed. Footsteps sounded in the kitchen. "Daddy! I'm home."

"In here, lamb."

Clara skipped into the living room but stopped in the doorway. "Lainy!" She ran at Elaine and gave her a tight hug, then turned to Grandma. "Grammy!" Clara climbed onto her lap.

"Grammy?" Judah's eyebrows rose. "Why did you call Mrs. Kent that?"

"I already have a nana and a grandma, but I don't have a grammy yet." Clara looked around the room. "Where's Aunt Sally?"

Judah shook his head with a low chuckle.

Grandma pointed into the kitchen. "She's on the counter, dear."

"I ran right past her." Clara giggled. "Want to see my room?" She didn't wait for an answer before taking Grandma's hand and pulling her down the hallway.

Judah stood. "I'll take Sally Ann and Wanda's bag to my room, then check on Clara. I'll be right back."

He disappeared, and Elaine sat on the edge of the love seat perpendicular to the couch. A flat screen TV sat on the mantel of a stone fireplace. Leather couches. A mahogany coffee table in the middle. Everything upscale and everything cream and plain. The bare walls called to her like an empty canvas, and her fingers itched to for her paint brushes.

When Judah returned, he sat beside Elaine. "Making yourself at home?"

"Have you?" She scooted to the back of the couch, but she couldn't relax against the cool leather.

"What do you mean?"

"There's nothing personal here. No pictures on the mantel or art on the walls. Where's the pile of junk mail you plan on going through but never will? Or a jar of odds and ends that you don't dare throw away in case you need them?"

He laughed. "I don't generally keep clutter, but I do have a junk drawer in the kitchen. I keep my mail in my office. It's the first door down the hallway."

"What about Clara's toys?"

"They're in her room."

"All the time?" She'd never been able to keep Marcus's things in one room.

"No, but she puts them back when she's done. Wait"—he swiveled to face her—"do you disapprove of my home?"

She shook her head as she tried to think of a polite way to describe the room. "Not at all. It's a very . . . elegant house."

"Elegant?" He narrowed his eyes. "Tell me what you really think."

"I think it's elegant."

"But?"

Elaine fidgeted as he watched her. "It's a bit . . . plain."

"Plain?" He glanced around. "I guess. You'd probably paint all the walls a different color and fill it with antiques."

"That would certainly reflect my personality, but your home should reflect you. I know you're not this boring."

He shrugged. "Decorating isn't my thing. I haven't a clue where to start adding personal touches."

"Pictures are personal. One of Clara and maybe one of you both." She turned to the plain wall behind her. "You could put a collage of pictures over there."

"I don't have any recent pictures of Clara."

"None?" There were hundreds of photos of Marcus in her basement.

"They're on my phone. I never print them out."

"You need to. And a picture of both of you."

"All I have are selfies that Clara took."

Elaine smiled. "Then I'll need to take some of you."

"Daddy!" Clara ran into the living room and jumped onto the loveseat, landing haphazardly across Elaine and Judah. "Grammy and I want pizza for dinner. Can we have pizza?"

"We ordered last night. We were supposed to cook tonight."

"But we want pizza."

"Clara, what have I—" His phone rang, interrupting what Elaine was sure would be a lecture. "It's the office. I need to take this."

"Go ahead. I'll take Clara into the kitchen and show her how to make pizza."

"Yay!"

Judah cringed. "I'm not sure we have the ingredients, but you're welcome to try." He put his phone to his ear and walked into the other room.

Elaine looked down at Clara. "Can you show me where Daddy keeps your food?"

"Sure." The girl took Elaine's hand and led her to the pantry. Cans of soup, fruit, and vegetables, boxes of macaroni and cheese, and dry cereal lined the shelves along with various baking supplies. No pizza sauce, pasta sauce, or even canned tomatoes. Not sure what Judah had in his refrigerator, she picked up a box of mac and cheese. "Would you like mac and cheese pizza?"

Clara jumped up and down. "Two of my favorite things together!"

"You take this and I'll get the rest of it." Elaine put the ingredients on the island and rummaged around for a pot, then started the water to boil. After she found measuring cups, she helped Clara measure the flour and baking powder, then gave her a spoon to stir it.

While they were mixing, Judah walked in wearing jeans and a snug navy t-shirt. "What can I help with?" She pulled her gaze from him before he caught her gawking at his fine frame. She cursed her warm cheeks, hoping he wouldn't notice her embarrassment.

She glanced at their work. Flour coated the counters and most of Clara's cheeks. Elaine swept the flour into a pile "Sorry. We're making a mess. I'll clean it up." She held her breath, hoping he didn't mind the wait.

"I'm sure it can be cleaned up later." He dipped his finger in the flour and wiped it on Elaine's cheek.

She froze. Where were the insults or the anger? Before she could ask, he dipped his finger in the flour again and raised an eyebrow. He wasn't her mother or Caleb—how long would it take her to accept that? When he smiled at her, she breathed out her relief and wiped her cheek with a towel. "Because of that you can make the mac and cheese."

He cocked his head to the side. "I thought we were having pizza."

"We are. Mac and cheese pizza!" Clara spread her arms wide, flinging flour onto the floor.

Elaine laughed. "There wasn't much to work with, so we're improvising."

Judah's half-smile triggered the butterflies in her stomach. "You're good for her. And me."

She hoped so, but she couldn't admit that yet. Instead, she dipped her finger in the flour and smiled at Judah. He narrowed his gaze. She lunged at him, her flour-coated finger aimed at his cheek, but he stepped back. With a shriek, she fell toward him. His hands steadied her as he pulled her to his chest.

"Get her, Daddy!" Clara giggled, wrapping her arms around Elaine's leg.

Judah scooped his daughter up, sandwiching her between him and Elaine in his tight grip. "Now I've got you both where I want you."

Their laughter colored the house in ways paint never could. And for the first time in a long time, Elaine started to feel at home.

****

After Clara and Wanda were tucked into bed and Elaine had retreated to the downstairs bathroom, Judah stepped into the utility room. He opened the cabinet above the washing machine and pulled a box off the top shelf. The one box of mementos he'd kept from before. Apprehension seized him. He hadn't looked inside since he'd packed up his Texas home, for good reason.

Before he could change his mind, he carried the box to the downstairs family room, then sat on the blue cloth couch. There'd been so much turmoil and anxiety in Texas—what if opening the box let it out in his new home? As long as the lid stayed shut, all that pain stayed inside. But so did the happy times, like Clara's birth. Her first steps. Her mother. Despite the arguments he and Whitney had had, he'd never doubted her love for Clara, and Clara needed to see that. She needed to see pictures of him and her mom, of their life together.

Something rustled in front of him.

Judah looked up and found Elaine watching him in tight, short pants and an oversized t-shirt that hung to her knees. He smiled. "Would you like to join me for a bit?"

"Sure." She sat beside him, close enough to touch but with enough space between them to be modest. "What's this?"

He took off the lid of the box. Picture frames filled one side and trinkets were piled next to them. He pulled out a stack of frames and handed one to Elaine. In it, Judah stood behind Whitney in front of their brick, ranch-style home. He wore a blue, button-down shirt and Whitney wore a soft yellow sweater, her short blond hair flipping up around her ears. She held baby Clara, with little wisps of blond hair and Whitney's button nose.

"Where's this?"

"In front of our house. It was taken a week after we brought Clara home."

Elaine touched Whitney. "She's pretty."

Not sure how to respond, he handed her a picture of Whitney in a rocking chair cradling Clara. Love shone on Whitney's face.

"How old is Clara there?"

"Six weeks, I believe." Then he handed her his wedding photo. He liked how he looked in a black tux, but Whitney stole the spotlight. The white satin flowed down her slim figure, simple but elegant.

In the photo, he stared at her with adoration. Had he felt that much love for her then? Guilt turned in his stomach. He never talked with Clara about Whitney because all he could remember were the fights, but something new churned inside of him. No, not new—buried. When had he buried those feelings?

"What was your wedding like?"

Judah sat back, trying to remember. "It was fun. Whitney wasn't like one of those bridezillas you see on TV. She wanted all the guests to have a good time. We got married in the park near the softball diamond where we met and had the reception at the local community center."

Elaine looked at him. "Did you have fun?"

"I did. There was lots of dancing. Several guys from the PD did a choreographed dance to I WANT IT THAT WAY." Judah laughed, thinking about their awkward moves. "It was awful but hilarious."

"What did you and Whitney dance to?" Elaine pulled her legs up and laid her cheek on her knees.

"'A Thousand Years.' I played it at her funeral too." The lump of emotion in his throat surprised him. With a frown, Elaine squeezed his shoulder. He didn't want to turn this into a sob fest so he wracked his mind for a lighter subject. "You would have loved all the colorful flowers we had."

Her face brightened. "Tell me about them. I love flowers."

"So did Whitney. She had a bouquet of tiger lilies, orange roses, some little white flowers, and sunflowers. And I think there were lilacs tucked in there too. I'm not sure what colors go together, but it looked nice."

"I bet it was beautiful."

"It was. What about your wedding? I'm guessing you had even more flowers than we had."

She shook her head. "Since we were married right out of high school, we didn't have much of a wedding. I did have a bouquet though. It was a surprise from Caleb because I didn't think we could afford fresh flowers. It was a big bouquet of Gerber daisies—purple, yellow, and pink. I loved it."

"Where did you get married?"

"In my grandma's church. I wore her wedding gown, which was a simple but very pretty, cream satin dress. My great-grandma had embroidered pink roses along the neckline before Grandma got married."

As she spoke, Judah played with one of her curls, straightening it and watching it bounce back in place. "I bet you were a gorgeous bride." He loved the blush that invaded her cheeks. "Please tell me your grandma and Sally Ann sang a duet."

She laughed. "No, thankfully, but Grandma did play 'The Wedding March.' Aunt Susan's husband, Will, walked me down the aisle, and my mom even came. Then, afterward, we went out for dinner." She grinned at him. "It was simple, but I was so happy. I didn't feel like I was missing out. I'll never forget the look on Caleb's face as I walked toward him. He had his problems, but in his own way he loved me."

Judah nodded as he developed an unexpected kinship with Caleb. "I feel the same about Whitney. We had problems, but there were great times too." His hand shook as he passed the final picture to Elaine. Whitney in her police officer's uniform with her hair pulled back and a bright smile on her face. An American flag hung in the background. "We displayed it at her funeral." He took an unsteady breath as the buried sorrow scratched its way up his throat. This picture was the hardest to look at.

"She looks happy."

"She was. She loved being a police officer. It was her dream since she was a kid. After one of many domestic violence incidents between her father and mother, the police arrested her dad and they never saw him again. She said they were her heroes and they probably saved her mom's life that day."

Tears filled Elaine's eyes. "She died a hero."

Her face, so full of sympathy, soothed the ache in his heart. "And she should be remembered as one. Leaving these memories boxed up doesn't give her the honor she deserves."

Judah pulled out the framed folded flag from her memorial. "We've been here for almost a year, and Whitney's been gone longer. I want Clara to be able to see this and her mom's police picture whenever she wants. I have Whitney's badge, but I'm going to keep it in a safe place until Clara's older."

Elaine picked up the wedding and family photos. "Where should we hang these?"

"We have plenty of empty walls to choose from. I'd like to hang them down here." Judah looked around the plain room. An oak counter with a sink ran along the wall next to them, and a wood burning stove and stone back splash were the only things in the room. It could be a cozy room if he tried. Maybe Elaine could help. "I think I should get a pool table or ping pong table and definitely a big screen TV to watch football on. Turn it into a game room. What do you think?"

"Now that would reflect *your* personality. I think it would make a great art studio."

Maybe one day it will be. Her cheeky grin tempted him. With Clara and Wanda upstairs, he leaned in and touched his lips to her soft ones. One taste was not enough. A lifetime of them wouldn't be enough. He plunged his hands into her mass of curls, deepening the kiss. His pulse sped as heat rose in him until he sat back, gazing into her blue eyes. He wouldn't be the guy who took advantage of the situation, no matter how tempting she was.

He cleared his throat as he tried to shake off the effects of her kiss. "So, where should we hang these?"

She blinked a few times, then glanced around the room. "Maybe between the two windows over there." Her husky voice about did him in.

He stood before he gave in to temptation. "I'll go get my tools."

By the time he reached the utility room and grabbed his toolbox, his heartbeat had slowed to normal. Back down in the family room, Elaine was kneeling on the floor. She had arranged the pictures in a diamond pattern with the flag on the bottom, Whitney's police picture above it, the wedding picture on the right, and the family picture to the left.

She looked up at him, her brows tight together. "What do you think?"

"Looks great, and I know Clara will love that she can see her mom's picture anytime."

Elaine held out the picture of Whitney holding Clara. "I think this should go beside her bed."

Judah took the picture and touched Whitney's face. "That's the perfect spot for it." A deep ache seized his chest and tears blurred the picture. "She loved Clara more than anything."

Elaine rose and stepped close to him. "You're allowed to feel sad you know."

"How can I grieve when I have to help Clara through her grief?"

"Maybe by talking with a friend. Like me." She laced her fingers through his.

"It was nice to talk about Whitney and our wedding."

"It was. I always dwell on the hard times I had with Caleb, but there were great times too."

"There were more good moments than I'd realized. Even if she and I had problems at the end, she gave me Clara. Eventually, I'll tell her about our struggles so she can learn from them, but not for a long while."

Elaine kissed his cheek. "I love how you're always thinking of Clara's needs, even when it could be hard for you. Not all parents are like that."

He gazed down at the remarkable woman beside him. He hated the sadness reflected in her eyes. "I'm sorry your mom wasn't that kind of parent."

Blinking tears away, she nodded. "Thank you." She wiped under her lashes then sat back on the couch. "What else is in this box?" She pulled out a picture of Judah in his air force uniform in front of the American flag. "You look good in your uniform, but your hair is so short. I like it better now, with a bit of wave."

He chuckled. "Me too."

"We should put it right . . ." She moved Whitney's picture over a few inches and set his to the left of hers. "Here. Are there any other framed pictures?"

He leaned over the box. "I don't think so."

"What else is in there?"

"Just some of my air force stuff." He pulled out a fan and opened it. A traditional Japanese lady in a pink kimono rested in a garden. He fanned himself, blowing cool air across his face. "You should take this for when I make you blush."

The mere mention of blushing made Elaine blush, which warmed Judah in a completely different way. She really had no idea how tempting she was, but he did, and he didn't want to scare her. "And on that note, I think we should go our separate ways."

"What about the pictures? Aren't we going to hang them?"

"I'll get them later. I don't want the pounding to wake Clara or Wanda up."

"Then I'll haul myself to bed too." She kissed his jaw. "Good night, Judah."

"Good night." He watched her walk to her room, waiting for her to close the door before bending over and picking up his wedding picture. The ache of grief tightened his chest. He hadn't shared it with anyone . . . until tonight.

Setting the photo aside, he looked back into the box. In the corner sat a black wooden box with cherry blossoms on the front. He'd forgotten all about it. He opened it and touched the smooth half globe with cherry blossom branches floating in it. He'd never understood what made him buy it. Something about the colors appealed to him, but it wasn't Whitney's style and it seemed too old for Clara. After the funeral, he'd tucked it into the box with no idea what to do with it. Now he could imagine how beautiful it would look around Elaine's freckled neck.

CHAPTER 25

Judah stretched his back as he rolled over on the hard mattress, rubbing his eyes before staring at the ceiling. Not his ceiling. The guest room ceiling. Because Wanda was in his bed, and Elaine was down the hall. He couldn't stop smiling as he remembered their night with the photos.

Wondering what she was up to now, he climbed out of bed, slipped on a USAF t-shirt, and grabbed his phone. He wandered upstairs to the sound of laughter and the scent of bacon. In the kitchen, he found Clara at the counter eating pancakes. Wanda sat next to her while Sally Ann perched in her cage on the stool beside her. Elaine's back faced him as she stood at the stove flipping pancakes.

His skin tingled as he watched a scene he'd always wanted for Clara. Forcing the desire back, he said, "What do we have here?"

Clara dropped her fork. "Daddy!"

"Hi there, lamb. Whatcha eating?"

"Pancakes with chocolate chips!" She grabbed her fork and took a huge bite.

Elaine, with her red curls floating around her, brought him a plate of pancakes and two pieces of bacon. "Would you like eggs too?"

"No, this is plenty. You found all this food in the kitchen?"

She laughed. "Not a chance. I was up before everyone else so I made a quick trip to the store."

As he sat on the last remaining stool next to Clara, his phone rang. He didn't recognize the number, but that didn't necessarily mean anything with his patient load and schedule. "Excuse me. Hello, this is Dr. Demski."

"Dr. Demski, this is the Black Hills Animal Clinic."

His stomach seized, hoping for good news.

"Sheba had a good night last night. Her vitals are strong, but the doctor would like to keep her another couple of days to make sure she's going to be OK."

He exhaled in relief. "Yes, of course. Thanks so much for the update."

"We'll call you tomorrow with another update."

"Thanks."

He hung up and smiled at Clara. "That was the vet clinic. Sheba's going to be OK."

"Yay!" She bounced on her stool. "Can we go get her now?"

"In a couple of days. She needs to rest and recover before she has the energy to play with little girls." He tickled Clara's side. "You finish your breakfast, then go get dressed."

"Let's hurry up, Grammy. I have stuff to show you."

As Clara attacked her pancakes, Elaine sighed. "What a relief. I thought about her all night."

"I did too." Among many other things. "I should let Zoe know." He opened his texts. *Vet called. Sheba's ok. They'll keep her a few days.*

He only had time to cut one piece of pancake before the phone pinged. *Thanks.*

He stared at the single word. That was possibly the most civil conversation he'd had with his sister-in-law since Whitney's death. Grateful for the reprieve, he focused his energy on happier things—an amazing breakfast, his chatty daughter, and his pretty houseguest. He bit into a piece of bacon, savoring the rich taste as Elaine fluttered around his kitchen. She flipped pancakes, refilled Clara's chocolate milk, took her grandma's empty plate, and even baby talked with Sally Ann.

When she faced him, her gaze connected with his. Something about the flush in her cheeks and the smile on her face hit him in the heart. It had taken him over six months to feel more than attraction for Whitney, but those feelings didn't match the intensity and depth of the emotions he had for Elaine. His throat tightened at the realization.

Elaine set the syrup next to his plate, her brow creased. "Is everything OK?"

"Fine," he said, his voice cracking.

"Would you like coffee or chocolate milk?"

"Can I have both?"

"Together?"

"Why not?"

She smiled. "That's a splendid idea."

After filling his mug, she grabbed a cloth from the sink and washed Clara's face and hands. "You're ready to get dressed now."

Clara took Wanda's hand. "Come on. I'll show you my favorite princess dresses."

"I can't wait to see them."

After they'd disappeared down the hallway, Judah faced Elaine. The lightness of the morning was dampened by the conversation he knew they needed to have. "I don't suppose I can convince you to close the store today."

"You know I can't. I'm already opening later than usual. But last night I was thinking. I don't usually have many customers after dinner. I can close early, but I need to open."

Judah nodded, already prepared for that answer. "Let me text the sitter, then I'll get changed. We should be able to leave in thirty minutes."

Elaine set a plate in the dishwasher before looking at him. "What are you talking about?"

"I told you yesterday. I'm going to work with you today."

"Clara—"

"Loves her babysitter and will be thrilled to introduce her to Wanda and Sally Ann."

"You expect the babysitter to watch my grandma?"

He crossed his arms, willing to fight this battle. "Do you want your grandma at the store if Wallace comes back?"

She pursed her lips then shook her head.

Judah grabbed her hips and pulled her close to him. "I know you need to open today, but I need to know that you're not alone. Please, let me do this for you."

She wrapped her hands behind his neck, sending shivers through him. "OK, but your next day off I get to treat you and Clara to a fun date."

"Deal." He pressed his forehead to hers, and her lilac scent calmed his racing pulse. "Thank you for letting me help you today. You mean a lot to me." His throat tightened. "Is it too soon to name these feelings?"

She stood on her toes and kissed his cheek. "Maybe, but I feel the same way."

CHAPTER 26

Two hours after the store opened, Elaine rang up another customer as Judah wrapped and bagged the wooden figurine. They'd worked that way since opening the doors and people still filled the shop.

Judah handed the antique to its new owner, then smiled at Elaine. "I'm glad you decided to open the store today. I can't believe you usually do this by yourself."

"It's not always this busy, but now you can understand why I needed to open."

The next customer set down her purchases before turning her attention to the small selection of necklaces Elaine had finished and displayed. The woman picked up the rose quartz beaded necklace. "This is stunning."

Elaine smiled. "It's South Dakota's state mineral."

"You're kidding. What an elegant way to remember our time here. Do you have any more like it? My sisters had to leave early, but I'd love to bring them both one."

"I don't have any more, but I can make two more if you're OK with me shipping them." Elaine reached under the counter and pulled out a receipt book.

"That would be perfect."

After taking the customer's payment and information, two more shoppers stepped up to the register. So did Bridget. "Hey. How's it going?"

Elaine smiled. "It's been crazy busy, but I'm not complaining."

Bridget looked around the store. "This is a bad time. I should have called first."

"Is something wrong?" Her stomach quivered.

"Nothing new. I just have some news that I wanted to share in person."

Judah touched Elaine's back. "Go ahead."

She looked at the line, then remembered the extra work Judah had left the last time he watched the store.

He laughed. "You look like you just ate sour candy."

"Sorry. I was thinking about . . ."

"The last time? I've been helping you for the last two hours. If anything happens that I can't handle, I'll go get you."

"Or I can come back later," Bridget said.

That wasn't an option—Elaine would spend the whole day wondering what was going on. She picked up the baby monitor before smiling at Judah. "Thank you. We'll only be a few minutes."

He gently pushed her toward the kitchen as he reached for the next customer's basket. "Did you find everything you wanted?" he asked.

Elaine led Bridget to the kitchen, where they sat at the table. "Is everything OK with Jules?"

"It's as OK as it can be. She and Ginny are in a tough position. Legally, they're still juveniles, but they've experienced so much. Most foster families treat them like children, but it's hard to come out of that lifestyle and care about bedtimes and homework."

"It breaks my heart to think of all they've been through. I can't imagine what it must be like."

"Few people can."

"I wish there was something I could do to help them."

"Actually, that's why I'm here."

"Oh?" She fidgeted trying to relieve the unease she felt.

"Jules and Ginny are trying to adapt, but they're struggling. They're both in therapy, but trust—especially trusting adults—is hard for kids like them. Yet somehow you connected with Jules, which is amazing. I thought it might help her if she got to see you.

Maybe they could come over here a few hours a week and you could teach them how to make jewelry to sell here."

Happiness and caution bubbled up in her. "I would love that, but what about my felony?"

Bridget smiled. "I spoke with their social worker, and she said as long as I accompany the girls, there won't be a problem."

"You don't mind doing that?"

"Not at all. I'll bring my computer and work on my never-ending stack of paperwork. My boss said it was OK."

A dozen ideas and questions buzzed through Elaine's mind. "We can do it right here at the table. I can't pay them much. Do you think they'd be happy earning commission?"

"I wasn't thinking you'd pay them at all, so a commission would be great. I'm more interested in what this will do for them emotionally and mentally. Maybe learning to make jewelry will give them a sense of value and purpose."

"It would give me one too. When do you want to start?"

"How about next Tuesday at two?" Bridget chuckled. "The girls aren't early risers."

"I'd love that." A rush of emotion hit Elaine and she wiped at her tears. "I'm sorry. I'm just so thankful that you trust me this much. I know you're doing it to help the girls, but . . ." The reality of the situation pushed fresh tears into her eyes. "It's expanding my dreams in ways I never realized I wanted. Does that make sense?"

"Sure does. Like I said, I believe in second chances." Bridget winked. "I'll let you get back to work. Before you do, you might want to check your makeup."

As Bridget disappeared into the store, Elaine rushed to the bathroom. Mascara darkened her eyes and ran down her cheeks, which only made her cry more, but she didn't mind. For the first time in longer than she could remember, she wiped tears of joy from her face.

* * * * * *

At six, Elaine locked the front door and leaned against it, exhausted. The day had been so full of customers that she'd barely talked with Judah. And, despite her initial hesitation, the day had gone well. She loved the way they worked side by side.

"I have to admit, you were right." Judah stood behind the counter adding up the day's profit.

"About what?"

"Opening the store today."

She stepped to the counter and leaned over her iPad so she could see the final numbers. Giddiness zinged through her. After adding this figure to the rest of the money she'd made this week, she'd have extra money to buy a few more jewelry-making supplies for Jules and Ginny. If she'd done her math right, and if people signed up for her classes, the sales and class fees would multiply that money. Then she could *really* help the girls.

But why should she wait? "Will you calculate ten percent?"

"Sure. Why?"

"I think I'll give it to a charity that helps trafficking victims. I'll ask Bridget which organization she recommends."

Judah's eyebrows rose. "Can you afford that?"

She shrugged. "My finances might be tight, but I have more than Jules and Ginny and the other victims. Even if I have to get a second job delivering pizzas, I'm done worrying about it. I'll be OK."

Judah walked around the counter and pulled her into a tight hug. "And this is another reason why you're so amazing. Once you get that information from Bridget, let me know. I want to match your donation."

She squeezed her arms around him. "Thank you, not just for the donation but for all your help today. It would have been madness without you. I should cook dinner since you worked so hard on your day off."

"Not a chance. How am I supposed to impress you with my culinary skills if you cook? Besides, I had a blast."

She laughed. "We should get going. We need to relieve the babysitter and my feet are killing me."

Judah released her. "I have to stop at the store first, but you can stay in the car."

"My feet thank you."

At the grocery story, Judah parked and sprinted inside. While she waited, Elaine slipped her feet from her sandals and stretched her toes. Outside, the sun reflected off of the metallic bikes that filled the parking lot. Their loud mufflers rumbled around her.

She'd never liked the rally, with all the noise and crowds everywhere, but this week had given her a new appreciation for it. While she'd be thankful when Sturgis returned to a peaceful, quiet town, she'd actually look forward to the rally next year.

Beside Judah's car, a woman with a sunflower tattoo on her arm sat on a Harley. The details in the tattoo—the colors and movement—were more realistic than some of Elaine's own paintings. The tattoo, she noticed, matched the sunflowers on the motorcycle. As Elaine waited, she examined the stylistic choices of the other bikers. She'd never paid attention to the unique colors and patterns of each bike—they were a moving art gallery.

As she admired the art work, she spotted Mitch on the other side of the parking lot talking to a young woman with long brown hair. He leaned close to her ear, then turned his face and kissed her. Relief filled Elaine.

Mitch had moved on. Judah was going to make dinner for her. And with the rally ending, either Wallace would move on or the police would be available to offer her more protection. It was turning into one of the best nights she'd had in weeks.

CHAPTER 27

Judah stirred the bubbling spaghetti sauce, then glanced over his shoulder at Elaine as she chopped carrots. A bowl full of lettuce and other diced vegetables sat in front of her on the counter, a pile of scraps beside the bowl. When she looked up, she caught his gaze and smiled. He couldn't help smiling back. He'd never enjoyed cooking a meal so much in his life.

"Watch me!" Clara, in her pink tutu and leotard, danced around the great room, twirling a baton with purple ribbons on each side.

"Bravo!" Wanda clapped from her place on the couch with Sally Ann on her shoulder.

"How's the sauce?" Elaine asked, forcing his attention back to the kitchen.

He dipped a spoon into the pot. Garlic, sage, fennel, and a touch of rosemary blended together with the spicy Italian sausage. His momma would be proud. "Just about there."

The water in the pot beside him boiled so he threw in the noodles. The aroma of garlic bread made his mouth water. He hurried to the oven and pulled out the foil-covered bread, then laid it on the granite counter.

"That smells amazing." Elaine leaned against his shoulder blade.

His heartbeat accelerated. "All I did was heat it up."

"I'm sure it will be delicious." She squeezed his middle then turned from him. "Grandma, dinner's ready. Put Sally Ann back in her cage. Then can you help Clara wash up for dinner?"

Wanda stood with the bird still on her shoulder. "I'll race you."

Clara squealed as she ran ahead with Wanda walking swiftly after her.

Judah chuckled. "They've become best friends. Clara's always been a happy child, but never this happy."

"I don't think I've ever seen my grandma smile so much. They're good for each other." Judah and Elaine worked together to get all the food on the table by the time Clara skipped back into the kitchen.

"I'm hungry." She climbed onto her chair as Wanda joined them. "I love pasketti."

Elaine kissed Clara's head, pushed her chair in, then sat between her and Wanda. Judah sat on the other side of Clara and dished up her food.

"Can I have more?"

"Why don't you finish this helping first, then we'll see?"

"Don't forget to cut it small, Daddy. I don't want to choke. Jamie said we have to eat very small bites so we don't choke."

His hand froze. "I've told you that a gazillion times. Why is it more important when she tells you?"

"Cuz she's smart. She knows everything."

Judah smiled at Elaine, who was covering her mouth with her napkin while her eyes sparkled in amusement.

Clara went on to tell them everything she and Wanda and Jamie, her babysitter, had done that afternoon. Judah and Elaine dutifully asked questions and oohed when appropriate. Everyone settled into a comfortable dinner.

Halfway through the meal, the doorbell rang. "I'll be right back." Judah hopped up to answer it. Zoe stood on the front step. Before he could ask why she was there, she pushed past him and walked into the house.

"Aunt Zoe!" Clara jumped from her chair with spaghetti sauce all over her face and ran over. "Are you going to eat with us?"

Zoe smiled as she picked Clara up. "Not this time. I need to talk to your dad, but I wanted to squeeze my favorite niece first."

Clara giggled. "I'm your only niece." She wiggled until Zoe set her down. "If I eat fast, I can show you Sally Ann after you talk to Daddy."

"Who's Sally Ann?"

Clara pointed at Wanda. "Grammy's bird."

Zoe's nostrils flared as she looked from Wanda to Elaine to Judah. "We need to talk."

He sighed and shot a look at Elaine. Worry etched her face. "I'll be right back."

He followed his sister-in-law outside. She marched down the porch steps and to her car before spinning around and glaring at him. "You've moved your girlfriend in with you?"

"Yes, on the advice of your fellow officers. They didn't want her staying at the shop."

"That doesn't mean she needs to stay here! What if Wallace shows up? What if something happens to Clara?"

"I have an alarm system, and Wallace doesn't even know who I am. I appreciate your concern, but you're not the only person who can protect Clara."

"Like Sheba protected Elaine? Look how that worked out."

"That's not a fair comparison. You're being irrational." Despite Zoe's different hair color and complexion, everything about her expression and stance reminded him of the arguments he'd had with Whitney. There was no use trying to reason with her now. "Did you want something, or did you come all the way over just to yell at me? If so, I'd rather go inside and have dinner with my daughter."

Zoe yanked open the passenger door of her car. She pulled out a plastic bag. "For Sheba. When she comes home."

"Thanks." He grabbed the bag, then headed for the house.

"I've been speaking with a social worker."

She did what? He turned slowly to face her.

"If anything happens to Clara, I'll sue for custody."

Disbelief paralyzed him. "You've got a lot of nerve. I moved back here so Clara could be around you, and this is the thanks I get."

"But she's not around me, is she? She's inside having dinner with a convicted kidnapper."

Anger slashed through him. "Keep threatening me, and we'll move away." Turning his back to her, Judah stormed into the house. The door slammed, followed by the squeal of tires.

The group at the table froze. Clara's mouth hung open a bit wider than Elaine's eyes. Wanda kept her head down as she moved the pasta around on her plate. He took a breath to calm his racing pulse.

Elaine's chair screeched against the floor as she stood. "Is everything OK?"

"It's fine. Excuse me. I've got to make a call." He kissed Clara's head when he passed her. "Your Aunt Zoe brought some toys for Sheba. You can look through them when you're done eating." He set the bag on the counter and proceeded to his office.

After plopping into his chair, he pulled out his phone and scrolled through his contacts until he found his sister-in-law's number.

"Hey, how's that sweet niece of mine?" Mollie asked as someone cried in the background.

"She's great. Listen, I may need your professional services."

"Wait a second. Asher, can you take Grayson?"

Judah took several deep breaths, trying to calm down. People mumbled on the other end of the line before the crying stopped.

"I'm in my office. What can I do for you?"

"Remember when I called about that friend who was on probation? Well, it's a bit more complicated than that." He explained his relationship with Elaine and the developing situation with Zoe. As he explained, panic replaced anger. "Zoe is threatening to sue for custody of Clara. Can she do that?"

"She can, but I don't see that she'd win. While Elaine's felony doesn't look good, it isn't a reason for the state to take custody. When did you start dating?"

"A little less than a week ago. I would never put Clara in danger, and Elaine would never hurt anyone. It's not like she went around snatching kids off the street. She ran away with the foster son she'd raised for three years. It was a stupid move, but not an evil one."

"What if she makes more stupid decisions? Ones that hurt Clara or you?"

"She learned her lesson and I trust her."

The silence on the other end made him nervous. Maybe he should have called a lawyer outside of the family, but he didn't know any other lawyers. Besides, Mollie was the best.

His sister-in-law sighed. "You're smart and you love Clara more than anything. I don't doubt that. If you think this lady is trustworthy then I believe you."

"So how do I protect Clara from Zoe? She said she'd sue if anything happened to Clara, but I can't control everything." Judah rubbed a hand across his neck face. "After what happened to Whitney, we should all understand that."

"Understanding and accepting are two different things. There's not much you can do to stop Zoe, but you can make it hard for her if she does decide to sue. Document all the interactions you've had with her, especially since you met Elaine. Be as detailed and honest as possible. I'll contact the state's attorney in that county and try to get ahead of any problems."

Relief instantly relaxed his tight muscles. "Thank you. Send me a bill."

She laughed. "I'm not going to charge you for legal services any more than you'd charge me for medical advice. That's what family's for."

Another reason to regret his decision not to move closer to his family, but maybe that could be fixed. "I get attorney/client privileges no matter what I tell you, right?"

"Of course, but if your mother finds out I knew about Elaine first, she won't be happy."

"There's nothing to tell her yet. It's been a week."

"An intense week."

"Yes, but that's not what I wanted to talk about. I'm planning on coming out for Clara's birthday next month, but if Zoe keeps harassing us, we might come out earlier," he said, wishing he could shake the unease that gnawed at him. "In fact, keep your eyes open for houses and jobs in the area."

"Will do."

"Thanks." After hanging up, Judah took a few minutes to calm his temper before leaving his office. When he stepped into the kitchen, Elaine sat alone at the table.

She looked at him as he sat beside her. "Clara finished and asked to be done. She wanted to put Sheba's new toys her in bedroom, so I told her she could. I hope that's OK."

"Of course." He motioned to her still-full plate. "I didn't expect anyone to wait for me."

"I thought we could eat together." Elaine tilted her head. "Is everything all right?"

"Zoe's meddling again."

"Is there anything I can do to help?"

"You can change the subject. I need to get my mind off it." He picked up a fork and took a bite of lukewarm spaghetti. "How are you doing?"

Her eyes lit up as she grabbed her phone. "I texted Bridget to see if she knew of any charities that help trafficking victims. She sent me the name of a few." She moved her chair closer to his and showed him her phone. "This one here is A21. Did you know there are more people enslaved today than at any time in history?"

"Really?"

"It says right here." She tapped the screen, then handed him the phone.

He scrolled down. "It's a hundred-and-fifty-billion-dollar industry?" The spaghetti churned in his stomach. He pushed his plate away. "That's sick."

"But they're offering hope too." She reached over and tapped another tab. "They not only help rescue victims, they also provide a place for them to go afterward and even relocate them to a safer place. They provide support to victims so that they can heal, and they give legal help too. They even teach classes to educate the public on how to spot a victim and what to do." She shook her head. "I wish I had known all this earlier. Even though I've learned a lot this week, I think I'll take one of their classes to learn more."

Elaine's passion inspired his own. "I'd be interested in taking that too."

"Really?"

He nodded. "Absolutely. I don't know why anyone wouldn't."

Elaine leaned in and pressed a kiss to his cheek.

He covered the spot with his hand, preserving the warmth. "What was that for?"

Her smile glowed. "For being you."

He wanted to do something for her too. "Wait here." He hopped up, ran downstairs, and grabbed the necklace box from the dresser.

When he returned to the kitchen, Elaine raised her eyebrows. "That was quick."

"I didn't want to lose the moment." A jolt of nerves shook his hand as he handed her the box.

Touching the lacquered finish, she smiled. "It's beautiful. I love cherry blossoms." She gently opened the box, her eyes widening. "What a gorgeous necklace."

"I got it when I was stationed in Japan, before coming to South Dakota. I want you to have it."

She shook her head. "You should save it for Clara. It's too special for me." She held the box out to him.

"I've saved all of Whitney's jewelry for Clara. This one's for you."

"This wasn't Whitney's?"

"Nope. I knew she wouldn't like it so it's been at the bottom of that box for a while. Now I think I know why."

A tentative smile formed on her pretty face as she nodded.

He picked up the dainty ends of the gold chain. She swiveled from him and lifted her glorious curls. When he clasped it around her neck, he kissed her nape before she let her hair down.

Blushing, she faced him. "Thank you. I love it."

"Now, don't you wish you'd kept that fan?"

She laughed, her eyes shining. "Yes, I do."

He sucked in a deep breath as desire consumed him. If she kept looking at him with that adorable expression, he wouldn't be able to think rationally anymore. Needing to focus elsewhere, he picked up her phone and cleared his throat. "It looks like they have benefit walks to bring awareness to trafficking."

Elaine leaned closer. "I saw that. They're in October. Fort Collins is the closes city, but I think I might try to go. I wish they had one in South Dakota, though. I'm sure we'd have enough people interested."

"Why don't you organize one for Sturgis?"

"Me?"

"Why not? Your excitement already has me excited to help. You'd be perfect."

She tapped her fingers on the table and she thought. "Will you walk with me?"

"I'd love to."

"You don't have to commit or anything. October's a long time away, and . . ."

He tapped the pendant where it hung around her neck. "I'm not going anywhere." He hoped.

CHAPTER 28

After Judah and Elaine finally finished their meal and cleaned up the kitchen, Judah went downstairs to take a shower so Elaine went in search of her grandma. She already knew Clara's opinion on their day, but she wanted to make sure Grandma had enjoyed it too. Elaine found her in the middle of Judah's large bed already in her pajamas and reading a novel.

She sat on the edge. "How was your day?"

Grandma set down her book. "Good. The neighbor girl played music on her phone and Sally Ann sang along with it while Clara danced around." She smiled for a second before it faded into a frown.

"What's wrong?"

"I miss my piano. When can I go home?"

Elaine took a deep breath. "I was hoping you'd move in with me for good. If you did, we could move your piano to your old house. Would you like that?"

The soft wrinkles on Grandma's face deepened. "Why can't I go home?"

The fact that she couldn't remember their previous conversation reinforced Elaine's desire—and her Grandma's need—to move in together. Putting on a warm smile, Elaine touched her grandma's hand. "I told you. I want to be able to take care of you every day. I don't get to visit often with you in Rapid City, and I worry that something will happen to you when I'm not there."

"Is it because of Misty? You don't want me to be her friend?"

"It's more than that. You hate leaving the house, even to get groceries, and most of the neighbors you used to know have moved. Plus, I think we're both a little lonely."

"I do wish more people visited me."

"So do I. If you move here, you'll have me, and maybe Clara will come visit too." Elaine hoped Judah would come, but even if things didn't work with him, he might still let Clara and Grandma continue their friendship. Not wanting to worry too much about that future, Elaine squeezed Grandma's hand. "What do you think? Will you let me take care of you here in Sturgis?"

Grandma's lips pressed into a line. "And you'll get me my piano?"

"I promise. Maybe you could teach piano lessons again. You used to love it."

Her eyes brightened. "I'd like that." This time she gave Elaine a genuine smile. "OK. I'll try to stay here."

Relieved, Elaine hugged her. "We'll have the best time."

"Maybe I could start by teaching Clara."

"That's a great idea, and Sally Ann could sing along." Elaine settled in next to Grandma, leaning against the headboard and stretching her legs out in front of her. "Let's look for a piano mover right now."

"You can do that?"

"Of course." She pulled out her phone and searched the internet. Grandma looked over her shoulder for a few seconds, then went back to her book. Elaine clicked on a few links and had to stifle her gasps. She had no idea it cost so much to move a piano. Maybe they could find one in town that wouldn't be so expensive. Maybe Mitch could help. He had a knack for finding what she needed. She sent off a quick text to him.

Looking for a piano. Know anyone selling one?

It didn't take long before her phone chimed. *I'll check.*

Grandma yawned.

Elaine glanced over in time to see her eyelids lower and her head tip forward. "You look tired. I'll let you get some rest."

"Will I get to go with you tomorrow?"

"Tomorrow, I'm closing the store so we'll have the day to hang out. I think we'll stay one more night with Judah then move back on Tuesday." She kissed her grandma's cheek. "Good night."

"Good night, sweetie. I love you."

"I love you too."

Elaine turned out the light on her way out and slipped down the hall. Giggling came from Clara's room, so she peeked in. Judah laid next to a tucked-in Clara reading a book.

"Oh my! I think I've lost my way!" he said in a falsetto.

Elaine leaned against the doorframe and listened as his voice ranged from high to low. Clara giggled some more. Elaine's heart melted.

"And the prince and princess lived happily ever after . . . until the kids came." Judah threw his head back. "Muwahaha!" Then he tickled Clara.

Elaine laughed at her giggles.

"Lainy!" Clara sat up. "Come read a book with me and Daddy."

Judah patted the bed next to them.

Elaine pulled up a little white chair with *Clara* painted in pink. "OK, I'm ready."

"Coward," he mumbled with a wink.

"Daddy, read!"

"You don't need to yell. I'm right here." He picked up a book with a bulldog on the cover. Then a frog book. Then another princess book. Finally, Clara's eyes started to droop.

Judah put the books on the floor. "Good night, my little lamb."

"Daddy, do you have to work tomorrow?"

"I do."

"I don't want to go to daycare. Can I go with Lainy? Please?"

He looked at Elaine. "Tomorrow is her day off. I think she's going to want to rest."

"I'll rest with her. Please, Daddy."

He leaned toward Elaine. "You can say no if you want," he whispered.

"I'd love to hang out with Clara. I brought over my beads. She can help me make necklaces."

"Yay!" Clara sat up in bed and clapped.

"But you have to promise to go to sleep now and be good tomorrow." Judah stared down at her with a stern look.

"I promise."

He kissed her forehead. "Love you, lamb. Good night."

"Love you too. Night, Lainy. Love you."

Tears sprung to Elaine's eyes. "I love you too." She slipped out of the room to compose herself. Marcus had been too young to talk when he came to live with Elaine, so it took years before he told her he loved her. She hadn't expected Clara's declaration, or the way it soothed her heart.

CHAPTER 29

Elaine dried and put away the last of their lunch dishes, then sat next to Clara at the counter. The little girl slid another large bead onto a thin wire. While she worked, Elaine rummaged through her supply of beads, picking a few more with large holes and putting them in a bowl for Clara.

Her phone dinged with a text message from Judah. *How's it going?*

Great. Making jewelry.

Jealous.

Lol.

See you tonight. I'll bring takeout.

No. I made a casserole.

OK. Give my lamb a kiss. I'm headed into surgery.

My pleasure.

Elaine kissed Clara's head. "That's from your dad."

She smiled then went back to the beads, sticking her tongue out as she concentrated on getting them onto the wire.

When Elaine's phone rang, she answered, "The Mother Lode Antique Shop, Elaine speaking."

"Elly. Why is the store closed?" Mitch asked.

She glanced at Clara, then walked onto the deck, shutting the door behind her. "The guy who chased Jules into the store last week came back on Saturday."

Mitch swore. "Are you OK?"

"I'm fine."

"Good. What rotten luck you've had lately."

"Yeah. It's been crazy. What can I do for you?"

"I found you a piano and it's a great deal."

She straightened, excited that he'd worked his magic so soon. "That was fast. What kind?"

"It's an upright with mahogany wood. The carving detail is awesome, but it needs some TLC."

"How much do they want for it?"

"A hundred, plus my fifty-dollar finder's fee. You'd still make a killing on it. Come check it out. You can negotiate with her if you want."

"Judah gets off at five. Can I meet you then?"

"They have another potential buyer coming at four. You can wait, but I can't guarantee they'll hold it."

"Let me see what I can do." She hung up and flipped through pictures of pianos online. If Mitch's was anything like the ones she found, it could be worth the trip. Plus, it would save her having to bring her grandma's piano up from Rapid City. But she hated to drag Clara all over town.

She called Judah, but it went to voicemail. Her phone dinged with a text.

Doc can't talk. In surgery. What do you need?

Found a piano. Can Clara come with me to check it out?

Sure. Booster seat in the garage.

Elaine jumped from her seat, excited for the possible deal. This could ease so many of Grandma's concerns. She texted Mitch. *I can meet you at the store in fifteen. Does that work?*

Yep. See you.

She slipped the phone into her pocket before going to get Clara. She found her watching TV. Elaine walked over and crouched down. "I have to go look at a piano for Grammy. Run and get your shoes on and you can go with me. I'll get my grandma."

Fifteen minutes later, Elaine pulled into her driveway with Sally Ann in the front and her grandma and Clara in the backseat giggling. The house was hot when they entered, so Elaine turned up the air conditioner.

"I have to go potty." Clara gripped her Cinderella doll and crossed her legs.

"OK. I'll be out front by the counter."

Clara ran to the bathroom.

Grandma started up the stairs.

"Grandma, where are you going? We're leaving soon."

"Where to?"

"To look at a piano for you."

"Can I stay here?"

"Don't you want to test it out before I buy it?"

She shook her head. "I want to take a nap."

Elaine sighed but wouldn't argue. It would be easier to negotiate the piano without worrying about Clara *and* her grandma. "I won't be gone long."

Grandma smiled, then took Sally Ann upstairs. The front doorbell rang and Elaine rushed to answer it.

Mitch stood on the other side, smiling. "It's just around the corner. We can walk if you want."

"Sounds good. Let me get some cash and Clara, then I'll be out."

"Clara?"

"Judah's daughter. I'm babysitting her today."

Mitch's gaze shifted back and forth before he shrugged. "Sure. That shouldn't be a problem."

She hurried to the cash register and stuffed some bills into her purse as Clara skipped into the parlor. She held on to her doll with one hand, so Elaine took her free one. "You're being such a good girl. Let's go look at this piano then maybe we'll get ice cream. What do you think?"

"Yes! Can I get a cone?"

"Of course." They joined Mitch on the porch, then set off down the sidewalk. "How did you hear about the piano?" Elaine asked.

"My friend's mom works with this lady's daughter. I went over this morning. It's a real beauty."

"Thanks for thinking of me."

"Sure." They walked around the corner as Clara chatted about everything she saw.

Mitch stopped at a small, ranch-style house with an overgrown lawn. The curtains were drawn, and one of the shutters hung at an angle. "This is the place."

"Are you sure?" The hair on her neck stood up.

"It's nicer inside." He headed up the walkway.

Elaine tightened her grip on Clara's hand and followed. He knocked, and someone opened the thick wooden door.

She squeezed Clara's hand. "This will only take a few minutes, then we'll get our ice cream."

Inside, the scent of smoke made Elaine choke. When her eyes adjusted to the dark living room, she noticed a young woman sitting on a faded floral couch. The girl cradled her head in her hands and her long brown hair covered her face.

What was going on? Unwilling to wait to find out, Elaine picked Clara up and turned to the door.

Mitch shut and locked it. "You're not going anywhere. Wallace, we're here!"

Wallace? "What are you doing?" Elaine's stomach churned.

"It's about time." A gruff voice came from the hall.

Elaine spun around. Wallace stood in the dingy dining room. He smiled. "We meet again."

Fear struck her in the gut. She turned to Mitch. "Let Clara go. She hasn't done anything."

He smirked. "She's worth more than you."

His confession nauseated her. "You're sick." She tucked Clara's head onto her shoulder as she searched for a place to hide.

A man with short salt-and-pepper hair approached from the hallway. He stopped next to Mitch. "We were about to leave without you." He scanned Elaine from head to toe. "She's older that the usual girls."

"I know, but she's perfect." Mitch grinned. "She'll be easy to break."

"Fine. I'll take her, but only because she comes with the girl." He handed Mitch a thick white envelope.

He thumbed through the cash. "Where's the other thousand? I brought you three."

"I guess we get these two at a deal." He reached for Clara.

Elaine backed away.

"Stop screwing me over, Brad!" Mitch stepped in front of the man. "You'll make a fortune off of them. I deserve my cut."

Brad pulled a gun from behind his back. "I suggest you cut your losses and move on. We're done doing business with you. We lost our biggest week because of you."

Mitch glared at him, then winked at Elaine. "I only regret that I couldn't sample your tricks first, but my loss."

Anger like she'd never experienced consumed her and she spit in his face. He backhanded her. Pain sliced through her cheek as she fell against the wall. Clara slipped from her arms, crying.

"Don't damage the goods." Wallace pulled on Elaine's arm. "It's time to load up."

Her body shook. What had she done? And why had she brought Clara? She couldn't ruin another child's life. She looked into Wallace's eyes, desperate to find a bit of humanity. "Please, don't take her. She's just a child."

"Move or you'll never see her again." His fingers dug into her skin.

Elaine leaned closer to Clara. "We have to do what they say. Can you be brave?"

She nodded, her eyes red and teary.

Elaine straightened on shaking legs. Wallace ripped her purse off her shoulder, took out her cash, then gave the purse to the other man. "Ditch 'em where no one will find 'em." He held out his hand in front of her. "Give me your phone."

She reached into her pocket and pulled it out. She tried to dial 9-1-1, but Wallace snatched it from her.

"Get her in the van," Brad said.

Elaine barely had time to lift Clara into her arms before Wallace pulled her through the dirty kitchen and into the garage.

The side door of a black passenger van opened and a large man with a long black beard got out. "Get in the back."

Clara cried harder. "I don't want to go with them. I want my daddy!"

"I know, sweetheart," Elaine whispered. She wanted to tell her it was going to be all right, that someone would rescue them, but who? How? No one knew where they were.

She carried Clara to the back and buckled her into the seat by the window, then took the middle seat as the car filled up with other women.

A teen with bright red hair and smelling like cheap perfume sat in front of Elaine. She looked at Clara. "Why she here?" she whispered.

"They took us."

The girl's eyes widened, then she faced forward. Beside them, a girl with tan skin and dark curly hair looked them over before sitting down. "How old is she?"

"Four."

She cursed. "She's too young."

Elaine put an arm around Clara and whispered, "How can we escape?"

"There ain't no way." The girl next to them raised her chin, bouncing her dark afro. "I'm Annie."

Elaine didn't know if she should tell them their names, but what could it hurt? "Clara and Elaine."

"Stop talking!" Wallace yelled from the passenger seat.

The garage door opened and the van rumbled out.

"Where are we going?" Elaine asked Annie.

"Not sure. Probably North Dakota. Lots of johns in the oil field and no women. It's a dream come true for . . ." She faced forward and laid her head on the window.

Clara quietly cried as she snuggled close to Elaine.

Elaine stared straight ahead as the town flew by the dark tinted windows. Panic clawed at her throat when they headed east. She had to keep a level head, find a way to escape, or at least save Clara. No matter what happened to Elaine, she had to be brave for Clara.

CHAPTER 30

Judah left the hospital at five o'clock, calling Elaine as he walked to his car. It went to voicemail. She and Clara were probably too busy playing to talk to him. Her text earlier that day had warmed him. He loved that they were getting along so well.

As he drove, he wondered if he could convince Elaine to stay one more night. Not only would he feel better knowing she was safe, but he was on call next weekend, so it would be two weeks before he could steal her away for a real date.

He pulled into the garage, but her car wasn't there. Maybe they had to run to the store. Inside, Elaine's beads covered the counter. He smiled. She certainly added touches of color to his life.

But where were they? He pulled out his phone and called her again. The voicemail picked up. "Hey, Elaine. It's Judah. I'm home and wondering where you and Clara are. I'll wait here."

Instead of watching the clock and waiting, Judah headed straight for his bathroom. He took his time showering, shaving, and even putting on his favorite aftershave. After dinner, maybe he and Elaine could walk down to the park with Clara and Wanda. Later, they could sit on the deck and watch the meteor shower. Anticipation quickened his steps when he walked into the living room.

He expected to hear Clara giggling or cartoons on the TV, but the house was silent. He peeked into Clara's room. Her stuffed princesses stared back at him. He checked the garage. Empty. Six thirty. They should be home.

He called Elaine again. Voicemail.

Was it like her to blow off plans and not answer her phone? He didn't know. Even if it was, she had Clara and Wanda with her.

Zoe's warnings flashed through his mind.

Judah pushed them aside as he grabbed his keys and headed to the garage. Maybe something had happened at the store. Or with her phone. Anxious and a little angry, he sped across town and parked in front of The Mother Lode. He jogged up to the door, but it was locked. He ran around to the back door. Locked. Elaine's car sat in the driveway. She had to be nearby. He saw Wanda through the kitchen window sitting at the table eating a sandwich. Relief filled him. When he banged on the window, she jumped.

"Wanda. It's Judah. Will you open the door?"

She scurried to the door and swung it wide.

"Sorry to startle you. I've been looking for Elaine." He stepped into the kitchen looking for signs of her. "Is she upstairs?"

"No. She went to buy me a piano. It's going to be lovely to have a piano again."

"I know. That was hours ago. Did Clara go with her?"

"I think so. She's not here."

Frantic, he whipped out his phone and called Elaine again. Voicemail. "Do you know where they went to buy the piano?"

"No. Do you want to say hi to Sally Ann?"

"I need to find my daughter!"

Wanda's eyes widened.

"I'm sorry, but it's almost seven. I haven't heard from Elaine in five hours." He ushered Wanda to the table. "Don't go anywhere. I'll see if someone can check on you." He ran to his car. He wanted to stay with Wanda, but he had to search for Elaine and Clara. What if they'd been in a crash? Were they in the hospital?

What if Zoe was right? What if Elaine took Clara?

He couldn't let his thoughts go there. *Please don't let them be hurt.*

Two hours later, having driven every possible route from his house to The Mother Lode and most of the streets in between, Judah pulled into the hospital parking lot and ran into the emergency department. When the triage nurse saw him, she buzzed him through.

He hurried to the nurse's station. "Have there been any car crashes lately?"

The nurse glared at him. "It's the end of the rally. There have been crashes all day."

"I'm looking for my daughter and girlfriend."

Her eyes softened. "There haven't been any kids brought in, but let me see if they're here. What're their names?"

"Clara Demski and Elaine . . . no, Mary Russell."

She punched a few keys, then looked up with a sad smile. "They're not here."

A vapor of relief came and went. They weren't hurt, but where could they be? "Call me if they come in." He gave her a business card then trudged outside. Darkness had descended. It was nine thirty and his baby was missing. With a convicted child kidnapper. Even if Elaine was innocent, one call could put her back in jail. But when it came to Clara, Judah would sacrifice anything.

He sat on the curb, pulled out his phone, and dialed 9-1-1.

"9-1-1, what's your emergency?"

"My daughter's missing." His throat thickened. "I've looked everywhere. It's been over eight hours. Please help me find her."

She might have an excuse, but the fact remained—Elaine had taken Clara. How could he have been so stupid?

****

Elaine hugged Clara close as she stroked her cherry blossom necklace. She had no idea how long they'd been driving north, but the sun had set a while ago. Judah was probably worried sick. Hopelessness clung to her.

They turned down a dirt road and bumped around for about a mile, finally stopping in the middle of nowhere. Elaine glanced at the dark sky. "Why are we stopping?"

"Potty break," one of the girls mumbled.

The sliding door opened and they filed out. Elaine unhooked Clara's seatbelt and helped her out of the van. They clung to each other as they followed the group of girls.

"Now's your chance to relieve yourself," Wallace said from behind her. "Stay in the light of the headlights or you'll be sorry."

Elaine scanned the endless pastures around them. "You want us to go outside?"

"Only choice ya got." He laughed then grabbed the girl with the long brown hair, pulling her into the dark field beside them.

Elaine gasped and quickly carried Clara over to the group of ladies squatting in the tall grass on the opposite side of the road. The beams from the headlights shone around them. She helped Clara then went herself.

A girl screamed. Elaine grabbed Clara and held her tight. Screams turned to crying. Elaine covered Clara's ears as tears fell down her own cheeks. What kind of nightmare had they been dragged into?

Annie leaned into Elaine. "Never let them see you cry."

She nodded silently as she wiped the tears from her face. She pressed her cheek to Clara's, humming a song she hoped would mute the crying.

"Everybody in!" Wallace yelled from the van. "Time to go!"

Elaine pressed Clara to her as she searched their surroundings. She had to escape. It was dark. Wallace would never be able find them in the field.

Annie pushed her toward the van. "Don't even think about it. When they catch you, they'll beat you. Then what do you think would happen to your girl?"

That thought literally shook Elaine. The closer she got to the van, the harder she shook. At the door, Wallace handed her two boxes of raisins, two granola bars, and two sodas. They climbed in. The girl Wallace had dragged away sat hunched over, her brown hair covering her face. Grass stuck to the tangled mess. When she glanced up, bile rose to Elaine's throat—it was the girl Mitch had been kissing in the parking lot.

Wallace pulled Elaine back and whispered in her ear, "You're next." His breath sent chills over her skin as his grip dug painfully into her arm. He released her with a shove.

She grabbed the seat to keep from falling and pushed Clara to the back.

"I want my daddy," she said as Elaine buckled her in.

"I do too. For now, let's listen to what they tell us to do and pray we can go home soon."

She buckled Clara into her seat and kissed her head before giving her some raisins. She put the rest of the food in her pocket for Clara to eat later.

With her distracted, Elaine looked at the girls around her. She had to form a plan. Annie sat beside her again. Maybe she would help.

Elaine leaned close and whispered, "How long have you been with them?"

"Three years."

Three years? She forced the dismay away. "Were you kidnapped too?"

"I ran away from foster care and went to a homeless shelter. I met a guy there. Promised to take care of me. As soon as he sold me, I never saw him again." Annie turned to the window and closed her eyes.

Panic tightened Elaine's throat. Three years. Maybe she deserved to be here, but not Clara. They were going to hurt her, and there was nothing she could do to stop it.

A sharp pain seized her stomach. She bent over and took several calming breaths. She had to focus. If she gave up, they won, and they were not going to win. She'd saved Marcus. She'd save Clara.

No matter how long it took, she'd never stop looking for a way to get Clara out.

Once her breathing returned to normal, Elaine stared outside, reading every street sign and mile marker and repeating them to herself as Clara slept against her. They traveled out of South Dakota through Dickinson, North Dakota. As far as she could tell, they were on their way to Bismarck. Why would they head east when the oil fields were west of them?

"Where are they taking us?" she whispered to Annie.

The girl turned her head toward Elaine but didn't open her eyes. "Probably to a truck stop."

"Not the oil fields?"

"We'll get there soon enough. They always take a bunch of backroads. Might as well make money on the way."

Hope sprung up. "Will they let us use the bathroom there?" She'd beg everyone and anyone to help them if she had to.

"No. They're not going to trust you around other people. Not until they've broken you."

She swallowed the fear threatening to creep up and leaned closer to Annie. "If I help you escape, can you take Clara with you? Her dad lives in Sturgis."

Annie's eyes popped open. "You would give up your girl instead of saving yourself?"

"I would do anything to save her."

"And you trust me?"

"I have to."

"Why?"

Elaine glanced at the front seats. "I think they'll expect me to try to escape. You've been here for three years. They won't expect you to run away."

Her eyes closed again. "They might. I tried before. Both times they caught me and almost beat me to death." She put her hand on her abdomen. "I can't risk a beating now."

What was left of Elaine's heart broke. "What's going to happen to the baby?"

Annie dug her fingers into Elaine's arm as she kept her face neutral. "They can't know. They'll punch me in the stomach until they kill it . . . and maybe me."

"What are you going to do?"

One silent tear slid down Annie's cheek. "I don't know."

Elaine did. "You need to get out. I'll help."

CHAPTER 31

Something nudged Elaine, and she woke with a gasp. Light filled the van. Hundreds of feet away, the truck stop shone like a football stadium. Between her and the convenience store sat at least twenty semi-trucks in five rows. If she provided a distraction, Annie and Clara could hide between and under the trucks until they made it to the stop.

The two girls in front of her snored. They should provide enough cover for her to tell the plan to Annie. She leaned sideways as Annie whispered, "We have a plan."

"What?"

"Shh. In a little bit they'll get us out to pee. We'll cause a distraction. Take Clara and run to the purple semi-truck with an American flag on the front. He travels with his wife. They should help you."

"No. You take her. Save your baby."

"Your girl don't know me. If she cries, they'll catch us."

Elaine searched the trucks for the purple one, but it was too dark to distinguish colors from so far away. "If you know they'll help, why don't you ask?"

"Because Wally knows that we know. He watches us. He won't expect you to go there."

She was right, but how could Elaine leave Annie and her baby? Her heart sank. She had no choice. She had to save Clara. "Thank you. I'll try to find a way to save you."

Without facing them, Annie squeezed her hand.

Elaine looked out the window, searching again for the purple truck. *Please let this work. Please let me find the purple truck.*

"Everyone up! It's time to earn your keep!" Wallace opened the door.

The dome light came on and Clara started crying. "I want my daddy."

"Shut her up!"

Elaine cradled Clara in her arms, stroking her hair. "I know you do. You're going to have to be brave and do everything I tell you. OK?"

She sniffled but nodded.

Everyone filed out of the van. Elaine hefted Clara into her arms and crawled out on shaking legs. The cool night air made her shiver, or was it her nerves? Her heart raced as adrenaline surged through her. Ahead of her, the girls grouped together in the field. Elaine carried Clara toward them.

A scream pierced the air. Then all the girls screamed. They ran around stomping their feet. "Snakes! Snakes!"

Clara cried louder. Wallace ran toward the girls. Elaine sprinted for the trucks.

Needle pricks stabbed her lungs, but she kept running, scanning the trucks. Her arms went numb so she put Clara down, grabbed her hand, then took off again.

"Come back here!" Wallace's shout echoed behind her.

Clara stumbled. Elaine scooped her back into her sore arms and kept running. Feet pounded behind them.

Where was the purple truck?

They reached the first row. Silver. Blue. Black. Red. She weaved through them, searching for the purple one. When her lungs seized, she slipped behind a trailer and leaned against the tire. Her chest heaved. Clara clung to her neck. Elaine's eyes never stopped moving. Where was the purple semi?

There! Fifty feet to the left.

Clara's grip tightened.

Footsteps pounded behind them.

Elaine's lungs burned as she sprinted. Past a silver truck. Her side ached. She sprinted to the purple cab and pounded on the passenger door.

"Help! Please help!" She put Clara down and beat on the door with both her hands. "Help! We need your help!" Why weren't they responding? Kneeling, she looked Clara in the eye. "Hide under the truck behind that tire. Stay there! Don't come out, not even if the bad man takes me. If you can, stand between the tires." She pushed Clara under the truck, praying the girl would hide herself well.

Someone grabbed Elaine's arm, yanking her back. "Now you'll pay." Wallace spun her around and smacked her face. "Where's the girl?"

Pain shot through her cheek. "She's gone. You've got me. Leave her."

Something squeaked behind Elaine. "Let that girl go."

"Mind your own business. The wife and I are having a disagreement is all." Wallace looked above her head.

She fought against his hold on her. "He's lying! I'm not his wife!"

Then a man stepped beside her. "Leave her and go or I'll shoot."

Wallace pulled her with him, dragging her stumbling feet across the asphalt. "My wife's off her medication. I need to get her home."

"I'm not his wife!"

The man cocked his gun. "Guess we'll have to call the cops to sort this out."

Wallace swore as he shoved Elaine away from him. By the time she sagged to the ground, he'd disappeared. Her limbs shook with relief. She glanced up at the truck driver, her throat tight with emotion. "Thank you."

"Come on, little thing. Let's get you inside, then I'll call the police." He lowered his gun.

"Wait!" She crawled under the semi. "Clara. It's safe to come out now."

"My knee hurts."

Her weak voice tore at Elaine's heart. "I'm sorry, but there's a nice man here now. I bet he has a bandage for you."

Something scratched against the pavement, then Clara appeared from between two tires. Black marks covered her dress. Elaine pulled the child into her arms, sobbing. They were safe!

"You OK under there?"

The kind stranger's voice brought more tears to her eyes. Taking Clara's hand, Elaine led them out from under the trailer.

The man held his hand out to her. She clasped it, allowing him to help her out without letting go of Clara. He looked to be a good decade older than her mom with a full brown beard. He tilted his baseball cap at her. "Name's Charlie. My Hannah will take good care of you."

He opened the cab door and motioned for them to climb in. Elaine sat on the passenger seat, then Charlie helped Clara up. As soon as she settled on Elaine's lap, he shut the door.

Someone turned their seat so they faced the living space of the cab. A thin woman with cropped brown hair smiled at them. "You poor dears. Is there anything you need? Something to eat or drink?"

Clara whimpered.

Elaine stroked her hair. "Can I have a bandage and ointment for her knee?"

"Of course." Hannah reached into a space above the driver's seat. She pulled down a first aid kit and gave it to Elaine. As she tended to Clara's knee, the driver's door opened.

Elaine's squeezed Clara to her.

Charlie climbed in and locked the doors. "I followed that jerk so I could get a description of his vehicle, but he pulled away before I could get close. I called the police. They're sending a state trooper. Is there someone you can call to let them know you're OK?"

Bless this sweet man! Her body relaxed into the chair. "I need to call Clara's dad, but I don't have his number. They stole my phone with all my contacts."

"The trooper will be able to find him. Just sit tight."

She nodded. She hated making Judah wait even another minute longer, but who could she call in the middle of the night? Bridget could find his number. "Maybe I could call the sheriff's depart—"

Charlie's phone rang, cutting her off. "Hello. Yep, I'm the one who called it in. We're at the Flying J Truck Stop west of Bismarck."

Elaine's hand reached for Judah's necklace, but it was gone. Sorrow filled her but only for a moment. She had lost his necklace, but at least she hadn't lost his precious child. Elaine stroked the girl's hair until her breathing deepened and steadied. Safe, warm, and comfortable, exhaustion consumed Elaine too. She laid her head against the seatback and closed her eyes, but Mitch's face appeared. Fear and anger forced her eyes open. How could she have trusted him?

Charlie tapped her shoulder. "What's your name?"

"Mary. Mary Russell."

"And your girl?"

"Clara Demski. Her dad is Judah Demski. We live in Sturgis. Will the officer let him know we're safe?"

His kind smile set her at ease. He repeated all the information into the phone, then hung up. "The trooper is almost here. He said he'd make sure to call Clara's dad soon as he gets here."

Elaine laid her head back against the headrest and closed her eyes. She forced Mitch's image aside and pictured Judah. She'd get Clara to him however she could.

Something squeezed Elaine's shoulder. Her eyes popped open. She glanced around the cab. Blue and red lights flashed outside.

Hannah knelt beside her. "Wake up, dear. The police are here."

The passenger door opened and a trooper in a tan uniform and broad-rimmed hat appeared. Her heartbeat increased.

"I'm Trooper Key. Please step out of the truck."

Elaine wiggled off the seat as she gently laid Clara on the chair, then slipped down from the cab.

"What's your name?" The trooper shone his flashlight on her face.

"Mary Russell. I go by Elaine now."

"Can I see your ID?"

"I don't have it. They took it from me in Sturgis. That little girl is Clara Demski." Elaine pointed over her shoulder. "Her dad is Judah Demski. He lives in Sturgis, but he doesn't know where we are. Can you call him and tell him? I don't have his number."

"Are you aware that there is a BOLO out for you?"

"No, but I'm glad you've been searching for us."

"An Amber Alert was issued for Clara."

Elaine nodded. "That's good, isn't it?"

"You're not the legal guardian of Clara and you brought her across state lines without her father's permission. You're under arrest for kidnapping. Turn around and put your hands behind your back."

Kidnapping? Numb from shock, Elaine turned around. The familiar click of handcuffs echoed in her ears. Her stomach sank as the metal tightened around her wrists. "This is a misunderstanding. I didn't kidnap Clara. I saved her."

The trooper led her to his patrol car. "Tell it to the detectives."

Tremors shook her body, but she refused to crumble. She had the truth on her side. They had to believe her. Didn't they?

CHAPTER 32

Judah paced in his living room while Zoe glared at him from the kitchen stool. He checked the clock again. It had been thirteen hours since Elaine's text message and two hours since the police had given him an update. He needed to do something.

Marching into the kitchen, he reached for his car keys. Zoe swiped them off the counter and into her pocket.

"I need to find Clara," he said.

"You're not going to find her. If you'd get that into your thick head and stay here, I could be out looking for her instead of babysitting you."

The doorbell rang. Judah ran to answer it. A detective walked in, followed by a sergeant whose name Judah had already forgotten. Officers Holt and McGuire filed in after them.

"Good news," the detective said. "We've located your daughter."

Judah's legs weakened and he grabbed the wall for support. Zoe appeared beside him. "Where is she?"

"They were found at a truck stop outside of Bismarck. She's fine. They're taking her to a foster home for the night."

Elated, he hugged Zoe's rigged form. She pulled away, but he didn't care. His baby was safe. He needed to get her. But then the detective's words register. "North Dakota? How'd she get there?"

"I don't know all the details yet. Mary Russell is on her way to the county detention center. She was arrested for kidnapping."

"Can I get permission to head up there to bring her home, Sarge?" Zoe asked, wiping tears from her eyes.

Judah stepped forward. "No. I'm going to get her."

The sergeant nodded. "You can go together."

"Sarge—" Zoe started, but he held up a hand.

"They'll need to release her into his custody in the morning anyway. I'll text you the social worker's information. You can contact her in the morning."

"Fine. But I'm driving." Zoe headed toward the door. Not wanting to argue with his sister-in-law, Judah hurried to his room and packed a bag, then he went to Clara's room and packed a set of her clothes. He stopped at her bed. Her favorite doll sat on top of the pink comforter. He picked it up, a sob rising in his chest. She must be terrified. He took a deep, shuttering breath and shoved the doll into the bag. The sooner they left, the sooner she'd be safe in his arms.

A horn honked. He hurried to the front door. Zoe sat in her Camaro and honked again. Judah gritted his teeth. After making sure he had his wallet and phone, he locked the door and jogged to the car.

Zoe took off as soon as his door shut.

He threw the bag in the backseat. "Let me know if you get tired and need me to drive."

She turned on the radio.

He pulled out his phone and pulled up a map. Bismarck was almost five hours away. His baby girl would be in his arms by the time the sun came up.

His phones buzzed.

What is going on??? I saw an amber alert for Clara. Call me, ASAP!!!

Mollie. Judah typed back. *Clara's safe. Can't talk. Riding with Zoe to Bismarck to get her.*

Bismarck?!?! How did she end up there???

Judah took a steadying breath before typing the words he still couldn't believe. *Elaine took her. She's arrested. Clara's in foster care. Worst nightmare ever.* He rubbed his eyes as three dots blinked on his screen.

Do we need to come out there?

He'd give anything to have Mollie and Asher with him instead of Zoe, but he didn't need more distractions. *No, but get the spare bedroom ready. Clara and I are coming.*
Stay as long as you need.
He laid his head against the headrest. The same question that had haunted him all night taunted him again: how could Elaine do this? She'd betrayed him. He wanted to shake her, yell at her, demand she explain. But he also never wanted to see her again.

****

Elaine glanced at the white clock above the two-way mirror in the interrogation room. One thirty in the morning and she was exhausted.

Detective Samuels sat across from her. He looked up from the yellow legal pad he'd been writing on. "That is quite the tale. You have a history of kidnapping and you want me to believe that you and the child were victims of kidnapping?"

She sighed. She didn't know how to convince him that she was innocent. Maybe she shouldn't have refused to have a lawyer there. "It's not like I kidnapped a random kid. My husband and I took off with a foster child I had loved for three years. I thought of him as mine."

"Do you think of Clara as yours too?"

"No, of course not. I know you don't believe me, and I don't blame you, but you're wasting time with me. Please try to catch them. There were four other girls in the van. One's pregnant."

"Is there anyone who could vouch for you?"

Elaine's head hurt just trying to think. She couldn't call Judah. He probably hated her for putting Clara in danger. If he didn't, he should. Maybe Bridget could help. "Bridget Smalls is the only person I can think of. She works for the Meade County Sheriff's Department. She knows all the details of my past dealing with both Mitch and Wallace. She also knows about my felony."

Detective Samuels wrote on his pad. "Let's say you aren't lying. Would you be able to give a description of the kidnappers and the other girls to our sketch artist?"

That would take too much time. She held out her hand. "Give me a pad and pencil, and I'll sketch them myself."

His right eyebrow rose. "You?"

"I was an art teacher for years."

"All right. I'll get you what you need. I'm also calling in the detective on the human trafficking task force. If you're sending us on a bootless errand, it won't look good when you're charged." The detective stood. "I'll be right back."

Elaine laid her head on her arms as the door clicked shut. Who would save her now? She closed her heavy eyelids as a familiar loneliness crept in.

Something banged and Elaine's head popped up. Sleeping five minutes at a time was making her jumpy, but she took a deep breath and willed herself to be calm. The detective sat across the table from her. "If you're too tired we can do this in the morning," he said as he slid a drawing pad and package of pencils toward her.

"I'll do it now, then you can start looking for them."

He nodded. "I issued a BOLO for the van you described. The sooner we get the images out to the officers, the better."

Two hours later, she had drawn everyone from the van. Detective Samuels left to issue BOLOs for them while she sketched Mitch's likeness. Her hand shook as she stared at the forming image. She had to get it right.

The door creaked and Detective Samuels walked in followed by a shorter man in a black polo shirt. A gun and badge hung on his belt.

"Mary, this is Detective Harris from the North Dakota Human Trafficking Task Force."

The detective sat across from her. She slid the picture across the table. "This is Mitch. I'm not sure if that's his real name, and

I don't know his last name. He's the one who lured us into the house."

Detective Harris picked up the picture. "Why did you go with him?"

"I've bought antiques from him before. He helped me at the store." Tears filled her eyes. "I trusted him."

"Why?"

"He flirted and flattered me. He helped me when I needed it. I thought he was my friend." Why hadn't she been more suspicious of him?

"Or were you working with him to sell Clara?" Detective Samuels asked.

Elaine gasped.

Detective Harris cleared his throat. "I interviewed the truck driver and Bridget Smalls. They corroborate your story."

Elaine sat straighter. He believed her. Bridget believed her. She wasn't alone in this mess. "Can I talk to Bridget? My grandma's all alone, and I'm worried about her."

Detective Harris pulled out his cell, pushed a few buttons, and handed it to Elaine. "It's calling her now."

"Bridget Smalls."

Bridget's beautiful voice, so calm and reassuring, overwhelmed her and she started to cry. "It's Elaine." Her voice squeaked.

"Are you OK?"

"I am now. I've never been so scared." She wiped at the tears running down her face. "I'm sorry to bother you so late."

"Like I could sleep after the detective called. I just got off the phone with Clara's social worker. They've got her tucked into a foster home. Sounds like she was already asleep before the worker even left the home."

Relief surged through her. "Thank you for finding that out."

"How can I help *you*?"

"Would you be able to check on my grandma? I left her at my house earlier today. I don't know—" Her voice broke as she imagined the worst. What if Mitch had gone back?

"I'll head over now. Let me know when you're done there. I can have someone pick you up."

"I will." She handed the phone back to Detective Harris. "Thanks."

He nodded as he put his phone into his pocket. "I ran your drawings through the system, and we were able to identify two of the three men. Is there anything you can tell us about Mitch?"

"Not really. He drives a silver Charger and he said his grandmother lives in Minneapolis. I'm sorry I can't tell you anything more."

Detective Samuels stood. "If you're done with Ms. Russell, I'll have an officer get her booked and taken to a cell."

"I'm still arrested?" Her stomach dropped. "I thought you believed me?"

Detective Harris winced. "I do, but there's nothing we can do about it until the state's attorney has a chance to look at the case. They don't open until eight tomorrow. I'll be there as soon as they unlock the door."

Elaine's hope fluttered away. She'd done the right thing. How could she go back to jail? Unwilling to give in to that fear, she took a deep breath. If Clara could sleep in a strange place, then so could she. Unlike Annie and the other girls, at least she and Clara were safe. As soon as Elaine got out, she was going to find a way to help them. She didn't know how, but she'd find a way.

CHAPTER 33

Judah sat on the black vinyl chair in the drab waiting room of the Department of Social Services and stretched his stiff neck. Two hours sleeping in Zoe's car hadn't been kind to his body, but he'd gotten some rest. He bounced his leg, anxious to have Clara back.

Zoe trudged back from the restroom and plopped down three seats away.

The locked door in front of them opened and a short lady in her mid-thirties entered. "Are you Judah Demski?"

He stood. "I am."

Zoe rushed to his side. "I'm Officer Zoe Charles. Clara is my niece. You'll be releasing her into my custody."

The lady's eyes narrowed. "No, I'll be releasing her to her father."

"But he allowed her to be kidnapped in the first place!"

"I got the full story from the detectives. It was an awful event, which could have had far worse consequences. Her father is her only legal guardian and the judge did not adjudicate at our request." She turned to Judah. "Clara is free to be released into your custody, and we will not be following up nor will DSS in South Dakota."

Relief poured through him. "Thank you. Where is Clara now?"

"She's on her way. The foster mom had a rough time waking her this morning. Poor thing was tuckered out."

Zoe huffed. "How can you release her without consequences?"

The social worker planted her hands on her hips. "We are not a punitive department. We don't hand out punishments for mistakes parents make. We feel Dr. Demski is capable of caring for Clara and keeping her safe. If you have an issue with it, take it up with social services in your county."

The glass door to Judah's right opened and a lady walked in carrying a sleeping child. He'd recognize that long blond hair anywhere.

"Clara." He rushed to her.

Her head popped up and she turned around so fast the foster mom almost dropped her. Clara's blue eyes widened. "Daddy!"

He grabbed her and crushed her to his chest, breathing in her strawberry shampoo. He squeezed his eyes shut to keep his emotions in check. His baby was back where she belonged. He held her until she squirmed, then he sat in the nearest chair and set her on his lap. He looked her over for injuries. A large Band-Aid covered her knee. "Are you hurt?"

"I hurt my knee." She laid back against him. "I want to go home."

"Me too, lamb. Me too." He gazed up at the smiling foster mom. "Thank you for taking such good care of her."

"It was my pleasure. Her knee is scratched, but it's not very deep. I cleaned it and got her a fresh bandage." She held out a blue duffle bag. "I washed the clothes she had on yesterday."

Judah looked down at the purple t-shirt and jean shorts Clara wore. "Are these your clothes? I can pay you for them."

The foster mom waved him away. "Nonsense. The state will reimburse me. I try to keep a few sets of clothes in different sizes for this reason." She knelt down beside them and put her hand on Clara's back. "You were such a brave girl. Take good care of your daddy, OK?"

Clara nodded.

"I put a picture of my family with our address on the back of it in her bag. I do it with all the kiddos who stay with us. Maybe drop us a note to let us know how she's doing?" She stood and waved. "It was a pleasure to meet you, Clara."

"I'd better get back to work," the social worker said. "The rest of my cases won't be this easy to resolve."

Judah grabbed the duffle bag. "Is that it? Anything else I need to do?"

"Not a thing. Have a safe trip back to Sturgis." She waved at Clara. "Have a good trip home."

Clara waved back.

Judah scooped her up and left the building, not waiting to see if Zoe followed. Driving together had made sense at one in the morning, but he wished he'd brought his own car so he could take Clara straight home. He leaned against Zoe's car as he waited for her. "We forgot to grab her booster seat. We'll have to buy one before we head home."

When Zoe reached them, she touched a shaking hand to Clara's back. "I'm so glad you're safe, Clara." Her voice wavered. She ignored Judah as she unlocked the car.

He reached across the rear seats and put Clara in behind the driver so he could see her as they drove. She grabbed his hand. "Daddy, will you sit with me?"

He glanced at the miniscule leg room at the other side. He'd be cramped but there was no way he was going to deny her anything. "Of course, lamb." He squeezed himself into the other seat, then buckled them both in. Clara reached over and took his hand.

Zoe backed out of the parking spot without a word.

"Where are we going?" Clara asked.

Judah squeezed her hand. "We're going to buy you a brand-new booster seat and get some snacks. Then we'll head home."

"Are we going to get Lainy?"

Judah's breath stuck in his lungs. "No. Elaine's not coming with us."

Zoe looked in the rearview mirror. "I'm sorry, but you can't ever see Elaine again. She put you in danger." Her voice shook—he didn't know if it was from rage or stress. For the first time in forever, he shared his sister-in-law's sentiments. "I hope she rots in jail."

Clara's face crumbled and tears ran down her face.

"We'll talk about Lainy later, OK?" Judah kissed Clara's hand.

Clara nodded. "Maybe she can visit me at home."

Zoe opened her mouth, but Judah caught her gaze in the mirror and mouthed *later*.

Why would Clara want to see Elaine? She'd crushed his heart. He had no desire to ever think about Elaine again, much less see her. What had she done to Clara to make her think she was still a friend? An hour ago, all he wanted was his daughter back. Now that he had her, he wanted answers.

****

A loud clang echoed in the cell. "Breakfast time." Overhead, fluorescent lights flickered on.

Elaine rolled to her side. Her breakfast tray sat on a ledge in the door. She sat up on the foam mattress, pushing the sheets and blanket off her orange scrub-like prison clothes.

Carrying the tray back to her cot, steam rose from the eggs, their scent causing her stomach to rumble. She hadn't eaten since lunch the day before. The eggs were bland and the sausage too salty, but she devoured them. She savored the sweet applesauce, then sat back, thankful to be full.

With nothing else to do, she put the tray back on the ledge before stepping over to the narrow window. The parking lot spread out several stories below her. She hoped Clara had slept soundly in the foster home. She hated that her sweet girl had to stay with strangers, but it beat the alternative. If she wasn't in her dad's arms yet, she would be soon.

Oh, Judah. How he must hate her. Sadness filled her again. She'd miss their talks and kisses, but she was thankful for their short relationship. It gave her hope. She could find love again, and despite her record, her escape with Clara made one thing clear—

Elaine was more than her past. She deserved a healthy relationship and, thanks to Judah, she had an idea of what one might look like. She leaned her head against the cool glass. When she got back to Sturgis, she'd move on. She'd start her art classes, take a martial arts class, and find a way to help Annie.

"Russell, you're being released." A female guard stopped outside the cell door. "Put your hands through the hatch so I can cuff you."

Lightness filled Elaine as she rushed to the door. Cold fingers tightened metal cuffs around her wrists.

"What time is it?" she asked.

"Eight thirty. Now, take a step back."

Elaine complied. The metal door swung open.

"Step out of the cell." The guard led Elaine past the other cells, down two flights of stairs, and through a long hallway. At another metal door, she pushed a button. A guard on the other side of a window nodded.

The door buzzed then opened. The guard led her to a counter and removed the handcuffs.

A male guard stood across from her. "What's your name?"

"Mary Russell."

He grabbed a file beside him and glanced at the top sheet of paper. "The prosecutor has decided not to file charges." He slid some papers across the counter to her. "Read these carefully and sign where indicated. If you don't understand something, I can explain it."

The words blurred and her limbs went numb. Soon the whole ugly ordeal would be over. She signed where indicated, then slid the papers back to the guard.

He put a white, plastic bag on the counter. "Look through the bag to make sure all your belongings are here. Then sign this form."

She rummaged through her clothes and shoes. Nothing missing. She signed the form.

"Officer Rose will escort you to the female change-out room."

Elaine nodded. "Thanks."

Once left alone, she quickly changed. Her dirty capris and yellow shirt had never felt so comfortable. She stepped out of the room, and the guard escorted her out of the processing room and into a waiting room.

"Elaine." Bridget's familiar voice caused tingles to cover Elaine's skin as relief and joy rippled through her. Bridget ran over to Elaine and hugged her. Elaine squeezed her tight, basking in the comfort of a friend's touch. They parted, and Bridget held her at arm's length. "Are you OK? That's some bruise."

Elaine touched her sore cheek. "I'm good now. Even better seeing you."

"I need to hear every detail."

"My thoughts are a jumble right now. Maybe after I've had a nap and a hot shower. Were you able to see my grandma?"

"I went over after we talked, and she was sitting at the kitchen table reading. Apparently, Judah had been there looking for you and Clara. She was pretty worried. I reassured her that you were OK and would be back by this evening. A social worker will be checking on her this morning and throughout the day."

The last of yesterday's tension slipped away. "That makes me feel better. Thanks."

Detective Harris strode into the building and toward Elaine. His dark hair, which had been neat the night before, was a mess, and brown spots stained his khaki pants. "Oh, good. You're still here. We've got a lead and need your help identifying the possible suspects."

After everything she'd been through, Elaine couldn't think of a better way to spend the morning. In fact, she couldn't think of a better way to spend the rest of her life. She smiled at Bridget. "Want to catch some traffickers?"

"Absolutely."

"Perfect." He led the way to the door. "My car is out front."

With renewed energy, Elaine followed. If they saved Annie and the other girls, then this would all be worth it.

After a quick drive to the police station, Elaine and Bridget were ushered into a room with several computers along one wall and a black leather couch along the other. A lady with a blond ponytail and a headset sat at one of the computers. A picture of a black van filled the two-foot-wide monitor in front of her.

"That's the van." Elaine rushed over to the monitor. A girl with an afro walked around the front of the van and looked into the camera before climbing inside. A lump formed in her throat. "That's Annie."

Detective Harris rolled over an office chair. "Take a seat. This video is from six thirty this morning, but it's the best footage we have. Can you pull up the latest footage?"

The blond nodded as she typed. A new video popped onto the screen. A highway appeared. Several cars drove by, then a black van. The video froze and zoomed in on the windshield. The picture was blurry, but Elaine recognized Wallace's bald head and the driver's dark hair. She sucked in an anxious breath.

"Do you recognize them?" Detective Harris asked.

"That's Wallace in the passenger seat. That other guy looks like the same driver from yesterday. I don't know his name." She sat on the edge of the office chair with her gaze glued to the screen. Another video of the van popped up time stamped eight thirty. Only twenty minutes ago. Hope sprung up in her. "It's them. Can you stop them?"

"We're working on it," the detective said. "This is already old footage, so we need to anticipate where they're going, then send units to intercept them. It's going to take time and coordination. Are you up for it?"

Hope soared. They were so close. She looked at Bridget who nodded as she sat in a chair beside her. Elaine took in a fortifying breath. She'd sit there all day if she had to. She'd made Annie a promise, and she meant to keep it.

CHAPTER 34

Judah fumbled to unlatch the booster seat from Zoe's car, feeling her glare on him as he struggled. As soon as he and Clara were away from her threats, the better. When he finally pulled the seat free, he gave his sister-in-law a farewell nod, then followed Clara to the front door.

"Come on, Daddy. I want to see Sheba."

"She's at the doggy hospital. Remember?" He unlocked the front door. "I'll call and see how she's doing. Why don't you go to your bedroom and get out your suitcase while I call?"

"Is Grammy here?"

"Not today."

Her face crumpled, but she ran to her room as soon as he opened the door.

Judah pulled out his phone and called the vet. "This is Judah Demski and I'd like an update on my dog, Sheba."

"She's made remarkable improvement. The doctor said she'll be ready to go home today."

A modicum of anxiety released. "Perfect. I'm headed out of town today and I'd like to take her with me."

"As long as you keep her calm for another week, that would be fine. That means no walks or playing ball or exercise of any kind."

"Thank you. When can I pick her up?"

"Give us an hour to get her ready."

"You got it." Judah hung up and smiled. He found Clara playing her in room, her princess suitcase on the floor beside her. "How about we go visit Uncle Asher and Aunt Mollie? Would you like that?"

"Yes!" She jumped up.

"Let's get packed. As soon as we can, we'll pick up Sheba and leave."

"Can I take my dolls?"

"You can take whatever you want." He'd make room for her entire toy box if he had to.

She unzipped her suitcase, so Judah rushed to the basement. He hauled up the boxes of mementos and important documents, then loaded them into the back of his SUV. While Clara continued packing, he called his boss, praying for favor but willing to do whatever was necessary to keep his daughter safe.

"Dr. Fleming."

"It's Judah. There's been a family emergency, and I'm going to need a couple of weeks off."

"I heard something about that. Is everything OK?"

"It is now. Clara was kidnapped yesterday." He cleared his throat as his voice cracked. "She's home, but she's having a difficult time. I need to get her out of town for a few weeks to help her recover." If his boss said no, he'd quit. He had plenty of money in savings. He could find another job.

"Let me look at the schedule, but I'm sure we can work out something. You take care of your little girl."

His shoulders relaxed. "Thanks."

An hour later, Judah picked up Sheba and settled her beside Clara. She licked Clara's face then laid her head on her knee.

Clara petted her. "Daddy, can Lainy come with us?"

Judah scowled. "No." He didn't want to push Clara, but he had to know. "Why do you want her to come? Weren't you scared with her yesterday?"

She nodded. "But she was scared too."

"Why would she be scared?"

"The bad man hurt her."

"What man?" Did she have a partner? "Did he hurt you?"

She shook her head.

He strangled the steering wheel. "Did he touch you at all?"
She shook her head again.
He sagged in relief as his phone rang. "Hello."
"Do you have her?" Mollie asked.
"Yes, and we're all packed. I'll call you when we stop for dinner."

* * * * * * *

Elaine sat on the couch next to Bridget. After four hours of looking through surveillance footage, her eyes burned. She hadn't realized how hungry she was until lunch arrived. She swallowed the last bite of her burger and smiled at Bridget. "Thanks for staying with me."

"I'm happy to. Catching these creeps would make my day. I still can't believe I didn't suspect Mitch. I've been around this enough to know the signs."

"I can't believe I let him in my home. I live there. What if Grandma—" Grandma! "Can I borrow your phone?"

"Of course." She unlocked it then handed it to her.

"I can't believe I forgot to call her." She dialed Grandma's cell. "How much should I tell her?"

"What do you think she can handle?"

"I'm not sure."

"Then tell her a watered-down version of the truth. It's better for her to get the information from you then someone else. She already knows something bad happened."

"Hello?"

The familiar voice brought tears to Elaine's eyes. "Hi, Grandma. It's Mary. I lost my phone so I'm using Bridget's."

"Are you OK, sweetie? Judah was looking for you and Clara. He seemed upset."

"I'm fine." She touched her cheek. "I hurt my face, but I'm good now and Clara's with her dad."

"When are you coming home?"

"I'm at the police station helping the detectives find the men who hurt me. It could be a few more hours, but I should be there tonight. Is the social worker still with you?"

"No. She left and another one is coming soon. Mary, I don't need a babysitter."

"I know, but with all the trouble we've had lately, it would make me feel better knowing you're not alone. Will you humor me?"

She sighed. "I guess. Do you want to talk to Sally Ann?"

Elaine laughed. It felt good to have some normalcy back in her life. The office door opened and Detective Harris came in. "I can't now. I have to go, but you can call this number if you need to get ahold of me. Love you."

Detective Harris smiled at Elaine. "We found them in Williston, thanks in large part to your drawings and positive identifications. I'm heading over there now. Do you want to come with me?"

Elaine hopped up. "Yes." Her legs shook with excitement as she followed the detective to his car. What would the girls be like when they found them? Had Wallace beaten them when she and Clara got away? Or had they been forced to . . . work at another truck stop? They'd sacrificed so much to help her. She needed to thank them and help them too.

Three hours later, they drove into the parking lot of a rundown hotel. Two police cars sat in front of an open door, their blue lights flashing. Harris parked behind them. "Stay here. I'll let you know when it's safe to come over."

Elaine squinted through the bug splattered windshield. Several uniformed officers walked around the parking lot and sidewalk. The empty, black van was parked across two spots. Then she saw Annie leaning against the hotel wall smoking a cigarette. Her hair was a bit wilder than yesterday, but thankfully there were no cuts or bruises on her face.

Adrenaline rushed through Elaine. She shot out of the car and ran between the police cars. Someone yelled at her. Annie looked up. Her face crumpled and tears ran down her face as she ran to meet Elaine. They collided in the parking lot, Elaine wrapping her arms around Annie as she sobbed.

"It's OK. You're safe." She held the girl until she stopped shaking. Cigarette smoke and cheap perfume had never smelled so good.

Finally, Annie sniffled and took a deep breath. "You came back."

"I told you I would. I just didn't think it would happen this fast."

Annie stepped back, her eye swollen with tears. "But you said you would and you did." Her lip trembled. "You didn't lie."

Annie's disbelief crushed Elaine. She pulled the girl close and hugged her again. "Do you have someplace to go?" She couldn't offer her home, but she'd find someplace for Annie.

Bridget stepped out from behind a car. "They're sending the girls to a safe house. While you were busy checking monitors, I got in touch with a victim's advocacy group in the area."

Annie broke away from Elaine and crossed her arms. "I'm not going to a home."

"It's not a foster home. It's a safe house. They've got counselors and doctors there to help you." She smiled as she nodded at Annie's stomach. "And your baby."

For the first time since Elaine had met her, Annie smiled. Her lips barely curled, but Elaine saw it, and it renewed her hope. She couldn't hold back her tears as she reached for Annie's hand. "The only reason I could help was because of what you did for me last night. We saved each other."

Ignoring the officers and detectives and spectators around them, Elaine held Annie and cried. She cried for what Annie had been through, for what she'd sacrificed for Clara, for the therapy and healing that each victim would need.

But she also cried for joy at their freedom. Somehow, the euphoria of that moment wrapped around Elaine and replaced the lingering shame of her felony. Her past was never going to hold her back again.

CHAPTER 35

Judah pulled up to his brother and sister-in-law's two-story farmhouse and rolled down his window. The setting sun cooled the hot summer air that blew over his arm. He'd never realized how safe he felt coming home until he knew what terrors were literally at his doorstep. The front door flew open, and three kids and two dogs descended on them. The laughter, barking, and shouts woke Clara up.

"I want out!" She pushed against the back of his seat.

While kids and dogs ran around him, Judah unbuckled her, then set her on the dirt driveway. She ran to her cousins as he headed toward the house. Asher stepped onto the porch wearing a plaid shirt, jeans, and a dirty Minnesota Vikings ball cap. He dipped his chin. "Hey, bro. Good to see you."

"Thanks for letting us visit."

"Anytime." He smacked Judah's shoulder and squeezed. "Mollie showed me the Amber Alert. After the kids go to bed, you can fill us in."

His nine-year-old niece ran over and gave him a hug. "Hello, Uncle Judah."

"This isn't Rosie, is it? You're practically all grown up."

She smiled as seven-year-old Charlene hugged his leg. "I'm growd up too." She wore her hair in a braid identical to Rosie's.

Ezra ran over next and pulled out a baby snake from the front pocket of his overalls. "See what I got?"

Clara ran her little finger over the snake's body. "She's cute."

Ezra's four-year-old face scrunched up. "It's not a girl. It's a boy."

"You had that snake in your pocket all this time?" Asher shook his head. "Mollie would have a fit if she knew. We're going to have to pat him down before we let him back in the house. After the girls, he's giving us a run for our money."

The screen door squeaked open and banged shut as Mollie stepped out holding eighteen-month-old Grayson. She gave him to her husband before pulling Judah in for a tight hug. "I'm so glad you're here." When she released him, she knelt down and hugged Clara. "I'm glad you're here too."

Asher pulled Judah aside as the kids got reacquainted. "How are you really doing?"

Judah rubbed the stubble on his jaw as he tried to figure that out. "I don't know if I'll ever be able to let Clara out of my sight again. I think this has scared years off my life."

Mollie screamed.

Judah tensed, ready to act, but Asher laughed.

"Ezra Micah Demski!" Mollie ran from her son. "Get that thing away from me!"

Judah snorted.

Mollie glared at him as she scrambled behind her husband. "It's not funny." She pounded Asher's back. "Control your son."

"It's only a garter snake. It won't hurt you." He put his arm around her, pulling her away from the kids.

Ezra followed, holding the snake up higher. "Come see it, Mommy."

"That's OK, sweetie. Go let it out in the pasture."

"I'll go with you." Clara held her hand out. Ezra took it and the four-year-olds walked over to the field and knelt into the grass. She pointed to the ground and giggled.

Her laughter soothed Judah's soul. He'd prepared himself to pick up a broken, traumatized girl. Over time, Clara would need to work through some things, but seeing her bubbly personality reemerge gave him hope for her future.

As the kids played, he gazed out to where the yellow fields of sunflowers met the horizon. Laughter mixed with the high pitch chirping of the cicadas and the fresh, wet, earthy scent of the nearby cottonwoods reminded him of his childhood. When they ran through the fields playing ghosts in the graveyard, and his mom's hug was all it took to soothe a hurt. He could sure use one now.

In the side yard, Asher stacked wood in the fire pit. By the time the fire was blazing, Mollie had all the fixings for s'mores laid out on the picnic table. The kids abandoned their games for dessert. Judah sat in a canvas chair and watched the flames dance as wisps of smoke floated away.

Maybe it was time to move back. Find some land where he could build a house. Clara would be happy living so close to her cousins and he'd be happy to be away from Elaine. He'd start looking for a job tomorrow.

CHAPTER 36

A t one o'clock on Tuesday afternoon, Elaine put a bin of beads on the kitchen table as her new cell phone rang.

"The Mother Lode Antique Shop, Elaine speaking."

"It's Bridget. I'm on my way to get the girls. I'm bringing another girl with me. She was rescued with you. Her name is Mandy. I'm hoping being around Jules and Ginny will help her open up."

Elaine couldn't remember a Mandy, but that didn't mean she'd turn the girl away. "Of course. I have plenty for everyone."

"Thank you. Have you heard from Judah? I've been trying to call him all week."

Elaine's face heated. "I haven't."

"I'm sorry. I guess I thought you two were close."

"We were, but I put his daughter in danger. I wouldn't want to talk to me either."

"None of this was your fault. Mitch is a professional. Men like him can manipulate and seduce anyone. Probably even Judah."

Elaine smiled at Bridget's fierce tone. "I'm not blaming myself. I promise. I just understand why he doesn't want to talk to me. I'd like to know how Clara is doing, but I'm not going to push him."

"He'll call when he wants to. By the way, did you lose a necklace with pink flowers on it? The truck driver found one on the floor of his cab. He and his wife didn't recognize it and figured it was yours."

A bittersweet feeling crept over Elaine. "It's Judah's."

"I see. Would you like me to return it to him?"

"I'll give it to him. I've got to get my stuff back from him anyway." At some point. She had what mattered—Grandma, Sally Ann, and Clara safe—but she would eventually need to pick up the clothes and crafts she left at his house.

"Sounds good. Listen, I'm at the group home now, so I'd better go. See you in a few minutes."

Elaine hung up and sat in the kitchen chair. She missed Judah. She hated what happened to Clara, but she didn't regret going with Mitch. Because of him, she'd helped Annie and Mandy and three other girls. She hoped one day she'd get to tell Clara about her part in saving those girls. Until then, she had an art class to teach.

She double-checked her bins of beads, wires, and tools before filling a pitcher of lemonade. She'd just set a plate of chocolate chips cookies on the counter when the front door jingled. A moment later, Bridget stepped into the kitchen with a black bag over her shoulder. She handed Elaine a clear bag with the necklace. Elaine shoved it, along with a pang of sadness at seeing it, into her pocket. It wasn't hard to forget the sadness when Jules followed Bridget into the kitchen

Elaine blinked back tears as she hugged the girl. "It's great to see you."

"Look at my new tattoo." She turned around and pulled her ponytail to the side. Where the barcode had been was a treasure chest filled with jewels. *Museum Quality* was written above it.

The vibrant colors not only covered the ugly barcode, it transformed it into a work of art. "It's amazing, like you."

"Remember Ginny?" Jules pulled Ginny in from the dining room. She'd cut her blonde hair into a bob and looked more like a teen without her heavy makeup.

"Good to see you, Ginny. I'm all set up over here." Elaine pointed to the table.

Jules linked arms with Ginny. They giggled as they sat and looked through the beads.

"I love hearing them laugh," Bridget said as she walked to the dining room doorway.

"Best noise I've heard in a long time."

She motioned for another girl to come inside. The brown-haired girl kept her gaze on the ground as she shuffled into the kitchen. "Elaine, this is Mandy." Mandy looked up, and Elaine sucked in a deep breath. Mitch's "girlfriend" from the parking lot.

Forcing her surprise away, Elaine smiled. "Hi, Mandy. I'm glad you're here. Would you like to sit?"

She nodded and sat beside Jules.

Bridget took a seat on the other side of the table and opened her computer.

When everyone was situated, Elaine picked up a clear cord and a small silver ring. "Today we're going to make necklaces. First, loop the cord around the ring and through the cord again, pulling tight." She picked up the needle-nose pliers and showed them. "Now you're free to add beads without them falling through." She added several small glass beads.

"How many do we add?" Jules asked.

"As many as you'd like."

"What if it looks stupid?"

Elaine tipped the cord over, spilling the beads onto the table. "You start over. There are no mistakes here. You can always start over and make it into anything you want it to be."

Jules and Ginny both got to work right away, but Mandy sat with her head down. When the other girls were about done with their first necklaces, Elaine moved to Mandy's side of the table and squatted beside her. "Would you like to try?" she asked.

"I guess."

Elaine handed her the supplies. Mandy's fingers shook as she cut the cord. She looped the end, then set it on the table.

"Did you decide which beads to use?" Elaine touched different bins to draw the girl's attention.

"I'm not sure it matters."

"It does matter." Elaine pulled a stool over and sat. "I find that when I create, it releases stress and anxiety. I don't know how it works, but when I'm focused on making something beautiful, it takes the focus off my pain and allows my heart to heal. That's why I love to paint."

"I'd rather paint than make jewelry." Mandy pushed the pliers aside.

"Maybe we can." Elaine swiveled to face their chaperone. "Bridget? Would it be OK if Mandy painted in my studio?"

"That's fine."

"Look." Jules held her necklace around her neck. She'd alternated green clay beads with brown crystals and tiny copper beads. The colors reminded Elaine of a sedimentary rock with a copper vein she saw in a museum once. Maybe she'd be Jules's first customer because she could think of a dozen outfits the necklace would look great with.

"It's beautiful. Give me a minute, and I'll show you how to put the clasp on." Elaine bent near Mandy. "Come with me."

Her face brightened as she stood.

Elaine led the way up the stairs, past her grandma's closed door, and into the bedroom she'd transformed into a studio.

Mandy's eyes widened as she looked from the painted tiger lilies on the wall to the roses then to the peonies. "It's like a garden up here."

"If only I was as good a gardener as a painter, I'd have the real things." Elaine stepped over to the stack of canvases and grabbed a blank one. She took a wisteria oil painting off of her easel and replaced it with the blank canvas. Before she could set the painting on the floor, Mandy moved next to her and tilted the painting up to look at it.

"That's beautiful. You painted that?"

"I've had a hard time sleeping lately. Painting relaxes me."

"How do you know which colors to use?"

"I don't. When I started painting it, I used a light green for the leaves. It looked awful so I tried adding highlights but that made it look worse. After several failed attempts, I decided to paint over the original color with this darker green." She pointed at the wisteria leaves. "If you look close enough, you can see some of the edges where the lighter color shows through. Technically it's a mistake, but I think it enhances the beauty.

"I think the trauma we experience can be like that. I can't change what happened to my husband, and you can't change what happened to you, but we can let it be turned it into something beautiful."

"How?" Tears glistened in her eyes.

"We talk to people who can help us. No matter how much it hurts, we believe it can get better someday. I never thought I'd get over my husband's death." Judah's face popped into her mind and she smiled. "But now I know that I can."

"How do we know who can help us?"

"Right now, we trust Bridget. She has lots of experience."

"Yeah, she told me her story." Mandy shook her head. "But it's too hard to talk about right now."

"You don't have to talk up here. My studio is open whenever you need to get away and paint. No talking necessary."

Mandy nodded. "Thanks."

Elaine leaned the wisteria painting against the wall knowing she'd give it to Mandy as soon as the paint dried. Then she pointed to the long table on the back wall. "The brushes are in the jars and the paint is lined up over there." She handed Mandy a smock and pallet, then turned on the CD player. Classical music floated around them. "Feel free to turn off the music or turn on a radio station. Do whatever works for you."

Mandy approached the supply table. Elaine stood in the doorway and watched as she smeared different colored paint blobs across her pallet. Then she stepped up to the canvas and brushed bright blue paint along the top of it. Not wanting to intrude on the healing moment, Elaine walked slowly back to the kitchen, the advice she'd given Mandy repeating in her own ears.

By helping Jules and Annie, Elaine had repainted the ugly leaves of her past, but she had a whole canvas to make over. Maybe it was time to put away the liner brush, pull out her wash brush, and start making some broad strokes.

CHAPTER 37

Elaine picked up the ballerina kitty that Judah had never bought for Clara. The familiar sadness stirred in her heart. She missed Clara almost as much as she missed Marcus. Opening her heart to kids had always been easy. It was adults Elaine struggled to trust. She'd trusted Judah, and he'd been silent for the last week.

She sighed as she put the figurine in a box with the others. After she emptied this last display case, she'd refill it with paints. Eventually. Between the lost inventory, repairs to the shop, and other unexpected expenses in the past two weeks, she didn't have the money to buy everything she needed for her classes, but she had enough beads to offer jewelry-making classes. She could build her paint supplies over time.

She carried the box into the other room. Bridget stood in front of an already-crowded cabinet. "Do you have room for these?"

Bridget scrunched her nose. "If we squeeze the vases together, maybe." She pushed the Amberina vases so they were almost touching. The bell over the door rang. "I'll finish this if you want to greet your customer." She took the box from Elaine.

In the foyer stood an older woman dressed in an elegant pantsuit.

Elaine smiled. "Welcome to The Mother Lode. Can I help you?"

"Are you Elaine Kent?"

Apprehension and curiosity battled in her. "I am."

The lady approached the counter and set down her black designer bag. She pulled a picture from one of the pockets. "Do you still have this?" She held out a five-by-seven picture of the ugly teapot Mitch had brought in.

"I do, but I haven't had time to price it yet. How did you know I had it?"

"My grandson mentioned this place once, and let's just say he has sticky fingers."

Chills rippled over Elaine's skin. *Mitch stole it.* She opened the closet behind her and pulled out the teapot. "I'm so sorry. He brought in dozens of items. I can't even remember all of them. I think I sold some of them, but you're welcome to look around the store and take anything that belongs to you."

The woman gently picked up the teapot. Her blue eyes glazed over with tears. "I'm the one who's sorry. I'm not supposed to contact you or any of the other victims, but I don't care." She set the teapot down and pulled out her checkbook. "I'd like to buy it back."

"Oh, no. It's yours. I never paid Mitch a cent for it."

She ignored Elaine and wrote on the check. "I made it out to The Mother Lode. Is that OK?"

"Yes, thank you," Elaine whispered. "But you don't have to."

She tore the check out and put in on the counter face down. "That should more than cover the cost of the teapot."

Doubt made Elaine leery. "I'm still going to testify against him."

"As you should."

"I won't lie on the stand."

"I would never ask you to."

"Then why come here?"

Mitch's grandma stroked the strange antique. "My husband bought me this teapot on our honeymoon sixty-seven years ago. It means far more to me than any dollar amount. And it's the least my family can do to make amends for the wrongs my grandson did to you."

Not sure how to respond, Elaine wrapped the teapot in several layers of tissue paper and put it in a bag, then handed it to Mitch's grandmother. "I don't hold Mitch's actions against his family."

"Thank you, child." She took the bag and held it to her chest. "For the teapot and for your forgiveness." She strode out of the store with her head held high. How could she possibly be related to Mitch?

When the door shut behind her, Elaine turned the check over and gasped. There were so many zeroes!

"Are you OK?" Bridget ran in holding a crystal vase in each hand. "What is it?"

"That was Mitch's grandmother." She held up the check. "She paid me ten thousand dollars for a teapot. *Her* teapot."

"What?"

"To make amends."

Bridget's eyes narrowed. "Did she ask you not to testify?"

"No."

"Threaten you?"

"No. I think she feels bad for what he did."

"Wow. What are you going to do with the money?"

"With this, I can buy my supplies." Elaine picked up her phone. "I have orders to make. And ads to design."

"When are you going to start? I can think of at least two deputies who would love to come. And reserve a spot for me."

"If we get enough people interested, we can get started as soon as the supplies come in." Excitement bubbled over and Elaine giggled—*giggled*—as her gaze met Bridget's. "Can Jules, Ginny, and Mandy come, if their social worker OKs it? Courtesy of Mitch's grandma."

Bridget winked. "It won't be a problem. I promise."

CHAPTER 38

After almost two weeks with his family, Judah didn't notice anything troubling about Clara. She hadn't had a nightmare since the first night, and she no longer asked about Elaine. He was lying on the carpet watching cartoons with his daughter beside him and Ezra on his back when Mollie walked in and laughed.

"Maybe I should hire you as my nanny."

"This is the life. Watching cartoons all day."

"I hardly let my kids watch TV all day."

The actual nanny stepped into the family room carrying a laundry basket. "I could hire him as my assistant."

Her red curls looked so much like Elaine's that his chest tightened. How could he miss someone who had hurt his child? What was wrong with him?

The nanny's eyes widened. "I was kidding. No need to scowl at me."

"Sorry. I was lost in thought."

"Hope you weren't thinking of me." She winked and headed down the hallway.

"OK, you two." Mollie turned off the cartoons. "It's a nice day. Ezra, why don't you go outside and find your sisters?"

Clara and Ezra ran from the room. Mollie turned to Judah, her eyebrows pulled together. "Can I talk with you privately?"

"Of course." His stomach rolled. "Is everything OK?"

"Yeah. It's just weird." She led him down the hallway and into her office.

He sat on one of the white leather chairs across from Mollie's desk. She sat on her office chair and rolled over to her computer.

"What's up?" Judah laced his fingers together in an effort to look calmer than he felt.

"I just got off the phone with the Meade County State's Attorney, and the good news is that Child Protection Services doesn't have an open case against you. In fact, there's never been a complaint filed."

Judah relaxed against the chair. "Zoe didn't call me in?"

Mollie smiled. "Nope, and I don't think it would do much damage if she had."

Relief coursed through him. "Thanks for handling this."

"That's not all. I did some checking on the kidnapping case and there are no recent charges filed against Elaine. In fact, she was never charged."

Surprised, he leaned forward, trying to see Mollie's computer screen. "That can't be. Did you check under Mary Russell? That's her legal name."

"I did. Nothing. She was arrested for taking a child not hers across state lines, but the prosecutor didn't file charges. She was released the next day."

Judah rubbed his temples. "That doesn't make sense. Did she strike a deal?"

"No. In order to make a deal, she'd need to be charged first. Here are the guys being charged." She flipped around her laptop. Wallace's mug shot filled the screen.

Judah clenched his hands into fists. "That's the guy who attacked Elaine. Why would he hurt her if they were in this together?"

Mollie took a deep breath. "Are you sure she was a part of the kidnapping?"

"She took Clara to North Dakota."

"She was found in North Dakota with Clara. Those are two different situations."

Judah sat back as he tried to process what Mollie was implying. "You think she was a victim?"

She shrugged. "The Meade County SA said he couldn't share too much about the case, but Elaine is a key witness. Nothing about this situation matches what happened with her foster son. If anything, Elaine resembles the girls that were rescued—petite, young, vulnerable."

The ache of Elaine's betrayal faded into confusion. "It doesn't make sense. Can I see the other mug shots?" She scrolled down. Mitch's face appeared and Judah almost fell out of his chair. "Stop!" A cocky grin stared back at him, making Judah want to punch the computer. "That's Mitch. What does he have to do with this?"

"Who's Mitch?"

"Some guy Elaine knows. He—" No. His throat dried. All that charm and constant flirting. Was it an act? "He was going to show her a piano the day of the kidnapping."

Mollie turned the computer around and started typing. "He's charged with conspiracy to commit sex trafficking by force and coercion of a minor."

The uneasy feelings he'd had around Mitch and Sheba's instinctual dislike of him—it all made sense. Mitch was in on the whole thing.

"I've got to find out what happened." He pulled out his cell, but who could he call? He couldn't ask Elaine—he still didn't know if he could trust her. Zoe? But she wasn't a detective. She might not have access to new information.

He tapped on his missed calls. Three from Bridget. Maybe she could help. He pushed her number.

"This is Bridget Smalls."

Nerves flipped his stomach at her voice, knowing she was his only link to Elaine. "It's Judah Demski. Do you have a minute to talk?"

"Yes, of course. I've been trying to get ahold of you. How's Clara doing?"

"She's good, all things considered. We decided to leave town for a while."

"That's great. Has she had any trouble sleeping?"

"The first night she had a nightmare, but since then she's slept through the night. I appreciate your concern, but I'm calling about the kidnapping charges. I'm confused. Why wasn't Elaine charged?"

"Elaine wasn't charged because she had nothing to do with the kidnapping. She was a victim too."

Judah sucked in a deep breath. "What? How?"

"Mitch. He'd been grooming her for a couple of months. That's why he was hanging out with her, trying to get her to go out with him. Then you showed up."

"What did I do?"

"She was more into you than him. It's his gig to lure young, vulnerable women into the sex trade. He might have succeeded earlier if you hadn't shown up."

Anger rippled through him. Why hadn't he punched Mitch when he had the chance? "How does Clara fit into this?"

"Collateral damage. She was at the wrong place at the wrong time. They were after Elaine, but they took Clara because they could."

"I had no idea." Judah moaned as bile rose up in his throat.

"Then you probably don't know that Elaine saved Clara too. She managed to escape at a rest stop and get help."

"I didn't know." He ran a hand over his face as he tried to process the new information.

"She also helped the police save five other women the next day."

Frustrated, he clenched his teeth together. "Why wasn't I told any of this?"

"I've been trying to get ahold of you for two weeks."

"I assumed Elaine was behind the kidnapping."

"Why would you assume that?" Her voice hardened.

He sighed. "Because I'm an idiot. You probably never doubted her."

"No, but it wasn't my child who was missing."

"What can I do? Do you think she'll forgive me?"

"It's not my place to give you advice. You need to talk to her about it."

"Can you at least tell me if she's OK?"

"I can't discuss her with you. You'll have to ask her yourself. While I have you on the phone, though, I need to tell you of the upcoming hearings. It's your right as a victim. Two of the perpetrators pled guilty. They have their sentencing on Monday. Mitch's preliminary hearing starts tomorrow."

Judah glanced at Mollie. "My lawyer said Elaine is a key witness. Does she have to testify?"

"She's on the list for tomorrow." Bridget paused. "Is there anything I can do for you and Clara?"

Despite his horrible judgment and unfounded accusations against Elaine, Bridget still wanted to help. He didn't deserve these people in his life. "Not that I can think of. Thanks for sharing this with me."

"Of course."

Judah hung up and let his phone drop to his lap. What had he done? He should have known Elaine would never have hurt Clara. He should have trusted her.

Mollie tapped her fingers on the desk. "That was an interesting conversation, at least the side I could hear. I gather things didn't happen the way you thought?"

"I've made a huge mistake. Elaine was kidnapped, too, and she saved Clara."

Mollie's jaw dropped open. "Wow."

How could he have doubted her? She was the bravest person he'd ever known, and tomorrow she'd face one of her kidnappers in court. He had abandoned her for weeks, but he had time to change that. "I've got to go to Sturgis. Elaine's testifying tomorrow. I need to be there for her."

"When are you leaving?"

He looked at his watch. "If I leave now, I'll get to Sturgis around ten. Can Clara stay with you?"

"Of course."

He felt energized for the first time all week. Elaine wasn't the villain Zoe said she was—he was. He'd believed the accusations, not the woman he knew. He wouldn't blame her if she hated him, but that didn't mean he'd walk away without a fight. He'd beg for another chance and spend the rest of his life proving himself worthy, because a life without Elaine would be a life without color.

CHAPTER 39

Judah opened the heavy courtroom door and slipped into the back row. The balding judge sat at the bench with the court reporter next to him. The jury box was empty. A tall man with curly brown hair sat in front of Judah, blocking his view of Elaine on the witness stand.

Shifting to an empty seat, his breath caught in his throat when he saw her. Even in a dull gray jacket with her hair pulled back in a headband, she was stunning. She sat tall in her seat and stared directly at the prosecutor.

"Mrs. Russell, do you have a felony record?" the state's attorney asked from his seat at the table.

"Yes."

"And what was the felony for?"

"Kidnapping."

"Who did you kidnap?"

"My foster son."

He looked down at his notes then back at Elaine. "Why did you take him?"

"My late husband and I ran away with him because we couldn't adopt him."

"Do you regret taking him?"

"I do. More than anything."

"Did you hurt the boy?"

"No." She shook her head so hard her headband slipped to her forehead. She pushed it back. "I would never hurt him. I loved him."

"Did you go to jail for the kidnapping?"

"Yes, for nine months."

"Why only nine months?"

"I was able to get a plea deal because I called the police when my husband kidnapped Marcus from his new foster mother."

The prosecutor nodded. "Tell me where you met Mitch Rosemont."

"I have an antique store here in Sturgis. He started coming in at the end of May to sell me antiques he said he bought at garage sales."

"How frequently did he come in?"

"Every two to three days."

"Tell me about the day of the kidnapping."

As Elaine recounted the details of that horrible day, Judah's anger at Mitch intensified, then simmered. He didn't want to think about Mitch. He wanted to focus on Elaine, and at that moment she was a superstar, boldly sharing every horrible detail.

"I begged Mitch to let Clara go, but he laughed at me." Her eyes narrowed as she stared at the defense table. "She's a child." Her voice cracked. "What kind of a sick monster are you?"

Judah squeezed the edge of his seat to keep from clapping.

"Objection." The defense attorney

"Please keep to the facts, Mrs. Russell." The judge smiled at her, which eased the tension in Judah's shoulders.

"I'm sorry, your honor."

The questioning continued for another ten minutes.

"Thank you, Mrs. Russell." The attorney looked at the judge. "I have no more questions at this time." He flipped through his papers.

The defense attorney stood and smoothed out his suit. He walked around the table and stopped a few feet in front of Elaine. Judah's nerves raced.

"Mrs. Russell. How old was the boy that you kidnapped?"

"Three."

"And Clara?"

"Four."

He stepped to the table and picked up a piece of paper. "Why did you kidnap Marcus?"

"Because I loved him."

"Did you love Clara?"

"I've only just met her."

"Yes or no, Mrs. Russell."

"Yes, then."

"Mrs. Russell, can you have kids of your own?"

Elaine gasped and looked at the prosecutor.

He stood. "Objection. Irrelevant."

"Your Honor. I'm about to prove that it is relevant."

The judge nodded. "I'll allow it."

"Mrs. Russell?" The attorney cocked his head to the side.

"No, I can't."

"And do you want kids?"

A tear flowed down her cheek. "Yes."

Judah gripped the arm rests.

"So you decided to take one again?"

Elaine's eyes widened. "No."

"No further questions, Your Honor." The defense attorney strode back to his table, sat, and shuffled through his papers.

"If there are no further questions, the witness is dismissed."

Elaine strode from the witness stand and sat in the gallery beside Bridget. The two leaned their heads together. Judah wanted to run up there and throw his arms around them, but he forced himself to stay seated.

"We'll take a fifteen-minute recess." The judge banged his gavel.

"All rise." The bailiff's voice echoed through the room.

Judah stood with everyone else, then plopped back down as soon as the judge disappeared through the back door. When Elaine walked out next to Bridget, he followed.

He rounded the corner and spotted Elaine at the end of the hall sitting next to a teenager. The prosecutor and Bridget stood in front of them. He leaned against the wall and waited for them to finish. He wouldn't interrupt their good work.

Finally, after several minutes of talking and nodding, Elaine looked over at him. Her eyes grew wide when she saw him, her face losing its color. He wanted to run to her, but he wouldn't force himself on her. Instead, he waited, letting her decide what she wanted to do. When she stood, he sucked in a breath. She stepped forward and his pulse raced. Her eyebrows lowered, she said something to Bridget, then frowned at him.

She walked over to him, fidgeting with a gold pendant around her neck. He wished it was the necklace he'd given her. "Judah."

Euphoria consumed him and he shoved his hands in his pockets to keep from embracing her and kissing her breathless. "Elaine."

"How's Clara? I've been worried about her."

"She's good. I took her to my brother's place. She's having a blast with his kids on the farm."

A delicate smile creased her lips. "Good. She deserves a bit of fun. I'm really sorry about what happened to her."

"I know you are."

"I never should have taken Clara with me. I'll never forgive myself for putting her in danger."

"You can't blame yourself. Mitch is the monster. You saved Clara from, from . . ." He couldn't say the words so he pointed at the courtroom. "You saved the other girls, too, and you're still trying to help them. You were amazing in there."

Her face sobered. "Thank you. It's good to see you, but Bridget and Mandy are waiting for me."

Panic rose in him. "Can I stop by your house later? There's so much more I need to say."

"I don't think it's a good idea." She started back toward Bridget.

It couldn't end like that. He'd never loved anyone like he loved her, maybe because he'd never met anyone as kind, selfless, and brave as her. He ran after her and grabbed her hand. "Elaine, wait. I don't blame you for what happened with Clara."

"I'm glad. I really have to get back to Bridget and Mandy though."

"After the hearing then. Please. Let me explain. I can bring dinner."

"Fine, but not tonight. Tomorrow at eight thirty. No dinner. It's not a date." She strode over to Bridget without looking back.

He ran a hand over his face. He had twenty-four hours to figure out how to win her trust again.

****

Elaine kept her head high as she walked away, but her chest ached. Seeing Judah when she was trying to be strong shook the walls she needed to keep up. After not talking to her for two weeks, he couldn't just show up at the hearing and expect her to drop everything to talk to him. She couldn't let her relationship with Judah distract her. She had to think about Mandy.

"I can't get up there and tell everyone about what happened." Mandy twisted her shirt around her finger. "I can't."

Bridget took Mandy's hand. "I understand. We can't promise that the defense attorney won't ask you about your assaults. All we know for sure is that Mitch was able to groom you and Elaine. None of his previous victims have pressed charges."

Mandy's head snapped up.

Bridget nodded. "He was expelled from college because of assault allegations. He was never charged because the girls wouldn't come forward. I'm afraid if we can't show probable cause, it will never go to trial and there'll be no chance that he'll be found guilty. He'll be able to keep hurting other girls."

"But what if I get on the stand and they ask me about my relationship with him? I slept with him. He didn't have to force me. What if they blame me instead?"

"Mitch was grooming you. All you have to do is tell them what Mitch did. I already testified that his actions are classic grooming techniques. Your testimony will support that."

Elaine sat beside Mandy. "I didn't sleep with Mitch, but I thought he was my friend. I trusted him. He needs to go to jail for a very long time."

The prosecutor knelt in front of them. "The good thing is that I get to ask you questions first, just like we practiced. I'll give you a chance to tell your side of the story before the defense attorney can ask anything. It's not a crime to sleep with someone."

Mandy trembled. "What if I get up there and cry or have a panic attack?"

"The judge will give you time to calm down," Bridget said. "He wants the truth, not to humiliate you."

"I started sobbing when I pled guilty to kidnapping my foster son," Elaine said, remembering the day. "They gave me a ten-minute break to get some water and collect myself."

"I can ask for a break at any time," the attorney said.

Elaine pulled a bracelet out of her pocket. "I know you're scared, but I also know you're brave. I made this for you to help you remember that." She handed it to Mandy.

Purple and green beads in different shades surrounded a thin silver plate with *Courage* engraved on it. Mandy took the bracelet, twirling it in her fingers. Then her eyes widened as she looked at Elaine. "These are the same colors as the painting."

Elaine nodded as she pointed to the lighter green beads. "This was the wrong color. But this"—she ran her finger across the darker green beads—"is perfect. And together . . ."

"They make the picture more beautiful." Mandy slid the bracelet onto her wrist and took a deep breath. "OK. I'm ready."

Elaine stood and held a hand out to Mandy. "How about we go in together?" They looped their arms together and entered the courtroom. Mitch swiveled around and frowned.

"You can do this," Elaine whispered. Mandy held her head high. Elaine had never been prouder.

CHAPTER 40

At exactly eight thirty the next evening, Judah walked into The Mother Lode and met the sounds of classical music and murmuring. He followed them into the parlor. Easels, canvases, and people filled the room. Bridget stood between a man and a woman he didn't recognize painting black trees over a large yellow moon. A dark blue sky surrounded it.

"Hi, Dr. Demski."

Judah turned at the voice of a surgical nurse. She and her daughter were painting the same night sky as Bridget. He waved because he wasn't sure what to say. There were at least eight other people painting the same thing.

"It's time to start cleaning up." Elaine walked to the front of the room. "You've all done a wonderful job. Leave the paintings on your easel to dry and you can take them home next week. Don't forget to spread the word. We had room for two more students tonight, but I can always open another class if there's more interest."

Judah watched her interact with her students. Her face glowed as she exclaimed over their paintings and showed them how to clean the brushes. Giggling erupted and he stepped farther into the room. Jules, Ginny, and Mandy flicked paint at each other's smocks.

"OK, girls. The paint's for the canvas." Elaine stepped between them, smiling. "Can you help me clean up the palettes?" She turned then and saw him. Her face turned pink as she approached him. "Sorry. I thought we'd be done by now."

"Don't apologize. This is amazing." He wanted to hug her but knew he didn't have that right anymore. He settled for admiring her beauty and strength. He couldn't be prouder of her.

"I can hardly believe it. And they're here because of word of mouth. I didn't want to wait, so Bridget and I made a few phone calls. I hope I'll be able to have several classes a week once I start advertising."

"I'm sure you will. Can I help with anything tonight?"

"Can you make sure all the supplies get put back? I have everything labeled on the table up front." She didn't wait for an answer before practically bouncing around the room, thanking everyone for coming.

Judah walked to the front and put everything in its place. Bridget set her brushes on the table, then winked at him before ushering Jules, Ginny, and Mandy away.

After the last student left, Elaine closed and locked the door. "We can talk in the kitchen."

He waited for her, then followed her to the table and sat across from her.

"How's Sheba?" she asked. "It's quiet without her."

"Good. It's hard to keep her resting. She wants to run after the kids. How's Wanda?"

"She's had a rough week. Ever since the kidnapping, she's been struggling with anxiety, and she's even more forgetful than before. We're going to Rapid City to start packing her stuff tomorrow."

"Do you need any help?"

She shook her head. "We're good."

Judah rubbed his sweaty palms on his pants. He couldn't think of anymore small talk. "I'm an idiot. When I couldn't find you and Clara, I freaked out and let myself believe Zoe's accusations. All I could think about was getting Clara back, then keeping her safe from Zoe. Then you."

"You thought I kidnapped her?"

He nodded.

Her eyebrows scrunched together. "How could you believe I would ever hurt her?"

"If I could go back, I'd search for you in Bismarck and let you explain what happened. Clara didn't want to leave without you. I should have listened to her. I should have trusted you and everything I know about you. From the minute we met, you've been sacrificing yourself for others."

She took a deep breath. "I'm not going to pretend that your disappearance didn't bother me."

"Do you think you can forgive me?" He held his breath, praying she'd give him one more chance.

"Of course, I forgive you."

Relieved, he reached for her hand, but she pulled away.

"But that doesn't mean we can start back where we were. I know it's only been two weeks, but this experience has changed me. I can't go back to the person I was before, and you might not like this new me."

He smiled. "Yes, I will, because she's the one I've seen all along. I've always known you were a strong, confident, and selfless woman. You're the one who didn't see it."

She blushed. "You forgot courageous."

"Oh no I didn't. I'm just getting started. Courageous and generous and beautiful and—"

She put her hand over his mouth. "That's enough. My face will never cool down at this rate."

He kissed her hand just before it fell from his lips. "I know I hurt you, and I know it's going to take time for you to see that you can trust me again. All I'm asking for is a chance."

"Honestly, I don't know if I should be dating anyone right now." She reached into her pocket and pulled out the cherry blossom necklace.

His excitement waned as she gave it to him, but he'd prepared himself for her rejection. He was ready to prove himself. "I understand, but do you think I could sign up for your art class? You said you have room, right?"

"I'd love for you to join us."

"How many classes are you offering? I'd like to join them all."

"Just the one, but Bridget and I are organizing a charity walk to raise awareness of and money for trafficking." Her familiar head tilt gave him hope. She was already warming up to him. "Would you like to help?"

"Yes, but not for you."

"Oh." She frowned.

"That came out wrong." He squeezed his eyes shut to compose himself before returning his gaze to her. "I want to earn your trust again and I want to date you again, but this hit way too close to home. Even if everything fails between us, I still want to help with this cause."

"I'd like that too."

"And I'd like to know the truth, about everything. I know what my sister-in-law told me and what Bridget told me, but you're the one I care about. How are you?"

A mix of emotions stirred inside him as Elaine told her story, but peace filled him as she talked about rescuing the girls. Excitement lit up her eyes. "Annie called me earlier this evening. She's enrolling in the CNA program at the community college. I'm so proud of her."

"And I'm proud of you." Wanting to share that pride with her, he handed her back the necklace. "I'd like you to keep this. No strings attached."

She leaned in and kissed his cheek. He closed his eyes as the scent of lilacs floated around him. "Will you wait for me?"

"Forever."

"I hope not that long, but a little longer. I've faced kidnappers and traffickers, but this"—she motioned between them—"I need a little more courage yet."

He smiled. She was one of the most courageous people he knew. He couldn't wait for her to realize it too.

Epilogue

Elaine taped the last piece of blue crepe paper to the kitchen ceiling, then stepped down and surveyed her handiwork. Alternating streamers in blue and purple hung from the chandelier to the walls. "How does that look?"

Ginny tied off a balloon and threw it to the ground among the other purple, blue, and yellow balloons. "It looks like a circus tent." Her shoulders sagged. "I wish I could move in too."

"If this works out, maybe in a couple more years. You like it at the group home, don't you?"

"I guess."

Elaine squeezed her arm. "You're welcome to come over whenever you like, after school of course."

Mandy walked in holding a canvas in one hand, an easel in the other. "I'm done." She set up the display for her garden scene, but instead of flowers blooming, jewels sparkled on the ends of the stems. Rubies clung to bushes surrounding a white bench on the left side of the canvas. Sapphires drooped as bluebells along the green hillside behind it. Diamonds clustered by a white gazebo with amethyst wisteria clinging to it.

A rush of emotion flowed from Elaine's heart to her throat at the light in Mandy's eyes. The painting was stunning, but the painter had blossomed into a far more beautiful masterpiece. "It's gorgeous."

"That's beautiful, Mandy," Ginny said.

"Thanks." Mandy smiled. "Elaine helped a lot."

Bridget walked in with a veggie tray. "Everything looks incredible. Jules is going to be so surprised."

Eighteen months ago, Elaine couldn't have imagined they'd all be standing in her kitchen waiting to surprise Jules. Now, she couldn't imagine anything else. Her phone vibrated, so she pulled it out and glanced at the text. "Judah says they're leaving. Why don't you girls go watch for them and let me know when they pull up?"

Ginny looped her arm through Mandy's and the two girls hurried through the arched doorway to the front of the house.

Elaine hugged herself. "Those two have come such a long way."

"We all have." Bridget nudged her. "Remind me. I have some news to share with you and Judah later."

"I hope it's good news."

"The very best. Do you want to catch a movie tomorrow night?"

"I wish I could, but Judah and I have a business date planned."

Her friend's face scrunched up. "A business date?"

"To finalize wedding details. It's only two weeks away, and his parents are coming next weekend."

"Fine, but don't forget that I'm stealing you away on Saturday so we can do some maid-of-honor things." Bridget winked.

"I definitely won't forget that. I can hardly wait for a girls' night out."

"I'm just glad we'll get to do more. How did you convince Judah to stick around Sturgis? Didn't he want to move closer to his family?"

"He still does, but I'm afraid Grandma would struggle with the move. And I couldn't leave Jules, Ginny, and Mandy just yet. They feel like my little sisters." She blushed. "And you. I've never had a best friend like you."

"Now stop all that mushy stuff." She wagged her finger at Elaine. "You'll make me cry."

"You never cry."

"I might."

Elaine laughed. "Anyway, Judah's looking at purchasing some land near the family farm, and we can slowly plan our home. Maybe in a few years we can move out there."

"They're here!" Ginny and Mandy ran into the kitchen.

Excitement bubbled in Elaine. "You girls go get Grandma. I'll be back in a few minutes."

Elaine rushed through the house and onto the porch. When Jules stepped out of Judah's SUV, Elaine ran down to hug her. "Happy birthday!"

Jules hugged her back. "Thank you. I can't believe I get to move in here. Are you sure you trust me to run the store?"

"Of course, I do. I'll only be ten minutes away at Judah's house—"

He cleared his throat.

Elaine beamed. "At *my* house and over here every day if you need anything." Elaine followed Jules to the back of the SUV to unload her things. Clara climbed out of the backseat and leaned against the truck pouting.

Elaine bent down to kiss her head, but Clara pulled away. "What's wrong?"

"Daddy says I can't come to the sleepover."

Judah rolled his eyes. "It's not a sleepover, lamb. Jules is moving into Lainy's house. And tonight is a school night."

Elaine crouched down to the six-year-old's level. "In two weeks, every night will be a sleepover at your house."

She folded her arms in front of her. "I don't want to wait. I want my new mommy now."

Elaine clutched the cherry blossom necklace over her heart. Joy sprang up as she looked at Judah and mouthed, *new mommy?*

He smiled. "She came up with that on her own."

There was nothing Elaine could do to resist her *new* daughter now. "Next Friday you can spend the night with me, Grammy, and Jules. How does that sound?"

"Yay!" Clara flew into Elaine's arms.

"OK, kid. Help me with my stuff." Jules handed Clara a basket filled with hair ties and scrunchies before grabbing a large tote bag and a pillow. "Follow me."

As they walked toward the house, Judah held Elaine back and kissed her. "I've been looking forward to that all day."

"Me too, but we better hurry or we'll miss the surprise."

They each grabbed a box and walked inside. They made it just in time to see Jules step into the kitchen.

"Surprise!"

Jules screamed, then laughed. Elaine stepped into the kitchen doorway as Ginny, Mandy, and Jules hugged and chatted. Grandma beamed at them from her place at the table. Their bright smiles, easy laughter, and happy chatter brought tears of joy to Elaine's eyes.

"The girls can help you carry up your stuff while we get the party started," Bridget said, turning to Elaine. "Where's the cake?"

"In the fridge. I'll get the candles."

By the time the girls came back down, the cake was on the table with eighteen flickering candles. They sang "Happy Birthday" and Jules blew out the candles. "I don't remember ever celebrating my birthday. Thank you, everyone."

After cake and presents, the girls went up to Jules's room and Grandma took Clara up to see Sally Ann. Elaine started picking up plates, but Bridget took them from her. "Can we talk first, while the girls are all upstairs?"

"Of course." She sat back down next to Judah.

"Law enforcement made a trafficking bust in Florida last night."

Judah nodded. "I saw it on the news. They were there for the Super Bowl."

"Twenty victims were rescued and five traffickers arrested. Among those arrested was Brad Baltic." Bridget tapped on her phone, then turned it for Elaine to see. His salt-and-pepper hair had grown out, but his familiar hard stare sent shivers across her skin.

So many emotions battled inside of Elaine. "He ordered Wallace to take me and Clara. Will I have to testify again?"

"If you're willing."

Judah slipped his hand around Elaine's and squeezed. "You can do it. You were amazing last time."

She shivered. She didn't want to relive that nightmare, but if she didn't testify and he walked, she would never forgive herself. "Of course, I'll do it."

"I'll call the prosecutor in Miami tomorrow and let him know." Bridget's phone rang, so she picked it up and carried it into the other room.

"I'm proud of you." Judah turned Elaine's chair so it faced his, then leaned forward and kissed her, sending sparks down her spine and heat to her face. He trailed a finger down her cheek. "I see you're still not used to my kisses."

"And I hope I never am." She laced her fingers through his. "Are you sure you're OK with Grandma moving in with us?"

"I've already moved my office downstairs, and Clara's super excited."

"But are you?"

"I am. Both of my grandmothers died before I was born. I've loved getting to know Wanda."

"And she comes with a bird."

"Well, there's that." He laughed. "And you're OK with Zoe coming to the wedding? Even though she apologized, she's not the nicest person."

Elaine smiled. "I'm glad she's coming. I can't say she's warmed up to me, but the few times we've met this last year she's been polite and professional. She may never like me, but for Clara's sake, I'm glad we're getting along."

Bridget rushed back in. "That was a detective. They've arrested a trafficker. I hate to split, but they need help with the victims." She raised her eyebrows.

Elaine turned to Judah, her mind and emotions battling. "I should stay. It's Jules first night here."

"And she would want you to go help the victims. I'll make sure she gets settled in, and I'll stay with Wanda until you get back."

"If you're sure."

"Of course I am. Go."

Fueled by adrenaline, Elaine jumped up and grabbed her purse from the counter.

"I'll meet you outside." Bridget left out the back door.

Elaine bent over Judah and leaned close to his smiling face. "Thank you for encouraging me to do this." She pressed a kiss to his lips. "And thank you for loving me."

"Thank you for bringing color into my life." He kissed her back. "We can continue this when you get home. Go, take care of those girls." He touched the bracelet on her wrist. "Go be courageous."

Elaine touched his fingers on the bracelet she'd made, the same style as the one she'd given Mandy, then Jules and Ginny. With more courage than she'd ever thought possible, she kissed Judah, then ran after Bridget.

If you enjoyed this book, will you consider sharing the message with others?

Let us know your thoughts. You can let the author know by visiting or sharing a photo of the cover on our social media pages or leaving a review at a retailer's site. All of it helps us get the message out!

Email: info@ironstreammedia.com

   @ironstreammedia

Brookstone Publishing Group, Iron Stream, Iron Stream Fiction, Iron Stream Harambee, Iron Stream Kids, and Life Bible Study are imprints of Iron Stream Media, which derives its name from Proverbs 27:17, "As iron sharpens iron, so one person sharpens another." This sharpening describes the process of discipleship, one to another. With this in mind, Iron Stream Media provides a variety of solutions for churches, ministry leaders, and nonprofits ranging om in-depth Bible study curriculum and Christian book publishing to custom publishing and consultative services.

For more information on ISM and its imprints, please visit
IronStreamMedia.com

Made in the USA
Las Vegas, NV
22 September 2022